WHITEWATER
A Thriller
William McGinnis

William McGinnis (signature)

WhitewaterVoyages.com

Whitewater: A Thriller

by William McGinnis

Copyright © 2012 by William McGinnis

Published by Whitewater Voyages
El Sobrante, California 94803
Phone: 800 400 7238
Website: WhitewaterVoyages.com
Email: fun@whitewatervoyages.com
Fax: 510 758 7238

First Edition

LCCN: 2012937303

ISBN: 978-0-9834370-2-4

Printed in Hong Kong

Cover and book design by:

Big Hat Press

To flowing rivers both within and without

Table of Contents

Chapter One: Entering Kern Canyon. 7

Chapter Two: The Swim. 13

Chapter Three: Hot Spring 19

Chapter Four: Guide School 25

Chapter Five: The Game 29

Chapter Six: Lower Kern 33

Chapter Seven: The Really Big Picture 39

Chapter Eight: The Hike 45

Chapter Nine: Dream Van 49

Chapter Ten: Town of Lake Isabella 61

Chapter Eleven: Indian Rock Resort. 65

Chapter Twelve: Petroglyphs. 71

Chapter Thirteen: Lake Isabella 75

Chapter Fourteen: Kernville. 85

Chapter Fifteen: You Are A River 91

Chapter Sixteen: Upper Kern 99

Chapter Seventeen: Airport 105

Chapter Eighteen: Giant Sequoias 111

Chapter Nineteen: Uncle Peace 117

Chapter Twenty: Sequoia Walk. 121

Chapter Twenty-One: Pot Farm 125

Chapter Twenty-Two: The Cliff 135

Chapter Twenty-Three: Forks Camp 147

Chapter Twenty-Four: Dog 151

Chapter Twenty-Five: Thimble Camp Morning 157

Chapter Twenty-Six: The Forks 165

Chapter Twenty-Seven: Vortex 169

Chapter Twenty-Eight: Westwall 179

Chapter Twenty-Nine: Carson Falls 187

Chapter Thirty: The Sheriff 197

Chapter Thirty-One: Crazy Man Shuttle 205

Chapter Thirty-Two: Dog Gone. 213

Chapter Thirty-Three: Kern River Preserve 215

Chapter Thirty-Four: Cartel Compound 223

Chapter Thirty-Five: Knucklehead 233

Chapter Thirty-Six: Blueberry Smoothie 235

Chapter Thirty-Seven: Confrontation 237

Chapter Thirty-Eight: The Flume 247

Chapter Thirty-Nine: The Big Swim 251

Chapter Forty: The Really Big Swim 257

Chapter Forty-One: Epilogue. 261

Disclaimer: Words of Caution and Encouragement . . . 263

Acknowledgments 267

List of Recommended Outfitters 273

CHAPTER ONE
ENTERING KERN CANYON

"Stay away from the Kern River!"

Peace's voice crescendoed via cell phone over the van's sound system as I hurtled toward the broad western face of the Southern Sierra.

"I've got to go in," I said. "I need you to tell me what you know."

"And help you get yourself killed like your mom and dad? No way!"

"I have to do this. I am doing this. With or without you."

"We've been through this a thousand times. It's suicide! Adam, you've got to let it go. I'm begging you, turn around now and come home."

"I'm going in."

I'm no stranger to fear. The dry mouth. The churning gut. The screaming need to empty bowel and bladder. I know them well. But instead of that long expected dread, I felt pure excitement as I, on that hot August morning, after half a lifetime of preparation, drove eastward on Highway 178 toward the deep-V mouth of the Kern River Canyon. Maybe it was my aroused state, but as I peered out through the bug-splattered windshield of my 4-wheel-drive camper van, the two canyon walls seemed to splay out like the craggy, tawny legs of some ancient earth giantess. Where the legs met, the Kern River beckoned, surging and pulsating in a geologic dance of rock and water—the rock hard and squeezing, the water ever moving and exploding in wild rhythms.

Somewhere in the canyon before me, my mother and father had been brutally murdered twenty-eight years earlier when I was a little boy five years old. Now I was back to find the killers.

Blasted out of the nearly vertical southern canyon wall, the road narrowed and snaked along, compressed between a ragged, dynamite-scarred rock face on one side and a sheer drop off with an intermittent guard rail on the other. Not far below, the leviathan Kern River surged through an earth-beat tango of smooth sensual glides punctuated by explosive whitewater cataracts.

After what seemed much longer—but was by my odometer only twelve miles—of twisting turns, the canyon opened and the narrow, constricted two-lane tarmac broadened into a full-blown, four-lane expressway. I remembered reading that, in one of the more bizarre anomalies of the US highway system, this major freeway from nowhere to nowhere sits locked away alone, largely cut off, deep inside the body of the Southern Sierra. I noticed with pleasure that the builders had taken care to blend this civil engineering marvel into the natural slope. Except for the road scar itself, high up the canyon wall, the original look of the place was intact.

To stretch my legs after my long drive from the San Francisco Bay Area, and to more fully take in the canyon towering around me, I pulled off the road and eased into a gulch. Prompted by survival instincts that had kept me alive through three tours of duty as a Navy SEAL captain, one in Iraq and two in Afghanistan, I hid my Sportsmobile van under a canopy of smooth-barked manzanita. Grabbing my binoculars, I locked the doors and started walking along the edge of the mountain freeway, and then onto a rocky promontory jutting over the river. In the brilliant mountain light, I gazed at the undulating river far below, the tree-dotted, boulder-strewn slopes, the majestic Greenhorn Mountains to the north—technically considered the southern end of the Sierra Nevada—and the Piute Mountains to the South.

The silence was absolute, as, through my binoculars, I studied the cathedral-like canyon. A thousand feet above, a California Condor, with wings spread incredibly wide, effortlessly floated on the thermals rising off the southern-facing rim, eyeing and apparently grooving with this slice of creation that had been carved out over the eons by the Kern River.

Sounds of screeching and crashing ripped me from my reverie. Louder and louder. Splitting the air. Metal resounding on metal mixed with the cacophony of imploding plastic and shattering glass. I spun to see a black humvee repeatedly side-swipe and rear end a white Prius, obviously trying to run it off the cliff. The Prius dodged this way and that, but despite the efforts of its driver, it could not outrun or outmaneuver the much bigger, more powerful jeep on steroids.

Frozen, I watched the two warring vehicles as they approached my promontory. Then the humvee exploded forward and rear ended the Prius in a homicidal acceleration that sent the small vehicle straight toward—and off—the edge just a few yards from where I hunkered.

As the Prius shot over the brink and out into thin air, the driver and I looked directly into one another's eyes. She—a raven-haired woman—was there for an instant, then gone.

Riveted, I watched the Prius make a short arc through the

air, land right side up, and slew wildly, skidding down the long scree slope. Dense clusters of bushes slowed the little car. Damned if the woman was not only keeping her wheels down, she seemed to be exercising some degree of control. I watched in admiration as she steered into soft bushes, avoiding trees and rocks which certainly would have killed her. Incredibly, she even had the presence of mind to aim for a gap in the dense tangle of trees lining the riverbank at the bottom. Whipped by bush after bush in its path, the hybrid slowed, then slowed some more. Still going way too fast, it swept through the gap in the riparian vegetation and slid into the water, disappearing below the surface.

The black humvee had skidded to a stop just before the cliff edge. And now two muscular men climbed out, one tall, the other short, both sporting square-edged, flat-topped haircuts and thick black shoes. Both gripped rifles with large scopes which they aimed at me, and I knew that, as their only witness, they intended to shoot me dead. I dropped my binoculars and flung myself down the steep incline. Shots exploded around me, two within inches of my right ear.

Dodging this way and that, I ran wildly, skidding, scrambling and sliding down the inclined plane of the canyon wall, avoiding the bushes, trying to put trees and rock outcroppings between me and the shooters, all the while praying the girl had managed to escape drowning. I slid, first on my feet, for a moment on my belly, then on my back. Finally reaching river level, I regained my footing, dodged through the gnarly, twisted trees lining the water's edge, and, right where the Prius had gone in, jumped feet first into the powerful current.

Submerged, my years not only as a SEAL but also as a kid swimming San Francisco Bay and the lakes of Northern California came rushing back to me. My senses sharpened,

I spotted the car below me and dove down. When I looked inside, the woman was not there. Had she been washed away? Knocked out cold, maybe drowned? I surfaced, gasping for air. Swimming at a right angle to the current, I stroked back to the bank and burst up onto a small grassy beach. The dripping-wet body of the woman was lying in the shelter of a huge sycamore trunk.

"Are you all right? Are you hurt?" I rushed to her.

CHAPTER TWO
THE SWIM

"One fit babe," I thought, *"but is she alive?"*

As I leaned over her, first one blue eye, then another looked up at me. "Are you okay?" I asked.

She gave a small moan, "What a ride. The air bag saved me."

Bright red blood oozed from her left forearm and from her right leg above the knee. A real trooper, she had clamped her right hand over the wound in her left arm and with her left hand was staunching the flow from her leg, but the bleeding continued.

"We need to stop that," I blurted as my military first-aid training kicked in. I pulled off my t-shirt, tearing it into strips. Pressing the patches of cloth over her wounds, I had her hold them in place while I checked for broken bones, concussion, and spine and neck injuries. As I did this, I couldn't help feeling the woman's magnetism, and noticed my heartbeat speeding up.

I stammered, "You were amazing! Making it down that slope! And getting your car through that narrow gap in the trees! It's a miracle you're alive."

"Yes, I was lucky," she gave a shadow of a smile. "Thanks. What about you? How'd you get down here so fast? You okay?"

"It was either stay and get shot, or tumble down the slope and rescue you. I'm good," I couldn't help grinning as I finished my examination. "Except for these cuts in your arm and leg, it looks like you came through okay."

As I tied more strips of cloth to secure her bandages and set her hands free, I said, "We need to clean and redress these wounds. But this'll have to do for now."

Gesturing with her thumb toward the highway far above, she said, "They've got sniper rifles, telescopic scopes. They'll stop at nothing, and'll kill you too. We have to get away."

Careful to stay hidden, I peered around the massive sycamore trunk up at the two guys who were now out on the promontory scanning the canyon for some sign of us. Seeming to read my mind, she said, "We'll have to swim the rapids. We've got no choice. You okay with that?"

"Definitely, but first I'm calling the cops." I pulled my waterproof cell phone from my pocket.

"No don't," she sat up, glaring at me, and gripped my hand so hard I almost dropped the phone.

"You've got to be kidding. Why the hell not?" I pointed toward the highway with my other hand, "Two pro killers gunning for us in broad daylight. They've got the high ground and the guns. It only makes sense to equal the odds a bit by calling in some cavalry."

"Big mistake," she said.

Flabbergasted, I was about to object when, taking both of my hands in hers, she interlaced our fingers, saying, "I'll tell you why later. But now we've got to go."

Despite misgivings, my objections melted and I sighed, "Okay, let's get out of here before we die like sitting ducks."

I helped her to her feet. With her wet, faded-red t-shirt

and shorts clinging to her body, she brushed her hair back and drew a deep breath. "I know this river," she pointed. "Our best line through this first rapid will be right of center where we should be hidden by the trees."

Although she limped slightly, she moved toward the water with animal grace. Lightly touching my arm, she ushered me forward, saying quickly and quietly, "Float feet downstream, toes on the surface, using your feet to push off rocks."

She paused and shook her head as though to fight off a moment of dizziness, then continued, "To miss submerged trees, swim perpendicular to the current. Because we don't have life jackets, we'll be mostly underwater in the rapids, so breathe whenever you can. Okay?"

I smiled inwardly, wondering what this woman might feel if she knew of my countless rough and tumble missions as a Navy SEAL. Then, as I looked downriver, it dawned on me that whitewater rapids were a whole new challenge. I was glad, then, that she seemed to know her stuff.

As we eased into the strong current, she grinned, "By the way, my name's Tripnee. It's been nice knowing you."

"I'm Adam. I guess you must be a river guide?"

"Yes, among other things."

Staying close to the right, where the dense willow, alder and sycamore trees lined the bank screening us from the riflemen above, we silently floated downriver.

Back in the water, after years away from it, I experienced an upwelling of my old love of swimming in nature, plus a new sensation. This woman kindled a spark. It wasn't so much how she looked—though her strong form looked just fine—it was the aliveness that flowed through her. *"Beware,"* something whispered within me.

As the current carried us, I became aware of a dull roar growing louder and louder. Tripnee moved into position directly ahead of me. I became mesmerized by the rhythmic stroking of her sculpted arms. As the current swept us toward the horizon line just ahead, she assumed a feet-downstream, toes-at-the-surface position, and I followed suit. Moments later Tripnee rose briefly, lifted by an upwelling in the water's surface, and then disappeared from view. Picking up speed toward the brink, up to my neck in this rushing river, I could see nothing but spray and mist thrown up by the cataract into which I was about to be hurled. With the speed of a projectile launched from a catapult, I shot down into a wild orgy of sucking, squeezing currents, probing fingers of foam, and thrusting tongues of limb-bashing whitewater.

Tumbling submerged, everything seemed pretty much fine, except for the no-breathing part, when suddenly my right foot caught in a slot between two rocks on the river bottom. I hung by my ankle face down, stretched out in the driving current like a Raggedy Ann doll in a hurricane. The harder I struggled, the tighter my ankle wedged into the vice-like grip of the rock crevice. Desperately I tried to move back upriver to free my foot, but the current was utterly relentless and overpowering. With my lungs screaming for oxygen, my strength waning, and my mind starting to black out, it occurred to me that I was going to join my mom and dad very soon.

Suddenly, amazingly, I felt Tripnee pushing me back upstream. While I was immobile underwater, she must have realized I was in trouble, swum for shore, run back up the bank, figured out where I was, and dived down to catch the small underwater eddy created by my entrapped body. Now she was under me, facing me, with her head pointed upstream and her feet somehow braced on the riverbed. She pressed her body against mine, held me tight, and somehow propelled me little by little, inch by inch, back against the current. My ankle loosened. As soon as I was free, Tripnee unbraced her feet and we shot off down through the rapid. Frantically, I stroked for the surface, where I filled my lungs again and again with delicious, life-giving air—each lungful a treasure beyond price.

Soon we were sucked under again—and still again. When at last I surfaced below the rapid, I looked around for my rescuer, but she was nowhere to be seen. House-sized boulders of salt-and-pepper granite glided by on both banks. The Kern rounded a bend. The riflemen now had to be out of visual and rifle range. But no Tripnee.

Then, there she was, rising to the surface at my side. In that same instant my vision shifted and I was struck by the greens of the willows and alders, and the blue of the sky. Tripnee's brilliant smile, her glistening, tanned skin, the curve of her neck meeting breastbone—all took on a rich vividness. I turned away.

"Are you okay?" she asked. "I want to look at you. Can you swim to the bank?"

As I said, "I'm fine," I realized my lower right leg didn't feel quite right.

"Humor me. Let's take a look."

We were in a long, quiet calm, and stroked for the right bank, the one nearest the highway, where we would be most hidden. In the shallows, I stood up and winced as a throbbing pain radiated up my leg. My entire right ankle was chafed raw and bleeding.

"Now it's my turn," Tripnee removed and tore her t-shirt into strips, using it to expertly bandage my wounds and stop the bleeding.

Seeing this woman in her nicely filled out red bikini top and matching shorts further eased my pain. "If this keeps up," I joked, "At some point we're going to run out of bandage material."

Tripnee just smiled and ran her tongue back and forth over her slightly lopsided lips.

Feeling a wave of shyness, we both looked out over the calm. Etching the river's surface, ever-changing patterns of swirling bubbles formed a series of masterpieces.

We eased back in. Neck deep, slowly treading water with extended leisurely strides similar to the motions of a cross country skier, I ignored the ache of my injury, and inhaled long, slow, full breaths. Taking in my immediate surroundings—Tripnee's bobbing head, the magnificent canyon towering around me, the growing roar of the oncoming rapid—I wanted to laugh out loud. Despite the fact that we were fleeing from crazed gunmen and our lives were in extreme danger, I experienced something that was rare for me: A sense of rightness, a sense that this was where I wanted to be.

We floated around several more bends and swam more roaring, electrifying, body-blasting rapids. I could tell Tripnee knew the river like the back of her hand. She led and I followed down through rapid after rapid. Some were too dangerous to swim, and needed to be walked around. Unfortunately I inadvertently swam a few of these anyway, because at times we got separated. But somehow we survived and kept going.

CHAPTER THREE

HOT SPRING

Tripnee and I floated into a meandering reach of the river where willows arched from bank to bank forming a tunnel-like canopy. Beams of sunlight filtered through the lush green dome, and here and there were big patches of blue sky. Wafting on the air came the smell of deep earth minerals blended with sulphur. We climbed out of the water to find a natural hot spring nestled between elephant-sized serpentine boulders hidden in a dense thicket of shimmering Fremont cottonwoods.

Unsure whether or not we had eluded the gunmen, we decided our safest option for the time being was to take refuge in this secluded little paradise. The mineral spring was a staircase of stone pools. Climbing among them, I found that the highest, the one being filled directly by scalding water that gushed from deep within the earth, was scorching. Each pool below, fed by the overflow from the one above, was slightly cooler.

Tripnee eased into the coolest, the pond closest to the river, and I settled in beside her. The steaming water took my breath away, and was the perfect followup to our long swim. Tripnee stretched, opened her eyes wide, and seemed to tune in to and absorb not just the healing heat, but also energy that emanated from the spot. Despite the tension running through me, I relaxed. We looked at each other.

"Hey," I intoned.

She responded in kind with an elongated, melodious, "Heyyyyyy."

"If not for you, I'd be dead."

"If not for me, you'd be in no danger at all," she replied.

"I'm not so sure. But, what's going on? Who are those guys and why are they trying to kill us?"

Tripnee replied, "One goes by the name Mack Dowell, the other Hektor Torrente. They're part of a drug cartel using the Kern Canyon to grow pot, and fly in heroin and crystal meth."

"Whoa! That figures. And you got involved with them how?" I asked.

Tripnee turned toward me, looked squarely into my eyes, and said, "Adam, right now, I just need you to trust me. When I can tell you more, I will. Do you understand?"

As I met her gaze, her calm sincerity—and the fact that she had just saved my life—prompted me to set aside my doubts, nod, and say, "OK. For now." But after a moment, I asked, "Why not call the sheriff?"

"Just between us," she said, "although it's not ironclad, there's strong evidence that local law enforcement is in league with the drug cartel. Calling the sheriff could catapult us from the frying pan into the fire."

She put a hand on my knee and said, "I have a question. You said you might be in danger even without me in the picture. Why's that?"

Following my gut, I decided to go to the next step in

trusting this woman. "I rarely share this, and I want you to keep this strictly between us."

She nodded, "Of course."

"My parents were murdered here on the Kern many years ago when I was a little boy." A searing pain flared just then in the old scar on my left shoulder. Covering it with my right palm, I continued, "I've come back to track down whoever did it. No doubt they're not very nice people—a lot like our friends in the humvee. My poking around is sure to be dangerous."

Tripnee winced, "That must have been very, very tough for you." Then she reached over and brushed back the hair on my forehead and, amazingly, the pain in my old wound subsided.

"Would you mind telling me about your parents?" she asked.

"The thing is I know so painfully little about them. Their names were Sarah and Abraham Weldon. She was a rancher and he was a school teacher. That's about all I know."

Tripnee's brows went up, "But how can that be?"

"From my earliest memories, I lived in the Bay Area with my uncle Peace." I said, "Peace is a zen monk, a school librarian, and completely goofy. He made the whole subject of my parents and their murder strictly taboo. So my family and anything having to do with it were never discussed."

"What was the man thinking?"

"Peace believed—and still believes—in non-attachment to the things of this world. I know, I know he meant well and was trying to protect me, to detach me from the horror of the murder. But I never got to come to grips with it."

"That must've been incredibly hard for you," said Tripnee.

"No kidding!" I said. "Never learning about my mother and father left a void and made it worse."

"How did you cope?"

"I went through phases of pleading—hell, demanding—that Peace tell me about my family. But he flatly refused. Never budged. At times, I tried to follow his advice and let go. But I think I've always known that I'd have to come here to the Kern. Not only to find out what really happened and see justice done, but to unearth my own roots."

"So why have you come now, after all these years?"

"A month ago I mustered out of the Navy SEALS." I said, "Over time, what gradually brought things to a head for me, was, during my deployments in Iraq and Afghanistan, seeing terrible things done to innocent families—families a lot like my folks and me—things done by my own buddies—but also things done to men in my unit—that I realized I'll never come to terms with, that I'll never be okay with."

As I talked, Tripnee scarcely blinked, taking in every word.

"So I was left with two choices," I went on. "One to retreat, shrivel up, hide in a hole and die either fast or slow. The other to engage life, and bit by bit, little by little, come to grips with the world as it is, with my eyes wide open, and, even though it might sound corny, try to make a positive difference, heal the wounds of violence—especially those done to my own family—and somehow, in the process, maybe heal myself."

Tripnee and I sat there quietly side by side, chest deep in the warm spring, with arms and legs touching, careful not to bump wounds.

After a while, nodding slowly, she said, "I respect and admire your quest."

We fell quiet. Something inside me withdrew from her kindness. Had I said too much?

Then suddenly I stiffened. My god, up there, through the willows, I saw the black humvee! Holding my breath, I prayed not to be seen. Following my gaze, Tripnee saw it too. Statues, we watched as the vehicle prowled along the Old Kern Canyon Road high up the southern slope. It kept going and we began to relax. Then we heard the distant sound of a door slamming. A moment later we both pointed backward. Smiling grimly and nodding at how we thought alike, we moved deeper into the hot spring grotto where we would be better concealed.

"Be ready to run," I whispered, and we tensed in silence, waiting for the first shot which would send us bolting for deeper cover.

"Yeeaaahh!" That single yell cracked the stillness. Then came laughter and happy shouts as, one by one, four tan-colored inflatable rafts crewed by people in orange lifejackets burst into view.

CHAPTER FOUR
GUIDE SCHOOL

As though popping out of a separate universe, the boats swept toward us exploding with vitality. These people were having the time of their lives.

While most of the lifejackets looked bright and new, I noticed at least one in each boat that was faded, older, and odd-colored. The people in the older jackets looked more sun-baked and grizzled than their generally younger, fresh-faced companions. Clearly these were the guides, but they weren't guiding. Each boat had about five to seven people aboard. Everyone sat perched along the sides, with feet inboard, facing the bow, gripping canoe-type paddles. Near the stern of each a peach-faced novice squealed out commands: "Forward," "Right turn," "Stop," and "Oh no, I meant left turn."

From the lead raft, a woman wearing a faded yellow lifejacket and a tan visor bearing the words "Fulfillment Voyages," called out: "Hi Tripnee! Great to see you!"

"Hi Becca!" Tripnee shouted and energetically waved them on downriver. "Don't stop! Float on by. Please! I'll explain later."

Becca responded with a dismissive hand motion, and her raft continued to glide straight toward us. As its bow tube touched the smooth, water-worn stone lip of the hot spring pool, she sprang lightly onto the rim, and tiptoed along the edge, moving toward Tripnee and me.

Coming close and speaking in a low tone audible only to the three of us, Becca said, "What's wrong. I can't just float on by. What's up?"

Tripnee whispered, "Oh Becca, there's trouble. It would've been better to keep your group out of it, but now that you've stopped there's no way to do that. The cartel ran my Prius off the cliff into the river. Now they're stalking us!"

Becca's mouth formed a big O.

I pointed toward where we had just seen the humvee on Old Kern Canyon Road, "We saw them right up there just a minute ago. They've got sniper rifles and shoot to kill."

"Oooohh!" said Becca again softly, drawing the corners of her mouth back in a grimace. After a deep breath, she said in a stage whisper, "OK. I see your point about not stopping. But we're here now," she swallowed and then grinned, "and I'm glad. There's safety in numbers. You're coming with us."

"You sure, Becca?" I asked. "We could endanger your group. The cartel snipers—they're in a black humvee—could be drawing a bead on us right now."

"I sure can't leave you here," said Becca, taking off her visor. Adjusting the Velcro band, she put it on Tripnee. "If you blend into our group, and we all keep moving, I think we'll be okay."

Tripnee and I looked at each other, and found ourselves mutually nodding assent. Then Tripnee stood up, stepped out of the hot mineral pool and hugged Becca, saying softly, "You're the best!"

I clambered to my feet, and was surprised to see that Tripnee was almost a foot taller than Becca. Drawing the three of us together, Tripnee quickly said, "Becca, this is my new very special friend Adam. Adam, Becca."

Slim and almost tiny, yet exuding confidence and athleticism, Becca momentarily took my proffered hand in both of hers, and calmly said, "Good to meet you, Adam."

"The feeling's mutual," I said. "I can already tell that you truly are the best—and that Tripnee probably is always right."

We all chuckled.

Returning to a whisper, audible only to Tripnee and me, Becca said, "By the way, let's keep this between us. These are great people, but groups can behave like herd-animals. Let's not spook'em."

The other boats had gathered in the hot-spring eddy, and Becca announced to the assembled group, "Everyone, this is Tripnee and Adam. They're going to be joining us. Tripnee is a senior river guide and trip leader with Fulfillment Voyages."

There was a welcoming murmur of people saying hi and hello, and I marveled at their obvious warmth and camaraderie. It reminded me of something my old Navy pal Bruce used to say, "In the heat of battle, we're all buddies." Probably the shared risk of rafting melted barriers and inspired this bonding.

Becca jumped lightly down into her waiting raft, unclipped two lifejackets, and passed them up to Tripnee and me. As we buckled and adjusted them, she motioned us to join her. With a big smile lighting up her emerald eyes, she said, "Welcome aboard, you guys!" She handed us both paddles, grabbed one for herself and sat down. "So, Adam. Have you rafted before?"

"Played around with one in the surf a little—which turned out badly—but never on a whitewater river," I replied, remembering with an inward shudder an amphibious night landing on a rocky coastline that killed my best buddy.

"Later I'd like to hear that story, but something tells me you're going to do just fine," she said with a wink. "We normally give newcomers a safety talk, but instead, right now, we're gonna boogie."

"Sounds good," I said, but inside I was in tumult: One part of me screamed, 'For Christ's sake, let's get moving! We could be shot any second!' Another was reliving that terrible night my SEAL team rafted pounding surf onto black, deadly, barnacle-covered rocks. While a third faint voice trembled, *This has to be better than swimming rapids with no lifejacket.*

"Hey, where's Dog?" yelled Becca.

I fought back my inner riot and sense of urgency. I understood from a decade in the military that even in life and death situations, groups move at their own lumbering pace. But it was driving me crazy! As the newly arrived guest, though, I had to respect and adapt to my host group's rhythms.

Waiting there in that enforced lull, some fractional chunk of my mind registered the words painted in bold letters on our boat's bow: "Saying Yes To What Is." Noticing my interest, Tripnee nudged my ankle with her toe, and pointed out the names on the other boats: "Happy to be a Hot Dog," "Mostly Just Air," and "Unfolding Perfectly." Balanced across from me, Tripnee looked very much at home and, to all appearances, completely carefree, her eyes glowing. We exchanged smiles, and for a moment the rest of the world, including my inner cacophony, receded and it was just the two of us.

"Hey, here's Dog!" someone yelled.

A young latino with a bulldog neck, tree-stump of a body and flat, dull expression, jumped nimbly into the stern of our raft. Then, one by one, our four-boat flotilla eased out into the powerful downstream current of the Kern River.

CHAPTER FIVE
THE GAME

Dog directed the crew with a voice that was at times barely audible and at other times loud and quavering. I sat on the right side of the boat near the stern, and matched paddle strokes with the paddlers in front of me. Our young captain's commands of "Left turn," "Forward," and "Stop," though a bit erratic, did a reasonable job of keeping the boat in the main downstream current and away from the numerous low willow limbs extending from both banks.

"So, Adam and Tripnee," said Becca, who sat on the left stern. "We're on the second day of a seven-day river guide school. Everyone here is training to paddle captain by plunging in—sometimes literally—and rotating, a rapid at a time, through the captain's seat."

"Learning by doing," I said, "Sounds good."

"Yes. It can be overwhelming," Becca increased the volume of her voice to be heard throughout the raft, "but this crew, you guys, are all doing great! Hey, everyone, both to introduce ourselves to our new companions and to have some fun, I have an idea. While we float through this long pool, let's go around the raft, say our name and briefly reveal something new, something as yet unknown to the group, about ourselves. Who'll volunteer to go first? Then we'll go clockwise."

I was impressed. Sniper slugs might rip into us at any moment, and we had no way to escape anytime soon. Yet Becca had the presence of mind to act as if everything was normal, and even play a game with the crew. I'd worked with many a leader who could've learned from her.

"I'll start," said Tripnee. "I'm Tripnee. As a teenager I walked around stooped over, partly because I was always curled up with a book, but also because I was trying to be inconspicuous, invisible. Looking back, I realize I was wrestling with a lot of confusion and low self-esteem. Anyway, in college and the years following, I managed to straighten myself up, and claim and enjoy my full height."

"And what glorious height you've got!" Becca beamed up at her friend, who sat directly in front of her.

The blond Tarzan-like young man in front of Tripnee said, "I'm Mark. In high school, I wrestled, got in lots of fights, was sort of a tough kid I guess. But a new side of me is coming out on this guide school. I'm learning to accept and give positive strokes."

The petite Asian woman in the left bow went next: "I'm Toni. Yesterday when this guide school start, I terrified to just climb into raft. But now I have new passion: rafting!" With this she flashed a broad smile around the boat, and then shared a fist bump with Mark, which left them both grinning ear to ear.

Hair stood up on the back of my neck. Sensing sniper scopes following our progress, I studied the tree and boulder strewn canyon slopes above us but saw no sign of the shooters or their humvee. Unable to shake the feeling they were up there watching, too cagey to be seen, I kept an eye peeled for trouble even as I became increasingly intrigued by my boat mates.

The fresh-faced kid with the wild mop of red hair in the right bow, who had turned to face the center of the raft, said, "I'm Reddy. That's short for Redwood. Yes, my parents were hippies. I was going to say only that I was the president of my high school chess club. But now I'm gonna say more: Until a few years ago, I had a debilitating fear of water. Just being here represents a big step for me, but I go in and out of shear terror and I have a long way to go." I noticed that as he spoke, Reddy didn't once take his eyes off Becca. Becca leaned across the boat and gave Reddy's knee a reassuring squeeze.

The young blond woman who sat behind Reddy and in front of me went next: "I'm Ludimila. I gave up my job, my relationship, and my apartment in New York to come to California to pursue my dream of being a river guide. The thing is, right now I'm overwhelmed by how much there is to learn, and I'm wondering if it was a mistake to take this plunge and burn all my bridges."

Forgetting our stalkers for a time and feeling that tremor of excitement that precedes going onstage—even this modest "stage" quickened my pulse—I went next: "I'm Adam. Thanks for your warm welcome! Well, as a kid I was incredibly shy and took refuge in books and long walks— and swims—along the creeks and lakes near where I grew up across the bay from San Francisco. In high school, I started to come out of my shell by playing football, learning kung fu and especially by joining the public speaking club. By the way, I have to say I'm impressed by everyone's openness with one another after just two days together. Reminds me of the closeness I felt with my long-time buddies in the Navy SEALS."

Our sullen-faced student captain then said, "I'm Dog. My dad owns half this valley and I'm gonna inherit." As he spoke, Dog's alert but guarded eyes first scanned the group, and then settled rather fixedly on the striking and shapely Ludimila.

Lastly, it was Becca's turn, and she said, "So, I—Surprise!—am Becca. When I was seven years old, my entire right side was paralyzed for six months. For much of my childhood I was the clumsy, awkward kid—and was painfully self-conscious. But over time I managed to overcome this and danced for six years with the Joffrey Ballet."

At this point there was a pause, and then Reddy exclaimed, "Hey, we've come full circle!"

Becca tousled Reddy's hair. There were some big smiles and high fives all around.

Becca said, "Like Adam, I'm blown away by the bravery and openness! I'm so glad I'm here with you guys right now!"

Toni said, "A big amen to that!" The mood in the boat soared.

Dog said in a surprisingly steady voice, "OK, we're getting close to the next rapid, and I'm captaining, so get ready!"

CHAPTER SIX
LOWER KERN

The long pool grew shallow, the current picked up speed, and our boat slid toward the rapid. Like bumps on a toad, round stones the size of grapefruit covered the river bottom. The sleek shape of a massive trout glided past headed upstream. House-sized granite boulders dotted the banks, and riparian willow, sycamore and alder crowded the gaps in between. The sun, brilliant and reassuring, shimmered on the diamond water. Ahead, a steep cascade appeared as a horizon line across the river. As our raft drew near, first Dog and then I stood up to get a better view.

Standing with my feet spread wide on top of our boat's perimeter tube and my paddle braced against a cross thwart, I peered over the horizon. The river screamed down a long, twisting, plunging runway of huge waves and giant holes, then leapt through a series of enormous standing waves—each evenly spaced, each high and peaking, each with the ferocious flow slowing slightly at its crest then accelerating down its back side. Finally, at the far bottom, I saw the stampeding main current crash, like an ongoing cataclysmic train wreck, in perpetual, white, foamy thunder upon a mid-river boulder!

Moments later, as the boat dipped over the brink, the entire boiling cascade swept into everyone's view. Dog called,

"Right turn!" and at the same time dug in his own paddle to help point the bow straight into the first big hole. In response, Toni, Mark, Tripnee and Becca, on the left side of the boat, paddled forward, while on the right side Reddy, Ludimila, and I back-paddled. Once we were squared up to the enormous back-cresting wave, Dog yelled, "Forward! Forward! Need ya now! Dig! Dig through this hole! Forward!!" In the bow Toni and Reddy threw themselves in unison into big, deep, plunging forward strokes, and behind them the rest of us followed suit matching their frenzied rhythm. Like a blast from a cannon, the raft shot forward and down along a smooth bulging V-tongue straight into the huge hydraulic alive with upwelling mountains of erupting popcorn foam. Exploding spume overwhelmed, stalled and knocked our boat for a loop, inundating the raft, slamming and lifting our bow paddlers. With adrenaline pumping, hearts pounding and paddle blades slashing through the froth searching for purchase, we stroked like demons, all the while struggling to stay braced. And this was just the first hole!

Our craft slogged forward on out of the stopper hole, on into one sticky reversal wave after another. Each slammed, blasted, and pummeled both us and our boat. With just the right balance of calm and urgency in his voice, Dog spurred us on. As the boat twisted this way and that, he called turns to point the bow into the next big wave or hole, and we responded as one. Sucked along in the howling tumult, our boat alternately staggered over the crests and raced down the smooth faces.

In one particularly huge standing wave, our bow plowed through, not over, the crest. Inundated, buried in lather, we all held our breath through the peak, then sucked in big lungfuls of air in the trough beyond, yelling, hooting, gasping. At that instant, two things happened: I looked down along the grain of the current, and dead ahead saw the giant midstream boulder, the train wreck, and realized we were headed straight for it! Also at that moment Ludimila lost her footing and rolled overboard.

Becca yelled above the rapid's roar, "Pull her in!"

I jumped, reached and grabbed Ludimila by the shoulders of her lifejacket, and hauled her into the boat. Because we needed all the power possible, I bounded back into my paddling position and resumed following Dog's commands. Ludimila lay on the raft's inflated floor half curled into a fetal position, trembling, hyperventilating, eyes unfocused and welling with tears.

Becca yelled, "Are you OK?"

Ludimila nodded groggily. With muscles quivering and teeth digging into her lower lip, she slowly clambered up, struggled back into paddling position, braced her feet and resumed matching strokes with the rest of us.

"Way to go Ludimila!" Becca yelled. "You've got grit, girl!!"

At that moment, Dog, who seemed a bit overwhelmed, saw the midstream rock racing toward us. He screamed, "Right turn!!!"

But it was too late! The raft washed broadside onto the boulder!

Just before impact, Becca yelled, "High side! High side!"

Everyone, except me, instantly jumped to the side of the raft nearest the rock. An instant later I realized what 'high side' meant and followed suit. This lightened and lifted the upstream tube—and let the current rush under rather than into the boat. The whole crew sat elbow to elbow and, amazingly, the boat settled on top of the boulder. We bounced around a bit, but seemed pretty stable.

Catching everyone's gaze, Becca yelled above the roar, "Everything is OK, and we're doing great! The river has pushed us up onto the top of this big rock. The current is going around the boulder—and around our boat, not into it. We're hung up, not wrapped. So take some long, slow, full, deep breaths! Look at this fabulous place we're in!" We all breathed deeply and took in our surroundings. As our heart rates slowed, we savored the sudden contrast between the tranquility of the rock and the tumult of the rapid. We marveled at the indigo sky, the verdant woods, and the magic of the foam surrounding us.

Two of the other boats, like bucking broncos, hooting and yelling, leapt and dove down the rapid and flashed past, each narrowly missing the boulder on top of which we perched. The last boat, our sweep boat, eddied out above us.

Becca said, "So Dog, now that our boat is anchored in place, we can take some time to reflect on what just happened—and then come up with a plan."

"First," Becca said, "You're doing great! Your commands are loud and clear, and I like the way you're using your crew—by calling turns—to point the bow into the big waves and holes and—by calling forward—to punch through the big ones. But how could you have avoided hitting this boulder?"

Dog replied, "I could have looked and planned further ahead. I got totally focused on the waves and holes immediately in front of me, and forgot to look near, medium *and far*."

"Wow! Well said!" said Becca, "I do want to acknowledge that your right turn call was the right idea, it just needed to come earlier—and it needed to be followed by a strong forward to get us out of the water hitting the boulder. Still with Ludimila going overboard—and by the way, that was a great rescue Adam and a gutsy recovery Ludimila!—even a veteran guide could have easily done the same thing. It's a very understandable error. Not really an error at all, but a great learning opportunity! For the second day of a white-water school, Dog, you are doing just great! I'm impressed!"

Dog beamed and looked abashed—both at once.

Becca asked, "Now, what do you think we should do to get off this rock?"

Dog said, "The boat is still floating on the surges, and doesn't seem to be stuck all that tight. I think, if we're careful to keep our weight mainly on the high side—the boulder side—of the boat, we might be able to put four people in the bow and have them grab enough current with their paddles to pull us off the rock."

"Dog, are you sure you're not a veteran guide masquer-ading as a novice? That's brilliant!" chortled Becca.

Dog's plan worked like a charm, and we twirled off the boulder and back into the main current. Soon the waves became smaller and finally disappeared altogether. Our boat slowed, we'd arrived. We floated in a deep, emerald pool. Dripping, breathing deep, watching water drain out of the self-bailing floor, I reflected that no one had been lost, the raft was intact—and I had gotten so caught up in the excite-ment that for a time I even forgot about our stalkers.

Our sweep boat came through the rapid bringing up the rear. The other rafts pulled out of eddies, where they had waited in rescue position while we were hung up on the boulder, and resumed their places in the middle of the flotilla. There was an overall feeling of relief and exultation released in chatter and bursts of laughter.

CHAPTER SEVEN
THE REALLY BIG PICTURE

As our raft floated in the calm, Reddy asked, "Hey, Becca. What was it you were saying last night at the campfire about something called the little and big picture?"

"Sure, Reddy," said Becca. "Well, the little picture, in river guiding, concerns one's own personal comfort, health and safety. For example, a guide needs to get enough sleep, avoid sunburn, drink enough water, and stay warm or cool enough."

"And what's the big picture?" asked Dog.

"That," said Becca, "has to do with the overall trip. For a river voyage to move smoothly, guides need to take care of hundreds of details, everything from boat rigging to safety talks, from rescue gear to food and so on."

As Becca talked, droning on a bit, I studied the canyon slopes. Some sixth sense again told me we were being watched, probably through crosshairs.

Toni, in her accented English, asked, "So what about really big picture? You mention last night but not say more."

Becca leaned forward, "A subject dear to my heart. And by a stroke of luck we happen to have with us someone who is famous on the Kern as a shaman of just that very thing." Becca's eyes lit up, "Tripnee, you've been graciously quiet, letting me play the instructor role here. But I—and I know everyone—would love to hear from you."

"But you're doing a fabulous job!" responded Tripnee, "I'm impressed! And enjoying myself! This is your boat, your school…"

"Aw come on, Tripnee!" interrupted Reddy, "You're the shaman!"

Smiling, Tripnee said with a wink, "Well, if you insist, first of all, the really big picture is, well, really big. I'm not sure I should launch into it without a groundswell of interest."

"I'm really interested," said the Tarzan-like Mark.

"Me too!" said Ludimila.

"And me too," said Dog.

"Groundswell! Groundswell!" chanted a grinning Reddy as I cringed from the hokeyness of it all. The entire crew, except me, took up the chant with goofy smiles, "Groundswell! Groundswell! Groundswell!"

For my part, I found the whole thing extremely embarrassing.

"OK then," said Tripnee, chuckling, "The really big picture has two big chunks, two huge things to be aware of simultaneously: On the one hand, we humans are immensely gifted beings living on this beautiful planet. We have so much going for us, and we have so much potential—both within and without—that in some ways we are almost god-like."

Tripnee had everyone's rapt attention—except mine. I rolled my eyes at the thought of a long lecture and half tuned it out. A cold chill gripped my gut, and I couldn't shake the feeling enemy eyes were fixed upon us. How could she talk about the subtleties of river guiding at a time like this? Then it struck me: *What could be better?*

She continued, her words mixing with the rippling current, "So, often, there is something about this planet, this universe, that seems to assist us. When we seek, we find. When we knock, it gets opened unto us. We only have to look around us right now, with this awareness that we share, to know that this world has the potential to be—and in a deep sense basically is—paradise."

I looked around and damned if the faces around me weren't all lit up with something I didn't feel. When I thought about it, though, the very fact that I was finally in the Kern Canyon with these engaging people was, in fact, some kind of miracle.

"Yet, on the other hand," Tripnee's rich, full voice continued, "at the very same time, often, life can seem overwhelmingly difficult. We humans frequently experience so much fear, sadness and pain that all this beauty and vast potential can even seem hollow and empty. Every newspaper, every TV newscast is full of examples of people behaving in unthinkable ways towards one another, doing unimaginably hurtful things."

Now she was starting to make sense.

"Unfortunately, this fear, sadness, and pain is something we all experience. It's part of being human. Each of us wrestles with these things pretty much daily. I see even now—from your eyes that hold so much emotion right now—that each of you knows whereof I speak."

Why did I feel she was speaking especially to me? She swung her fingers in a circle, indicating all of us.

"So, you and I are blessed with almost infinite potential and a planet of wealth and beauty, and at the very same time, we live with so much pain, fear, and sadness that all this beauty and potential can seem meaningless."

As she paused, I again looked around at the entranced faces.

"There it is, the really big picture."

There was silence, only the babble of the river around us.

"Unfortunately, I do not have a solution. But I do have a suggestion." There was a surge of movement as everyone leaned forward pulling me along with them. "I suggest we keep all this in mind as we go forward in our lives. During you guys' time together on your whitewater guide school, in whichever ways feel okay to you, give yourselves and the people you are with acceptance and support; treat each other—and yourselves—with kindness, respect and appreciation; support one another's growth and learning; be both teachers and students to one another; forgive rather than judge; give yourselves and one another the benefit of the doubt; look for the positive, the generous, the beauty, and the depth in yourselves and one another. Then the worst rapids won't look so formidable when you come to them." Tripnee stopped and drew in a deep breath, her face glowing.

Despite my skepticism, I felt that a light switch had been flicked on inside me, bringing into view my darkest corners. I took in the luxuriant, infinitely varied greens of the trees, bushes and ground plants lining the banks; the ever-changing kaleidoscopic patterns on the river's living surface; the blue of the sky; the incredible aliveness of everyone in that boat— and it filled me with appreciation. I thought, *The world's not all bad.*

Too soon! At that moment, I looked back upriver and there it was: The humvee moving slowly along the Old Kern Canyon road. It had been tracking us the whole time. Tripnee followed my gaze, and we exchanged a grim nod.

Becca broke the pregnant silence, "Thank you so much,

Tripnee! Later I'd love to hear everyone's thoughts about all this. Right now, though, we're going to eddy out for a minute, drink some water, rotate captains and get ready to focus on the next rapid, which with good reason is called 'Compound Double Fracture!' By the way, just think about how each of us is a river."

As our boat eased toward the left bank, Tripnee and I nudged each other, confirming agreement that, for the safety of the group, we needed to leave pronto and somehow get out of there on foot.

With a wink I quietly said to Becca, "There are some things we've got to do right now." To the whole crew I said, "Thanks for the ride."

"I really enjoy you guys," Tripnee said to our boat mates. "Thanks. We've got to go now, but hope to see you all again."

We shook hands all around, shared a quick hug with Becca, then jumped onto a broad flat rock, and headed off into the trees.

CHAPTER EIGHT
THE HIKE

Tripnee and I had threaded our way through the woods only a short distance when, as we crossed a small clearing, I heard the thud of bullets hitting the ground around us. My war reflexes kicked in, and I hustled both of us in under a nearby cluster of California junipers.

"That was close," I breathed. "You okay?"

With her eyes dark and beads of sweat dotting her forehead, she nodded, "You?"

"I'm fine. Interesting, the shooters must be using suppressors, which completely hide their location. What's good is they're tracking us, and not the rafters."

Tripnee nodded, taking my hand. "What's not so good, though, is they're tracking us, not the rafters," she grinned. "Just kidding."

"Gallows humor," I said. "My kind of gal."

"Someone who appreciates weird jokes," she said. "My kind of guy."

"I've got an idea."

"I like ideas."

"It's better to be the hunter than the prey, or at least be an unpredictable prey," I said.

"Given the situation," said Tripnee, "I like this guy's ideas."

I noticed that her forehead was now dry and her eyes back to their normal color.

My plan, if you could call it that, was simple and based on ancient military wisdom: When in doubt, take the high ground. We started moving very carefully, slowly making our way up the canyon slope, all the while keeping to the deeper gullies and areas of dense vegetation. In the beginning, I led and Tripnee followed, but later we alternated. At times, in order to stay under cover, we crouched through thickets of manzanita and yucca. We often crawled on hands and knees squeezing along foot by foot beneath buck brush and Scotch broom. In other places, the canopy of California buckeye and juniper and scraggly live oak was high enough for us to stand and walk.

At one point, we made our way through a low forest of phallic statues. Some were 6 inches, some a foot, and a few three and four feet tall. Some were wood, some dried clay, and many concrete. All were unmistakable in their detail, shape and proportions. In the midst of these erect symbols of male potency and fertility, the foundation of an old hut—the hut itself having disappeared long ago—appeared to be a sort of ceremonial area—with well worn paths, altars and stone seating apparently used by the members of some strange cult.

I had read about cultures elsewhere in the world which openly worshipped the male phallus and paraded twenty-foot long erect male penises through the streets on their religious holidays, but I had not heard of any such worship on the Kern.

I said, "Whoever made these sculptures and hangs out here is likely a bit creepy and weird, but probably harmless."

Tripnee just smiled.

Intent on our mission, we kept moving.

Further along, we passed through an area of oddly shaped sycamore and live oak trees the limbs of which bore an uncanny resemblance to female torsos, breasts, hips, arms and legs.

Tripnee said, "Pretty cool. Maybe those phallus worshippers are onto something!"

We crossed the winding two-lane macadam of Old Kern Canyon Road and kept climbing until we reached a point overlooking the whole area. From this vantage point we studied the terrain downriver, upriver and below, but we could not see the gunmen. But what was that glinting down there a little ways below us in that wooded ravine? It was the cartel humvee! We waited to see if anyone showed up, and no one did. Since the best defense is often a surprise offense, we made a plan to play grand theft auto.

We agreed that one of us needed to stay put and act as lookout, while the other did the deed. Tripnee rolled her eyes at the suggestion that she be lookout and I play the thief. We flipped for it. I won.

So Tripnee kept watch, while I, questioning my sanity, climbed down into the ravine, which was crowded with grey pine and juniper, and also manzanita and buck brush. As I approached, a sudden frisson of fear shot up my spine. Some atavistic wedge of my brain stem conjured the image of a sniper at that moment centering the crosshairs of his rifle scope on my chest. Heart pounding, I went forward anyway.

The place felt spooky. Oddly, the wispy crowns and crooked, forking trunks of the grey pine brought to my mind John Muir's reflection that this pine is the only tree you can stand in the shade of and still get a sunburn. I reminded myself this was no time to think about John Muir. "This is real," I thought to myself. "Stay focused. Stay focused."

I had a hunch that even bad guys sometimes lock themselves

out of their vehicles and need a way in. So I checked the likeliest places for a magnetic key box. Rolling under the wide, high vehicle, I ran my hands over the frame and into the nooks and crannies. Not there. I got up and moved along the more protected side of the humvee to check the wheel wells. Not there either. Getting ever more nervous, I checked the front bumper and the wheel wells on the other side. Nothing! Maybe I wasn't so clever after all! Feeling exposed, with my back to the mouth of the gully, I was just starting to run my hands along the inside flanges of the rear bumper when I heard a loud crunch behind me! I turned slowly, half expecting to be looking into a rifle muzzle. A grey pine cone rolled and came to rest. Whew! Taking some deep breaths, I looked around. Good, I was alone. I continued checking the rest of the rear bumper ... and voila! A magnetic key box. In the most obvious place!

I inserted the key into the door lock and turned it, opened the small door, and eased into the driver's seat. Heart racing and adrenaline roaring in my ears, I started the engine, put the tranny in reverse, and eased the big vehicle back along the track. As I passed out of the mouth of the gully, I gunned the motor and threw the wheel to the right, flipping the rear end westward. Simultaneously, I slammed the transmission into drive, spun the steering wheel, and stomped on the gas to send the humvee accelerating eastward upriver.

I raced around several bends, and pulled off into a thicket of live oak. Right on schedule, following our plan beautifully, Tripnee slid down a road cut a few feet away, and jumped into the shotgun seat. I again jammed the beefy tranny into gear, gunned the accelerator and guided the wide super jeep back onto the pavement. Within moments all four massive tires tore at the tarmac of Old Kern Canyon Road as we raced around bend after bend headed upriver—hopefully away from the gunmen.

CHAPTER NINE
DREAM VAN

The sun blazed low in the West as Tripnee and I drove in a huge half circle. We first wove our way eastward along the south side of the canyon past Miracle Hot Springs and Sandy Flat, turned left onto Borel Road, whipped around the ornate edifice of Borel Powerhouse, and then, on the north side of the canyon, headed west on the Hwy 178 four lane back toward where Tripnee had earlier that day been forced off the road and into the river. We were mindful that much of 178 was visible to anyone searching for us on the south side of the canyon, but we figured—and hoped—that the cartel hit men were still miles downstream, so we stopped to pick up the binoculars I had dropped earlier. Stepping to the cliff edge, we looked down the route of Tripnee's long descent.

"Holy bejesus!!" Tripnee exclaimed. "It really is a miracle I survived!"

"Yeah!!" I said. "You were amazing!"

She looked at me with a twinkle in her eye.

An unexpected shiver of delight flowed up my spine. As I walked over and picked up my binoculars, I grinned and managed to say, "It seems like a lifetime ago, but it was just this morning."

Back in the Hummer, we drove on. Tripnee said, "Adam, I feel it's time for me to share something big with you, but it has to stay just between us. OK?"

"Of course," I said. "But wait just a minute while I park."

We were near where I had stashed the Dream Van. I drove off the pavement and eased down a little-used dirt spur road deep into a shady grotto screened from the highway.

As I stopped the motor, Tripnee turned to face me. Then she said, "Strictly between us."

I nodded.

"I'm an undercover FBI agent working with the Forest Service. I'm investigating a cartel run by Mexican and local drug lords."

"All right!" I said. "Somehow I'm not surprised. Tell me about the cartel."

"Well," she narrowed her eyes, "these are very deadly people. And they're using Kern Canyon and Sequoia National Forest not only to grow pot plantations and run powder meth labs, but also as a hub for smuggling heroin and crystal meth. They run their operation with military precision, and think nothing of killing anyone who stands in their way or causes them the slightest trouble."

"So, they blew your cover?" I asked.

"Possibly. But I don't see how. Maybe they sensed I was a problem and decided to arrange an accident. A lot of people around here have been disappearing and turning up dead under very strange circumstances."

I said, "What's clear is you're in danger and you need to call in your FBI team."

"Not me! I've been here for an entire rafting season. I'm this close," she held her right thumb and forefinger an inch apart, "to cracking this case and identifying the cartel king-pins. If my bosses think my cover's been blown, they'll pull me out. And I'm not letting that happen."

"Don't be crazy. We've got to get you out of here."

"For eight years—EIGHT years!—ever since I was recruited at age twenty five, I've been on too goddamned many assignments where they've pulled the plug. Oh, we've got to bring you back in for your own safety," she said with her brows pulled together. "Well, not this fucking time!"

"Rolling up a cartel takes a team," I said. "Let your FBI team take over. You've given it a good shot, but now you've got to think of your own safety."

"Adam, I'm on the verge of bringing it all down. I'm so close I can smell it! I know teams are important. They're part of the DNA of the FBI just as they are of the military." She bared her teeth. "This is a vicious gang killing people and moving tons of meth every fucking day! Despite this, with all the budget cuts and focus on terrorism, I know what'll happen if they pull me out. It'll be years before anyone gets back here, if ever. And I'm not letting that happen. I won't be pulled off this case. I won't hear one more word about running away."

Even though Tripnee's disregard for her own safety irritated me no end, I admired her resolve. In fact, I'd never met anyone with so much fire in the belly. *God*, I thought, *I like this crazy broad*.

"Well," I said, "I'm part of your team."

We sat there regarding each other. It might have been only for a few moments, but the rest of the world receded and there was only us.

Tripnee touched my wrist, "Thanks, Adam. I like that.

But don't you want to get on with your own search for your parents' killers?"

"First of all, these goons, and their whole cartel, tried—and will go on trying—to kill us both. I take that personally, but in particular I take umbrage that they're trying to kill someone I've come to care about," I squeezed her hand. "Besides, things happen for a reason, and something tells me, in the small world of the Kern, there could be a connection between this cartel and my parents' deaths."

After a moment, I asked, "What about the sheriff? Are you absolutely sure we can't call him?"

"This entire canyon has only a single deputy," she said, "and he could be in league with the cartel. But even if he is clean, he'd be no match for those hit men. Sending him after them right now would be his death sentence. Besides, I'm after the kingpins, and don't want to spook them or drive them to ground."

"In that case," I said, "I think our next move is to see if we can trace the ownership of this humvee."

"Good thinking." With the hint of a smile, she asked, "Now why do I sense you're experienced with this sort of thing?"

"You don't miss much." I acknowledged. "I led a very special, little-known criminal investigation unit in the Navy."

"Definitely my kind of guy!" Her eyes sparkled and there went that tongue, moving left and right along that uneven upper lip.

I grinned and, looking around the inside of the humvee, said, "Let's see what we've got here."

As we talked, we went through the humvee's interior, looking for clues to its owner's identity, but didn't find much. There were detailed maps of Sequoia National Forest, some pamphlets written by a Reverend Reamer Rook, several boxes of ammo of various sizes and a book on veganism, but nothing indicating registration or ownership. Even the vehicle identification number on the door frame had been removed, but I crawled underneath and found it on the engine block.

A few minutes later, we headed for my extended-body, pop-top Dream Van. From the outside, my mobile home-away-from-home looked just like any other four-wheel drive van. But inside, concealed by blinds and darkened windows, was a decked out, tricked out mobile palace and state-of-the-art electronic communications center.

As we climbed in, I noticed Tripnee wince when her bandaged arm touched the door frame, and I said, "Are you hurting? Just a minute and I'll get you fixed up."

While I got out the medical kit and laid out supplies to clean and dress her wounds, Tripnee started exploring the van like a kid in a candy store. With just a cursory examination, she figured out and activated the mechanism which lifted the roof, providing seven-foot headroom the full length of the van. After testing the hot and cold water pressure at the sink and in the shower, she grinned. Peeking inside the fully stocked refrigerator, she nodded approval. Settling into one of the commodious captain swivel armchairs up front, she studied the adjacent electronics panel. "Solar power, I like it," she said, commenting on meters which indicated power flowing from solar panels on the roof to a bank of deep cycle batteries mounted under the vehicle. "Satellite phones, I really like that!" And finally she declared, "Ooooo, high-speed mobile internet wifi! I love this Dream Van!"

"Me too," I smiled. "Now, sit still and let me wash and dress those gashes of yours."

As I worked on Tripnee's right leg and left arm, cleaning and closing the wounds with butterfly bandages, I took my time, secretly wanting the process to last as long as possible. The more closely Tripnee's sky-blue eyes followed my movements, the more time I spent performing each little step. Amazingly, she never complained, and simply continued breathing deeply, her magnificent chest rising and falling.

Finally it was her turn to do my right ankle, and her gentleness was angelic. I was actually glad my ankle was raw and bleeding.

As she applied stinging antiseptic, she asked, "How do you happen to have the ultimate vehicle?"

"Well I figured the quest for my folks' killers would take some time. So, after mustering out of the Navy a month ago, I used some of my savings to buy and equip this van. I named it the Dream Van because I always dreamt of having something like this."

As the sting from the antiseptic subsided, I untensed my muscles. "Turns out this van's improved my sleep, my dreams. I still have nightmares—about war and my folks—but now when I wake up in a cold sweat I'm in my own safe place. I can get up, make a bowl of soup and ease down off my nightmare, knowing I don't have to go out on a mission the next day."

Tripnee's eyes were understanding as she nodded. Then she sighed and, putting away the first-aid supplies, said, "I think it's time to track down the owner of that humvee."

Firing up the van's com system, I said, "With this satellite internet hookup and your access to the FBI database, that shouldn't be too hard. While you do that, I'll make dinner. How do grilled ribeye steaks and fresh green beans sound?"

She treated me to one of her crooked smiles. "Fabulous. I'm seeing ever deeper meaning in the name Dream Van."

We both settled into our tasks. After awhile, as Tripnee looked into the laptop screen, she said, "Strange, the FBI computers access every government database. Plus I even tapped into the top secret national mega database, but I'm not coming up with anything for that vehicle number."

"Hmmmm," I said. "If you'll take over on dinner, which's just about ready, I'll see what I can come up with." By logging into my old classified military criminal investigation computer system and drilling into several secret, backup Department of Defense server farms, I found that the humvee had been used in Desert Storm in Iraq, had been shipped to Camp Pendleton and sold at a DOD surplus equipment auction three years before.

I returned to cooking, and Tripnee got back on the computer. I added the finishing touches and served our savory meal on the van's fold-out dining table. She was still using the auction details to cross-check several arcane, backups of backup databases.

"Hmmm," she said, "Says here the purchaser was Reverend Reamer Rook, who reported the vehicle stolen six months ago."

"Come eat," I said, "And who's this Reverend Rook?"

Tripnee said, "Rook owns Indian Rock Resort here on the Kern. Our next step will be to see what he knows about who stole his humvee."

"I like how you say 'our next step,'" I said as I popped open a bottle of Napa Valley Olivia Brion Pinot Noir.

We toasted our meeting, and sliced into our juicy steaks.

Tripnee asked, "What have you been able to learn about your parents' murders?"

"Damned little." I said. "The newspaper and sheriff's reports at that time were sketchy. Come to think of it, almost suspiciously so. And like I said, my uncle refused to talk about it."

I asked, "What do you know about Reverend Reamer Rook and his resort?"

Tripnee cut into her steak. "As far as I know, Indian Rock Resort is a thriving destination casino. People flock to it from Los Angeles and all over the country. Mostly rich, sometimes famous and at times notorious high rollers, as Rook calls them. In fact, most of the private jets flying into Kern Valley Airport are his clients."

I asked, "How is it that he's so successful?"

"I've met Rook a number of times when guiding his clients on rafting trips on the Kern. He's charismatic and shrewd, but strange. Except for drivers and security people, he staffs his resort entirely with tall women with big boobs who bend themselves into pretzels to achieve the goals he sets. I must say, though, that they do a great job and seem to keep the place fully booked." She held her glass out for a refill. "It also helps that the resort sits in the middle of Sequoia National Forest with some of the world's best white-water rafting, fishing, mountain biking, windsurfing, kite boarding, water skiing, birding, hiking, rock climbing," she paused for a breath, "you name it."

Intrigued, I said, "Not living here, I'm out of touch, but I've been researching the Kern for years, and it's odd that I haven't heard anything about Indian Rock Resort."

"You're not alone. Most of the people living right here haven't heard of it either. In the name of exclusivity, Rook maintains a veil of secrecy around his establishment, especially vis-a-vis the locals," replied Tripnee. "In fact, his only local business dealings seem to be with Fulfillment Voyages."

I gnawed the ribeye and sipped more Pinot, letting all this sink in. "How is it that he runs a casino, with gambling illegal in California?"

"Well, Rook is part Tubatulabal Indian. Sounds weird, I know, but that's the tribe native to the Kern," said Tripnee. "He managed years ago to get an Indian casino license in part based on his ancestry, but also probably by donating to the political campaigns of the right people. And, as I understand it, by promising to preserve Indian heritage sites. Rook's five-thousand-acre spread encompasses a slew of significant archeological locations including an entire cliff of Indian petroglyphs on the river."

"Ya' know," I observed, "A gambling casino would be the ideal way to launder drug money."

"Yeah," replied Tripnee. "I thought of that. I started out very suspicious of the guy, but for all my digging I haven't found any proof he's done anything illegal. The guy's a charmer and kind of grows on you. In addition to everything else, he's a very articulate preacher with a big following. Of course, you never know about his associates and employees."

With all this in mind, we made a plan about how much to reveal to Rook.

Outside it was growing dark and the day's heat began to dissipate. We cleaned up dinner and savored the last of the wine, which had to be among the best I'd ever tasted. Sharing the confined, womb-like interior of the Dream Van with this amazing woman was something else. Her long, lithe, muscular legs, tanned to perfection, sent me into emotional somersaults. Those lips, those cerulean eyes, her overall poise, and the supple curves of her neck, all set my senses on fire.

Standing side by side, facing the sink, we washed our dishes with hips touching. As she dried and put away the last plate, I brushed my lips against the back of her neck, and hugged her from behind. Enveloping her in my arms, luxuriating in her full length against me, I nuzzled her hair, kissed her head, and breathed in the smell of her. She turned toward me, wrapped her arms around my neck, and we kissed.

Crash, smash, kerplunk! The van rocked and reverberated from the impact of something big. Grabbing my two-foot-long metal flashlight and Glock pistol, I dashed outside to find that a tree limb, maybe sixteen feet long and six-inches in diameter, had dropped from a towering Grey pine. Climbing the rear ladder to the van roof, I heaved the branch to the ground and was glad to see that, except for a few small dents, the van was unharmed.

Relieved, I called down to Tripnee, "Nothing to worry about. Just a tree limb with bad timing."

When I went back inside, Tripnee said, "Ya' know, maybe that tree's timing is good. We're just getting to know each other, and I don't want to rush things."

"You're right, of course," I said, concealing my disappointment.

"I want you to know, though, that I really like where we seem to be going," she said. "But taking our time is best."

This perked me up a bit. In fact, it infused me with joy.

"Well, we need to get some rest," I said. "We're going to have a busy day tomorrow. You can have the bed and I'll sleep in this reclining chair."

I got out two sleeping bags, and we settled in for the night. At first, lying there, my imagination undulated with images of what might have happened had it not been for the intervention of that damned tree limb.

Then a storm of warnings whirled within me: Beware of

caring, they thundered, as I realized I could really like this girl. Don't start anything. Everyone always leaves. My folks, my best buddies all died. Gone. This gorgeous FBI agent, one way or another, would disappear as well. The world is a lonely place. Stay in touch with this fact, this reality. Forget this at your peril! Everything a man loves gets taken away. Everything!

CHAPTER TEN
TOWN OF LAKE ISABELLA

After coffee and a hearty breakfast of eggs over medium, sourdough toast and sliced grapefruit, we headed for Reamer Rook's Indian Rock Resort, which sprawled along the Lower Kern River in an area known as Keyesville. I drove the humvee, and Tripnee followed in the Dream Van, which, acting on my survival instincts, we left hidden, before driving the last few miles together.

Tripnee looked terrific in her red shorts and one of my t-shirts, but she insisted on swinging by her house in the town of Lake Isabella to upgrade her outfit for our appearance at the resort. I was glad I had put on clean khakis and a fresh shirt that morning. Our route took us along the four-lane main drag of Lake Isabella, past a busy lumber yard where building materials were being piled into pickup trucks, a spirited little-league game in a spacious park with a vintage World War II army tank out front, and a vast strip-mall parking lot where already a steady river of shopping carts carried goods out of shop doors to a sea of waiting cars. Near the Shady Lane Saloon I turned the humvee off the main drag and we rattled and jolted up a parallel dirt side street.

I parked in front of Tripnee's cottage, which was in between the Fulfillment Voyages guide house and the KRV

Recycling Center. While Tripnee was inside changing, I got out and leaned against the humvee, taking in the scene.

The yard in front of the modest, low-slung guide house was swarming with fit, upbeat spirits preparing for their day's adventures, which I gathered from bits of overheard conversations and from the gear being loaded, included everything from rafting, kayaking, mountain biking and kite boarding to fishing, bouldering, tai chi chih, and, for one buffed young man, just reading by the river.

The nearby recycling center, a lot crammed with shipping containers and mountains of plastic bottles and aluminum cans, was populated by people who clearly were of a different sort: homeless men and women probably wrestling with a variety of addictions, for whom life was a struggle. It struck me that both groups were probably truly of the earth and richly blessed with dreams and souls, the one soaring and transcendent, the other living down in the dust, with many slowly being crushed.

As I leaned on the humvee waiting for Tripnee, one of the homeless guys, a man with alert blue eyes and a push-broom mustache, stepped toward me and said, "Shit man, this is Mack's humvee! What's Mack doing?"

"Probably wondering where this humvee is right now," I said, "Because I stole it from him."

"No shit! Way to go!"

"You a friend of his?" I asked.

After glancing around to see if anyone was nearby, the mustachioed man stepped closer and said in a hushed tone, "That mean son of a bitch? Hell no!"

"In that case, I'm glad to meet you. I'm Adam," I said.

"Hi, they call me Brushy, 'cause of the mustache," he said, shaking my proffered hand.

"So, Brushy, what do you know about Mack?"

"Just that he's one dangerous bastard. He comes by here sometimes looking for people to do jobs for him."

"What sort of jobs?" I asked.

"Jobs where you don't ask no questions," said Brushy. "The trouble is the people who work for him don't come back."

"That figures," I said. "Know where I can find him?"

"Don't. He just shows up here sometimes," said Brushy. "Last time was maybe two weeks ago. Oh god, Bud! My best friend Bud Birdsong! Nicest guy you could ever meet. Sure he drinks too much and has a habit of wandering off. But he got into this here same humvee with Mack, and no one ain't seen him since!"

"Brushy, this is important: How long has Mack been driving this humvee? Longer than six months?"

"Six months ago, man, I was recycling cans in LA."

At that moment Tripnee emerged from her house looking drop dead gorgeous in designer black skinny jeans and a green top.

"Wow! Look at you, Tripnee!" whistled Brushy.

"Hi Brushy. How are you?" asked Tripnee.

"Not so good. Bud Birdsong ain't been seen since he got into this humvee with Mack," he said. "Tripnee, you got to be super careful. Mack finds out you've been in his humvee… I'm worried 'bout you."

"Thanks, Brushy. We'll be careful. Sorry about Bud. He may be on a drunk and hopefully will turn up," said Tripnee as she opened the humvee passenger door.

"Whatever happens, don't you tell Mack you been talkin' to me," pleaded Brushy, "Or I'll be next to disappear."

"Don't worry," said Tripnee, as she climbed into the vehicle. "Mum's the word."

"A piece of advice," I said to Brushy while getting in beside her, "When Mack offers you a job, don't take it."

Brushy saluted with blackened fingers, gave a little bow and turned back toward the recycling yard.

I started up the Hummer and headed for the resort. As we rolled up Hwy 155 towards where it crossed over Hwy 178, I was struck by an open meadow between 178 and the town of Lake Isabella.

Noticing my gaze, Tripnee said, "That's called Hot Spring Valley." Then she pointed a mile to the north, "Lake seepage under Auxiliary Dam up there, combined with natural hot spring activity, keeps the water table right at ground level all through here. That combined with an active earthquake fault has made this place rather notorious."

Wind rippled through the valley's reeds and green grasses like a great hand caressing an animal's fur.

CHAPTER ELEVEN
INDIAN ROCK RESORT

We continued north on Hwy 155, rumbling over a low ridge, crossing the river at the base of lake Isabella's Main Dam, and making a left onto Keyesville Road. Soon we turned onto a paved private road, and passed under a massive arch built of mortar and granite boulders that marked the resort's entryway. Security guards at the gate recognized Tripnee and waved us in. The manicured, mile-long entrance driveway, ubiquitous security cameras, seemingly endless gleaming white fencing, immaculately landscaped grounds, private lake, rolling green lawns, and colossal, beautifully-maintained hunting-lodge-style architecture throughout reeked of luxury and limitless money. To all appearances, Rook had managed to create a super-high-end destination resort which I thought very likely catered to both the savory and unsavory entertainment, political and business elite not only of nearby Los Angeles but perhaps also of North America and the world.

As we drove, threading our way between house-sized boulders and small rolling hills, I glimpsed a man. He wore thick black shoes. Holy bejesus! I recognized him! He was one of the guys in the humvee the day before. I turned to Tripnee and nudged her arm. "Look there's one of them!" But when I looked back the man had disappeared—essentially vanishing into thin air.

Tripnee said, "You're seeing things."

The resort was a compact city of private bungalows the size of small mansions, each artfully situated to both blend with and provide magnificent views of the rugged landscape. The main parking area overflowed with a blinding display of gas guzzling bling which both fascinated and repelled me. Among the Rolls', Bentleys, Mercedes and stretch limos, I spotted DeLoreans, Lamborghinis, and a Tesla.

We rolled right up to the main casino—which was, I had to admit, surprisingly tasteful—and reminiscent of the Ahwahnee Hotel in Yosemite Valley—but bigger. Tripnee led the way straight toward Rook's private offices and inner sanctum. Her charm got us past his personal receptionist, a six-foot blonde bombshell in a skimpy, shimmering outfit, and we barged into his executive suite.

Seemingly surprised at first, Rook quickly recovered and broke into a huge smile. Six-foot-six, slim and fit, with an almost perfectly round bald head, he came forward and warmly took her extended hand in both of his. "Tripnee my dear! It's great to see you. How are you, darlin'?"

"Good, Reamer," she said, smiling. "I'd like you to meet my friend Adam Weldon. Adam, this is Reverend Reamer Rook."

Another brief look of surprise quickly morphed into a broad smile, and Rook took my hand in both of his, stared me directly in the eyes and said in a low, mellow voice, "It's a genuine pleasure to meet you Adam Weldon."

Spreading his arms wide, he said, "Welcome to Indian Rock. If I know you, Tripnee, you're on a mission of one kind or another. How can I help you?"

"Thanks, Reamer," said Tripnee. "I'll go right to the heart of the matter: Six months ago you reported the theft of your black humvee. Do you have any idea who might have stolen it?"

"I'm afraid I don't," said Rook. "One day someone somehow broke into it and drove it away. My security staff reported the theft, did some investigating, but came up empty."

I asked, "Did your security cameras show anything?"

"You'd think our fancy surveillance system would show something," replied Rook, "But it didn't help at all. The humvee was stolen off a back, unlit parking area, and even careful study of the footage revealed zilch. But what's your interest in this?"

I could see the wheels turning in Tripnee's mind, reconfirming our plan regarding how much to reveal to Rook.

"Yesterday," she said, "Two men driving your stolen Hummer tried to kill me by forcing my Prius off a cliff into the river. It's a miracle I survived. Adam saw the whole thing. Now they're trying to kill both of us." Tripnee went on to describe how we'd stolen the humvee and traced it to him. "So, the good part is your humvee is back and parked out front."

"That's incredible, Tripnee!" exclaimed Rook. "How many people know about this?"

"Right now, just us," said Tripnee.

"Mr. Rook…" I began.

"Reamer," Rook cut in. "Any friend of Tripnee's is a friend of mine. Especially under these circumstances. Please call me Reamer."

"OK. Reamer," I said. "Well, I was going to say, I commanded a criminal investigation unit in the military. With the sheriff's department apparently stretched thin around here, we decided to do what we could on our own to track down these guys. After all, it's us they're trying to kill."

"Makes sense," Reamer responded. "I admire your gumption. Thanks for bringing back my favorite toy. How can I help with all this?" Turning to Tripnee, he said, "Darlin', do you need a vehicle to replace your Prius?"

"That's generous of you, Reamer. But no, I'm fine," said Tripnee.

"Well, just let me know what you need. Anything at all," Reamer said opening his arms wide.

I said, "So, Reamer. The fact that the stolen vehicle was driven past all those security cameras without any of them recording the driver's face suggests to me a well planned, inside job. Have you taken a hard look at this probability?"

"You're sharp, Adam," said Rook. "I like that."

I continued, "Something you should know: The two men who tried to kill us go by the names Mack Dowel and Hektor Torrente. I might have seen one of them on your property when we were driving in here a little while ago. I could be wrong, but I could swear I glimpsed him. I looked away for a moment, and when I looked back he was gone."

"This is serious, Adam. I'm very glad you told me. Those names don't ring a bell, but I'll launch a thorough investigation," said Reamer.

"Thanks," I said. "I must admit I'm curious about something else. Not many casino owners are reverends."

"I like your curiosity, son," smiled Reamer. "Of course, I need to maintain a certain separation between the resort and my church. But my sermons are not to be missed. You both should come, or at least listen in on the radio."

"You surprise me," I said. "A radio preacher!"

Beaming, he said, "I get right down to serious issues. As a long-time observer of our society, I am very concerned about a deterioration of the core fabric, the fundamental values of our country."

"For example?" I asked.

"Well, for example," said Reamer, "No one wants to take responsibility for themselves. Spill a cup of coffee on yourself in today's world and you sue and win a huge settlement. Defend yourself from a burglar in your own home and the burglar can sue you for assault."

Just as Reamer was warming up to a full rant, Tripnee and I rolled our eyes at one another and knew it was time to hit the road.

Tripnee interjected, "I'm afraid, Reamer, that we have a very busy day ahead, and we need to get on with it."

"Under the circumstances, you at least have to let me arrange a ride for you," said Reamer. "I'll have a limo pick you up out front and take you wherever you want to go."

"You really don't need to do ..." Tripnee began.

"I won't hear another word about it, darlin'," stated Reamer, "It's done."

Then to me he said, "Take care of this terrific gal." And then to both of us, "If there's anything you need, just let me know. Protection, anything."

We said our thanks and good byes. Then Tripnee and I walked out to the resort's grand main lobby, where we waited for Reamer's car and driver. Soft live piano music floated in the air. The voluptuous resort concierge cum spiritual counselor was locked in conversation with a guest—a minor celebrity of some sort who was herself a statuesque beauty—planning out a personal agenda for her stay that included spa treatments, yoga, private VIP invitational gambling sessions and a rafting trip.

In this opulent setting, Tripnee, jewel that she was, to me radiated not only glamour but also an integrity and generosity of spirit not much in evidence in the casino clientele.

As we soaked in the feel of the place, I felt an urge for caution. Looking out through floor to ceiling windows past a steady flow of casually elegant men and women, we saw the limo wheel up and the driver step out. An alarm went off in my mind when I saw that he wore thick black shoes.

With a hand squeeze, quick look and gesture, I signaled Tripnee the need for an immediate change of plan. To conceal my suspicions from Rook and for the sake of appearances, I asked the curvaceous concierge to extend our thanks to Rook and the driver—and to please tell them that we had made other arrangements for transportation. We then faded away deep into the crowded casino, and left by a side door.

CHAPTER TWELVE

PETROGLYPHS

Tripnee knew of a little-used path that led down to the prehistoric petroglyphs by the river. As we hurried past the spectacular ochre drawings on weathered granite protected under an overhanging cliff, I was gripped simultaneously by an uncanny sense of deja vu, a deep appreciation for the artistry on display and nostalgia for a vanished way of life.

Probably sensing my interest, and perhaps unable to resist playing tour guide, Tripnee, still keeping up the fast pace, said, "Ya' know, before the arrival of Europeans, the Tubatulabal Indians enjoyed a life of remarkable abundance and leisure. They were able to take care of all their survival needs in about two hours of hunting and gathering a day."

"What a contrast to the long hours most people work now," I said. "What did they do with all that free time?"

"Mostly played games, told stories, chanted in sweat lodges and did cliff art like you see here."

"I like it," I said as we dashed down to a little beach.

Stopping at water's edge, Tripnee unfolded a big ziplock plastic bag from her tiny fashion-statement purse. Shedding our outer clothes, I stripped down to my shorts and Chaco buckle-on sandals, and she peeled down to a mind-boggling black bikini and Jesus sandals. Then she sealed our stylish clothes in the waterproof bag.

We eased into the sensual current, this time to swim down a mild stretch of the Kern—a section with no rapids—which would take us back to the Dream Van. I checked again and again to see if anyone was following us, but saw no one. Despite my visceral fear that we were in danger, I couldn't help but savor gliding along in earth's bloodstream with this woman. The flow bent around a submerged boulder. Extending my arms, I cupped my hands in a swift jet of current, and enjoyed the pressure and strength of it. Together we drifted as though in a flying dream.

While we floated side by side through an especially long calm overhung with willows, I mused, "Reverend Reamer Rook is an impressive, very smooth guy, but something tells me he can be utterly ruthless, especially with anyone standing between him and something he wants."

"Just because a man is polished, charming and rich, doesn't have to mean he's hiding something," responded Tripnee. "If Reamer's a bad guy, he conceals it very, very well."

"You think I overreacted to the black shoes, then?" I asked.

Smiling and prodding my bicep repeatedly to punctuate her words, Tripnee said, "Let's put it this way: If we had taken the limo, we would have missed so much. I'm always impressed seeing the petroglyphs up close. And I'm loving this swim. I was hoping we'd come this way. Why do you think I brought the big ziplock?"

"I like the poking," I said as I thought to myself: *I really do like the poking!* Yet I couldn't shake the feeling there was something not right about Rook.

At one point we floated very close to a mountain lion

crouching to drink from a quiet pool in the shade of an over-hanging willow. Tripnee and the majestic beast shared a long, lingering glance, and some sort of mutual admiration seemed to pass between them—until, at last, the cat disappeared into the woods in a blur of smooth motion.

CHAPTER THIRTEEN
LAKE ISABELLA

Back in the Dream Van, as we again headed up Hwy 178 toward Lake Isabella, Tripnee said, "Ya' know, I think we can catch one of Rook's radio talks. Wanna hear it?"

"Sure," I said. "Might give us some insights into the guy."

"Exactly," she said. "But let's turn it off if it gets preachy or unbearable."

"Definitely."

Tripnee touched a few buttons on the dash. "Most of these talks must be pre-recorded. I think we're just going to catch the end of this one."

The mellifluous voice of Reamer Rook poured out of the van's Bose speakers: "'I believe in aristocracy ... Not an aristocracy of power, based upon rank and influence, but an aristocracy of the sensitive, the considerate and the plucky. Its members are to be found in all nations and classes, and all through the ages, and there is a secret understanding between them when they meet.'"

"I love this E.M. Forster quote," I said. "I'm impressed that Reamer is using it."

Tripnee smiled and nodded.

"They represent the true human tradition," Reamer's

voice continued, "'the one permanent victory of our queer race over cruelty and chaos. Thousands of them perish in obscurity, a few are great names. They are sensitive for others as well as for themselves, they are considerate without being fussy, and their pluck is not swankiness but the power to endure, and they can take a joke.' That, my friends, is a quote from E. M. Forster's 'Two Cheers for Democracy'."

I turned off 178, and then left on Hwy 155.

"Before criticizing or judging someone," the radio continued, "walk a mile in their moccasins. That way, you'll be a mile away and you'll have their moccasins."

Tripnee and I laughed.

"All joking aside, my friends, I ask you to practice kindness and look for the good in others."

Having passed over a low ridge, I peeled off 155 onto a spur road to the right, and headed up a parched slope toward Lake Isabella.

"Reach out to people, especially to people not like you—get to know folks, as we say, from different tribes. Learn to work with diverse people, collaborate with them. Do this and there is nothing you can not accomplish. Do this and you will not only build literal bridges and achieve lofty goals benefiting many—but what is more important, you will build bridges between people."

Just as the sermon ended, we crested the hill and the wide brilliant expanse of Lake Isabella came into view.

Tripnee turned off the radio and asked, "So, what do you think?"

"The guy's at the extreme high end of polished and persuasive," I said. I had to admit, there was nothing to object to, and I felt a bit won over. Even as I weighed these thoughts, my old star-shaped scar began to burn.

I could see rough, four-wheel-drive roads ringing the lake, snaking everywhere down to water's edge. Moving the Dream Van forward with an easy, rolling lurch, we followed a rutted dirt track out along a peninsula of low hills jutting into the lake between Main and Auxiliary Dams. According to Tripnee this cape is called Engineers Point, no doubt to commemorate the geniuses who built the adjacent earth-filled dam smack dab on top of an active earthquake fault.

I brought the van to rest on a small, level, decomposed-granite plateau. We grabbed some sandwiches, a thermos of piping hot goji berry green tea and binoculars, and, with the mounting excitement of little kids, climbed a nearby hill to take in the view. A foxhole-like indentation at the crest of the hill provided a comfortable backrest for the two of us, shelter from the wind and a sweeping 360-degree view of the surrounding lake and mountain panorama.

Lake Isabella's shimmering waters form the shape of a vast rough-hewn pair of pants. Both legs extend about six miles, the skinnier one running south to north, the stouter west to east. Engineers Point occupies the position of the zipper. Encircling the lake is a steep, boulder-strewn ring of saw-toothed mountains painted in muted earth tone tans, greens, grays, and yellows. Surrounding this inner ring is a seeming infinity of ever more distant jagged mountain peaks arranged in an apparently endless succession of concentric circles, each slightly paler than the one before.

Not far away a regatta of windsurfers glided over the lake's azure surface. Elsewhere kite boarders accelerated and jumped, power boats swung water skiers and wake boarders in wide arcs, and sit-on-top kayakers out for vigorous work-outs sent V wakes fanning out behind. Peppering the shore-line were parked cars and RVs, with their owners relaxing nearby in lounge chairs at water's edge reeling in fish and drinking beer. Overhead an incandescent blue sky lit up the entire scene like center stage in a Broadway musical. Not twenty feet away, a dozen canny jet-black ravens strutted to and fro on a shoulder of the hill eyeballing our sandwiches, their heads working forward and back in time with their steps.

As we talked and ate, I scanned our surroundings and noted with satisfaction that our hilltop afforded an excellent vantage point to observe anyone approaching from any direction. It also crossed my mind—sending a shiver up my spine—that our two noggins, visible above the rim of our comfy hollow, might be ideal targets for a trained sniper.

While using the binoculars to study something far across the lake in the direction of the Kern Valley Airport, Tripnee told me more about the drug cartel operating in the Kern River Canyon. Evidently, after big pot harvests, rather than pay their workers, the cartel often killed the poor Mexican campesino farmers they had brought in to plant and guard the pot plantations scattered through the forest. Also, although she had not yet been able to prove it, Tripnee said she suspected the cartel was using out-of-the way, off-the-radar Kern Valley Airport as a major distribution hub not only for locally produced drugs, but also for heroin and super-lethal crystal meth flown in from Mexico.

Suddenly, Tripnee exclaimed, "Heads up! My god! That plane! It's going down in the lake!"

I looked out over the broad, flat expanse of water in time to see an out-of-control aircraft cartwheel twice, then slam into the surface. "Whoa!" I blurted. "Look at that impact! That's one heavy plane!"

"The lake's shallow over there," said Tripnee, "Less than 15 feet. We gotta help."

"No boats, but voila," I said pointing to two nearby kite boarders who were just then sliding onto a beach directly below us. "You know how? I did it long ago."

"Sure thing. I know those guys!" said Tripnee. "Let's do some borrowing."

"Gonna be interesting!" I said.

I chased Tripnee down the hill, pausing for a moment to lock the binoculars in the van. When I reached the water, Tripnee had already talked with the boarders.

We quickly buckled on their quick-release waist harnesses, and were handed the control bars for the two big bow kites, which hovered aloft, forming blue and red 30-foot arcs against the sky. We hooked up our harnesses, jammed our feet into the stirrups of the oversize water skis, pulled back on our control bars to increase power, and rose up on our boards gaining planing speed. Within about four minutes, we were off and away.

It had been years since I held a four-string kite control bar, and I reviewed the basics in my mind: Push forward to reduce power. Do the opposite to increase power, but don't pull back too far or you flip the kite. Except when changing direction, keep the kite between one and three o'clock.

"Cool!" Tripnee crowed. "This keeps us undercover. That could be a drug plane."

"Yeah," I yelled back. "We're just curious kite boarders."

"If it is a drug plane, the cartel could show up any time, so we need to be fast," she called.

"This 15-knot wind guarantees that!" I yelled. "We'll fly!"

Because we were at the upwind end of the lake, the waves were small and the wind was behind us. Tripnee skimmed over the blue water smooth and fast, her board carving an unwavering, arrow-straight line directly toward the crash site. I wobbled and careened for at least the first mile, very nearly collided with a water skier in a dental-floss bikini, missing her by just a few feet, then my muscle memory returned, my wake straightened, and Tripnee and I glided and jumped along in parallel.

Both to look like ordinary adrenaline-junkie kite boarders and for the sheer fun of it, we started rotating our kites high to extend and heighten our jumps. Soon we were outdoing one another with jumps thirty and forty feet above the water and a hundred feet long. On one of the stronger wind gusts we flew through the air as one, soaring together, feeling the exhilaration, the pure rush of flight, for what had to be over a hundred and fifty feet! For a long moment I even forgot why we were there, and got completely caught up in the thrill.

Around the downed plane, amid much yelling and hubbub, milled a flash crowd of jet skiers, windsurfers, fishing boats, sailboats and boatloads of water skiers, all of whom must have witnessed the crash. Even though the airplane was clearly visible about five feet below the lake's surface, no one seemed to be diving to check for survivors. As we skimmed into their midst, dropped our kites and settled into the water right over the plane, I yelled, "Is anyone alive?"

A bevy of young women peering down at the plane over the side of a big glossy ski boat yelled back, "Don't think so." "Can't see anyone." "Oh my god!"

An old bearded hippie, apparently the ski boat captain, shouted, "Did you see that splash, man? What a crash! We called 911."

"Good," I called back.

In the center of that motley flotilla of curiosity seekers, while Tripnee dove, I stood chest deep with my feet on the slippery underwater fuselage, holding our kites and boards in the building wind. After she had been under for over three minutes, I grew concerned. When she finally surfaced, I felt tremendous relief.

Sucking in big breaths, she said, "Looks like there was just the pilot. He's still buckled in. Died on impact." And lowering her voice to make sure only I could hear, she continued, "This little Learjet is heavily—way too heavily—loaded—with drugs."

We traded roles and Tripnee took up a position chin deep on the downed aircraft gripping our kite boarding gear, preventing it from being driven away in the waves and wind. Diving down, I saw from the markings the plane was a five-passenger Learjet 35A. The tail and both wings were mangled and partially missing. The nose was smashed and the entire plane body tweaked, buckled and massively stove in. Peering through the hole which once held the windshield, I saw the pilot's crushed head oozing tendrils of still-quivering brain spaghetti. At the sight, I flashed back into my own nightmares, unspeakable Afghanistan memories. I was lost, as I had been so many times before, then somehow shook myself and came back. Swimming around and pulling myself in through the door, which Tripnee must have somehow pried open, I saw bread-loaf-sized plastic bags filling the small cabin from floor to ceiling. Hefting one of the bags, even underwater I could feel its dense weight. No wonder the jet crashed.

The moment I surfaced, gasping for air, I heard Tripnee yelling, "Quick! We've got to get out of here!"

I looked up. Sure enough, heading toward us was a houseboat with two familiar flat-topped figures visible on its bridge. The boxy craft was several hundred yards away, but its frothy bow wave showed it was coming fast.

Tripnee had already gotten our kite lines extended, and the kites airborne—how she managed to do this without tangling the lines—with two kites at once and with so many craft milling about—I have no idea.

The surrounding flotilla gave us some cover, but there was not a moment to spare. Tripnee slid my board toward me and handed over my control bar. I jammed my feet into the board's stirrups, seized the bar, powered up my kite, and initiated a water start.

I was just achieving planing speed when the awning of a crowded pontoon boat in full party mode popped out of nowhere, cut across my path and caught my lines. Oh nooo! Oblivious to the crashed plane and atmosphere of disaster around them, the revelers, with loudspeakers blaring rhythmic Indian sitar and tabla music, swept across from right to left twenty feet in front of me, dragging my lines further and further off course. My big wing flailed wildly in the wind. I was pulled to the left, and started to settle into the water—where I soon would be a sitting duck no doubt deader than a doornail.

Suddenly, like the great god Vishnu, a tall muscular olive-skinned man wearing a Hindu turban and tiny Speedo swim trunks grabbed my kite lines, pulled them around and above the party barge awning—and then released them—allowing them to spring high into the sky. My wing dropped for a moment then rapidly gained altitude. I stopped sinking, planed back to the surface on my ski, and rolled right to shoot off around behind the pontoon boat. Whew! That was close.

Looking around, I saw Tripnee just twenty feet away, slicing a wake as straight as a laser beam. We were just beginning to put distance between us and the chaotic regatta circling the plane body. Hopefully the milling boats were providing some cover.

I yelled to Tripnee, "I think we're OK. I don't think they know it's us."

Looking back over her shoulder, Tripnee yelled, "Like hell they don't!"

Glancing to the rear, I saw the houseboat turning toward us, giving chase! The wind, thank the universe, had been building and was blasting at a good 25 knots. Because our boards were fastest traversing the gale, which howled out of the west, we raced across toward Kernville and the mouth of the Upper Kern River at the north end of the lake. Leaping and gliding, at times jumping wildly 100 and more feet through the air, we seemed to be leaving the cartel houseboat in the distance. I thought, *We've got this wired! After all, what houseboat could catch a kite board?!*

But when I looked back, my jaw dropped. The cartel tug was closing the distance between us! Oh no! They must have some kind of Mad Max souped-up engine which thrust their shoe-box of a boat forward like a mammoth high-tech hydroplane. Now that we were away from other boats and they were getting close, they got out rifles and began shooting.

Desperate, we zigged, zagged and jumped, and redoubled our efforts to lay on speed. But it was a losing battle. Their super-powered houseboat drew closer and closer, and their bullets—which I noticed were shot with silencers—came ever nearer to the mark. One grazed my left arm, drawing blood! And another hit my control bar, snapping it in two, sending my kite into wild gyrations. Thinking it was the last thing I'd ever do, I gripped the two halves of the bar, and struggled to keep my kite powered up and pulling me forward. My heart sank when I looked back and saw the grim faces of the cartel men, now in sharp detail. I looked at Tripnee. What an amazing soul she was. And I felt a huge sadness.

Tripnee looked at me then with a giant smile. Surprised and puzzled, I saw that she was pointing excitedly ahead. I looked where she indicated and understood! We were racing toward the mouth of the North Fork of the Kern, toward a shallow rapid we could jump over—but that would block the houseboat! Making the 100-foot leap with a broken control bar took concentration, but somehow I made it. Looking south I saw the houseboat already having to slow to avoid running aground. They continued to pump off shot after shot, but we skimmed on up the Upper Kern toward the center of Kernville, soon rounded a bend, and were out of range.

CHAPTER FOURTEEN

KERNVILLE

Entering Kernville, carving and jumping along on our kite boards, Tripnee and I came to a riverside park of lush green grass and luxuriant shade trees. It seemed we had arrived at the tourist hub of the valley. The place overflowed with people picnicking, strolling, fishing, playing all manner of games and taking out rafts, kayaks and river craft of every description. Tripnee landed on the beach opposite the park, and I slid in beside her, somehow managing to drop my kite and step ashore without doing a face plant.

Looking at me, Tripnee exclaimed, "You're covered with blood!"

Realizing blood was splattered over my entire left side, but feeling OK, I said, "It's just a nick. Looks worse than it is."

I waded out, dove into the river, then popped up and waded back. The blood was gone, except for a fresh seeping from a shallow groove in my left triceps that stung like crazy. Tripnee insisted on bandaging my arm with her handkerchief.

"Not tearing up our clothes for bandages takes all the fun out of getting wounded," I quipped.

We gathered up our boards and kites and walked back through a spacious campground, which Tripnee told me was called Frandy Park.

A lively chess tournament was underway. All around us were hundreds of people gathered around chess boards on picnic tables. Many were serious and intent on their games. Some moved from table to table whispering to one another, while a few pranced in victory dances with upraised arms. I think we were both tempted to linger, but we had to get out of there and find somewhere to lay low. Cartel killers could show up at any minute.

In the far back corner of the campground we came to the Fulfillment Voyages Kern Outdoor Center. This, according to Tripnee, was the base of operations for all of their trips on the Kern. An acre or so of parking extended along the foot of an ornately landscaped knoll. On top were shaded gathering and changing areas, an office and store, guide housing and a huge gear and bus yard. On the front of the store, I noticed an engraved wooden sign with the words, "How can I enhance my own experience—and the experience of the people I'm with—right now?" And nearby was another sign with a similar message: "Be Excellent To One Another."

We had just put the kite boards in the gear yard, in the spot set aside for guides' personal stuff, when we saw Dog emerge from the campground shower building fifty yards away.

"Hey Tripnee! Adam!" he called.

"Hi Dog!" Tripnee called back as we walked over to him. "Good to see you!"

"Are you guys OK?" he asked.

"We're in a jam," I said. "We have to get away from here fast and lay low for awhile."

Tripnee added, "The thing is, we're being chased by some very bad people and it could be dangerous just to be around us."

With a calm that surprised me, he flashed a warm smile and said, "So that's what was going on yesterday too? I'm headed up to the guide school base camp right now. Nice and secluded. Why don't you come with me?"

"Sounds good!" I said.

"Thanks so much! I love the serendipity!" said Tripnee. She and I nodded and raised our eyebrows at one another, as though to say, 'Cool, huh, he's changing!'

"This is my car. Welcome aboard," said Dog, gesturing to a mind-boggling, apparently brand new, bright yellow Lamborghini Estoque four-door sedan twenty feet away. As we walked over and got in, I smiled, "Check this out! Dog, you scoundrel. You've got to tell us how you happen to have such a pimped out ride!"

"I know it's over the top. But it has a big trunk and gets me around. Can we save that story for another time?" Looking grim and serious, then brightening, he said, "I'd rather talk about rafting and the guide school."

"No problem. How's your paddle captaining coming along?" I said.

"Not bad!" said Dog. "In fact, my run with you was kind of a breakthrough! I have a long way to go, but so far it's not bad!"

"All right!" I said.

"As much as the river stuff, I like these people!" said Dog as his Lamborghini floated out of Frandy Park like a magic carpet with infinite power. "I grew up around mean, dangerous people," Dog continued. "Here, on the river, I'm getting positive strokes, real support, and I'm actually having fun! I guess you can tell, this is new for me!"

"I know you have it in you to be open to all this," said Tripnee. "I'm glad for you!"

I said, "I think I know what you mean. That run with you yesterday was an eye-opener for me too."

The Estoque hummed and purred, and we headed north out of Kernville on Hwy 155 along the Upper Kern River. I don't know if it was my awareness that the price tag of Dog's Estoque was eight times that of the Dream Van or what, but this fine automobile felt more like flying low in a luxury jet than riding in anything that could be described as a car.

"Hey you guys, we're coming to the KR3 penstock flume and powerhouse," said Tripnee. "Would you like to hear about it?"

Sitting in the shotgun seat, I saw Dog silently mouth "no" and shake his head. But thinking he was probably kidding, and sensing Tripnee felt it would be good to divert our minds for awhile, I said, "Sure. What's a penstock flume?"

"Hey, you know just how to treat a girl who can't resist being a tour guide. Now listen up," she said jabbing both Dog and me in the back of the neck.

"See?" she said pointing at two massive pipes coming down the hillside up ahead. "Those are penstock flume pipes. They're a lot bigger in diameter at the top than at the bottom where they enter the powerhouse at river level. The long, steep descent, combined with the diminishing diameter, speeds and pressurizes the water, blasting it into the massive turbine wheels with enough force to generate a ton of electricity."

Dog turned and rolled his eyes at me.

Tripnee punched his shoulder and continued, "Anyone unlucky enough to get sucked down one of those pipes would be totally atomized in a millisecond leaving zero trace that they had ever existed. What do you think of that?"

It seemed to me that Dog fleetingly looked pale and uneasy, but a moment later the look was gone.

I laughed and said, "Tripnee, I love how, despite everything, you can delight in what is essentially a big plumbing system."

Looking back at her in that luxurious leather interior, I saw that tongue slide back and forth along the wonderful moguls of her upper lip.

CHAPTER FIFTEEN

YOU ARE A RIVER

The guide school base camp was spread out on a river beach of white sand under a canopy of willow, alder and yellow pine. From both upstream and downstream came the muffled roar of formidable rapids, but here the river was smooth and calm, though moving fast. Between the camp and the road, spread among a forest of chest-high granite boulders was a diverse collection of old clunkers, luxury sports cars and pickups with camper shells plus some Fulfillment Voyages trucks.

A hundred yards from the main camp, Dog eased his Estoque into a niche between a pile of oblong, coffin-like boulders and a roomy tent, and said, "My little camp." He seemed subdued, like something was bothering him.

As we climbed out of the Estoque, Becca emerged from a green concrete Forest Service outhouse a ways off, saw us and called out, "Hey, Tripnee and Adam. Good to see you! You guys OK?"

Tripnee walked over to Becca, and I took the opportunity to say to Dog, "Thanks for the ride. I'd welcome the chance to talk more."

Dog looked at me strangely, I thought, and then said, "I'd

like that. Right now I've got to get into camp, but let's talk later."

I said, "Sounds good," and Dog hurried off.

As I joined the women, Becca was saying, "Stay here with us. There's safety in numbers. And if there is a problem, we've got ways for you to slip away fast."

As Tripnee gave her a squeeze, Becca said to me, "So Adam, I'm glad you're still alive! Welcome to our humble home. Come on in for dinner."

The camp overflowed with activity. At the upriver end of the beach, hula-hoop-sized pans of sizzling steak, chicken, rice and vegetables were about to be served on a row of counter-high tabletops by the dinner crew. Among this bunch, I noticed, were our former boat mates Ludimila, Toni, Mark and Reddy plus a wiry-looking, six-foot-six instructor who introduced himself as Sparky.

At the downriver end of the beach, a throng of students including Dog gathered around someone leading a seminar on unwrapping boats from mid river rocks. The focal point for the talk was a four-foot by six-foot panel on an easel illustrating a piggyback rig, a mechanical advantage system of ropes, pulleys and carabiners which multiplies a group's strength, enough to rescue rafts pinned to mid-rapid rocks by tons of force. This pig rig skills board, as it was called, was one of a long row of similar boards, each of which explained a specific emergency river rescue skill or technique.

A half dozen solid square picnic tables filled the middle of the beach. Something about them appealed to me instantly. I could see that their thoughtful design encouraged interaction: Instead of sitting in two long rows, as with most picnic tables, people sat two or three on each of all four sides. This put everyone closer together, and, I felt sure, enhanced sharing, talking and overall connecting.

The smooth surface of the big calm running the length of the camp reflected a huge golden sunset. Close in near the bank, the water was still and serene, while further out the powerful current streamed past. Around me energized souls young and old radiated excitement in the alpenglow.

A tall, lanky young man in his mid-twenties with glasses and a warm grin came up and introduced himself, saying, "Hi Adam! Welcome! I'm Cassady, one of the instructors."

I said, "Nice to meet you, Cassady. How's the school going?"

"Absolutely great!" said Cassady. "We had an excellent day on the water, though I did smash a pair of glasses in a flip. But everyone's doing well. Learning tons. And jump back, tomorrow we pack into the Forks, a challenging class 5 wilderness run upriver from here!"

"You think everyone's ready for class 5?" I asked.

"The instructors captain and row the class 5's," said Cassady. "The students take over in between for the class 3's and 4's. Of course, hands-on practice, the students doing it themselves, is the real teacher. But students learn a lot at this stage by watching their instructors. We call it teaching by example."

Tripnee sauntered over and listened in.

"I really liked our run with Dog yesterday." I said. "Someday I'd like to see the Forks. But I have to confess, just thinking about class 5 brings up some real fear."

"You and me both," said Cassady. "I'm always nervous going into the really big stuff. Our motto is: Be mindful of that fear, and use it to keep you on your toes. In fact, fear, by keeping us alert and careful, makes running class 5 possible."

Tripnee said, "You're an interesting man, Adam. I'm surprised. I didn't think you even knew the meaning of the word fear."

"What you might not realize," I said, "is that I'm used to people shooting at me, in fact I expect it, but I'm not used to getting pummeled and knocked around in whitewater."

There was that tongue on the lip again. Then she said, "I'm impressed you can talk about it."

"I wouldn't say this within her hearing," said Cassady to both of us with a grin, "but Tripnee is one of the best guides on the Kern."

"You might want to take that with a grain of salt," smiled Tripnee. "Cassady was my mentor when I worked my way through college years ago guiding summers on the Kern, and he's not exactly objective."

"No salt needed," I said. "I believe it."

"Seriously, Tripnee," said Cass, "You're a complete natural. You picked it up fast, and moved up the scale of difficulty to class 5 faster than anyone except maybe Becca. These days I learn by watching you."

Tripnee fairly beamed.

"One more thing about the Forks," said Cassady, "once you're in there, you're committed. Except for just a few very difficult escape routes, the only way out is downriver."

Dinner was announced, the seminar broke up, people heaped food on plates and flowed around the square tables. Sitting down with an abundant serving plus a tumbler of wine, I found myself packed in among Tripnee, Becca, a bunch of students and the instructor Kim who had just led the boat rescue seminar.

"Hey Becca," Reddy said, "Why is a person like a river?"

Becca beamed back at Reddy, obviously delighted. "Well, you really want to know? Okay, in healthy humans, emotions—joy, sadness, fear, you name it—morph, move and flow. They flow in, stay for awhile and then flow on through, a lot like a river."

"What's the big deal about that?" asked Dog.

"One big deal," responded Becca, "Is that, if this flow gets blocked, a person can feel uncomfortable, then miserable and even get sick."

"So how do you keep the flow from getting blocked?" asked Ludimila.

"Lots of ways," said Becca. "A key one is expressed in the old saying, 'If you can say how you feel to at least one other person, it can free you to feel something new.'"

"So, talking out our feelings keeps us healthy and free flowing?" asked Mark.

"That's my experience," said Becca. "Especially with a listener who is caring, attentive and accepting."

"Soldiers," I said, "recover from post-traumatic stress in part by talking through their feelings—as many times as necessary."

Dog, looking miserable, asked, "What if you know for a fact that you're not going to be heard or accepted?"

Becca took Dog's brown hand in both of hers. "Like the saying goes, all you have to find is one caring, accepting listener." Dog's compact, powerful body continued to look taut, drawn and in pain.

Toni, squinting, said, "This may be all well and good. I like river metaphor. But what does it have to do with being a river guide?"

"Well," said Becca, "Ya see, guiding is about so much

more that just getting boats down rivers. Clearly, it's vital to run the river as safely as possible. But that's just the beginning." Becca cleared her throat. "A guide's job," she continued, focusing on each of her student's faces in turn, "is to facilitate not just a physical journey from put in to take out, but also an emotional journey from fear to confidence to joy, from being a stranger to being a boat mate and buddy, from feeling maybe scattered and self-critical to feeling self accepting and whole, charged up and alive. From feeling cut off from nature to feeling at one with it." Becca drew in a deep breath, "A key skill that can help a guide achieve all this is good, non-judgmental listening. By the way, I want to thank you all for listening right now. Hey, this is a vast subject we'll come back to. But now, time for dessert!"

A sumptuous fresh-baked blackberry pie a la mode with hot herbal tea was served. Sensing that Dog could use some good listening, I suggested that he and I take ours down to a couple of empty chairs a little ways apart by water's edge at the downstream end of camp.

For a while we talked about our lives in general. He told me that he had recently graduated with an MBA from Stanford, that Toro Canino, his father, who he referred to a bit oddly by his first name, expected him to enter the family business, which was some kind of big import-export company, but that he wanted instead to be a river guide.

Then Dog, his massive neck spreading from his ears to the thick, bunched muscles of his shoulders, said, "What Becca said is brilliant and all, but me talking really isn't a good idea."

Dog silently finished his pie, then suddenly blurted out, "What kind of a father names his son Dog? Especially when his last name is Canino, which means dog in Spanish! In effect, naming me Dog Dog!"

I didn't know what to say, so I just put a hand on his knee and waited. I thought to myself: Everyone loves dogs. But I could feel the intensity of the young man's agony, and decided to be quiet and listen.

Dog hunched over as though punched in the gut. For a long time he just sat there, with his hands pressed to his face, silently shaking. After a while, with his eyes still covered, he continued, "Toro told me he did it to make me tough and loyal. Well, it did—but in his eyes I've always had a problem. I couldn't—and I still can't—help but feel for the underdog, the little guy. One of my troubles is that Toro thinks compassion shows weakness. He still ridicules me over this. So I hide my feelings—and put on an outward act of being a completely tough, callous asshole—which Toro loves and rewards. If I want to win his approval, all I have to do is be a hard ass and he showers me with money and what he thinks is praise—but his approval is gruff and, to tell you the truth, downright hateful—and some part of me has always known his way is not right."

He uncovered his face and looked at me, his eyes seeming to expand. Then he said, "Adam, don't get me wrong. I shouldn't be talking this way. I shouldn't be telling you these things."

At that moment Reddy came down to us and said, "Dog, your father and six men are up in the parking area looking for you." We both turned to look toward where he pointed. A hundred yards away a bunch of flashlights were panning around. In their wavering light, I saw, standing next to Dog's Estoque, fists on his hips, a physically powerful, barrel-chested Mexican man flanked by six very serious-looking cohorts.

"This is not good!" exclaimed Dog quietly. "That's Toro Canino!"

I could not be sure in the flickering light of the flashlight beams, but it seemed that the men wore thick black shoes!

Dog quickly ducked behind his chair, "I'm so, so sorry. I'll explain everything later, but right now you and Tripnee have got to get away!!!"

CHAPTER SIXTEEN

UPPER KERN

Grasping the situation—including the implication that Dog was turning a major corner in his own life—I immediately moved toward Tripnee, who was sitting at one of the square tables talking with Becca. Dog came with me, and I said to him, "You're an amazingly good man, Dog. You're doing the right thing. Thanks!"

To Tripnee I said, "We've got just seconds to get out of here."

Dog said, "I'll try to head them off. Now disappear, fast!" he then turned and, with his head high, walked toward the approaching men.

Instantly picking up on the situation, Becca pointed at two whitewater kayaks near the water twenty feet away, and said, "Take those and go!"

We ran to the long, narrow, plastic boats; grabbed life jackets; tossed in some paddles and stuff nearby; slid the boats into the water; jumped in; and in seconds glided off and away down the swift river into the night. We breathed a sigh of relief, and congratulated ourselves on having narrowly avoided a scene that could have endangered the whole group.

But moments later we realized that we had merely jumped from the frying pan into the fire. We had paddles but no spray skirts to seal the gap between waist and cockpit rim, which meant our boats were likely to fill with water in even mild rapids. My knowledge of kayaking was slim. And worst of all, we had major rapids to run but couldn't see anything in the dark! Rapids that would be a ton of hilarious fun in daylight with a good guide, boat and crew were for us full of peril.

Blackness closed around us. I could just make out the dark shape of Tripnee ten feet to my left. Roaring out of the inky void before us came a huge, broad, growing, frontal assault of white noise that had to be the first big rapid. Close around us, from all sides, came a macabre symphony of slaps, gurgles, hisses and blasting squirts like the body noises of some vast, unimaginable den of slithering monsters. Even heading for shore was a risk-filled option, because the banks were lined with bone bruising rocks and deadly strainers, sieve-like trees and bushes that allow the current to sweep through but pinned boats and boaters like spaghetti in a colander.

Humans, at least in my experience—both in and out of war zones—have within them an "I'm going to die" button. Probably centered below the lobes of the mind down in the depths of our reptilian brain stem, this on/off switch gets triggered by fear-inducing events both big and small, both real and imagined. At that moment, swept along in that kayak, I was gripped, overwhelmed, and on the verge of being immobilized by terror. Somehow, though, instead of freezing up, I managed to be mindful and present, aware enough to ascend to a meta level, to assume a vantage point above myself and to look down and say, *OK, going catatonic ain't an option, so how about saying 'yes' to this situation, accepting it, surrendering, going with the flow?* I took deep breaths, relaxed, and paid attention. I started noticing things. A certain concentrated source of white noise ahead on the right got closer and closer, slid past, and gradually receded. Probably a side stream confluence.

I realized that by plunging my paddle deep I could touch the riverbed. My blade slid tap tap tapping along the bumpy cobble of the river bottom. I realized I could gauge our pace by the rhythm of the taps, the faster the tempo, the greater our speed. I could also feel changes in depth. Increasing depth seemed to indicate more runnable routes, maybe even the main channel, which was good. Decreasing depth suggested the channel might be petering out, and was bad. I realized I was teaching myself how to paddle by braille.

My torpedo-shaped boat felt stable when hitting waves straight bow on, but tipsy taking them sideways. I began to create an inner map of the topography of the river's surface: The ridges and valleys, the mountainous standing waves and deep ravines in between. I began to anticipate waves and drops, and by dint of sheer trial and error, acquired a knack for gaining stability from my paddle deep in the water.

"Whatever you're doing, keep doing it," Tripnee yelled over the roar of the rapid. "So far, so good. Up ahead, go right."

We paddled right. The roar grew deafening. Everything speeded up. Something big and loud flashed by on our left— thank the universe for Tripnee's rock-by-rock knowledge of the river! Wave after wave swept over my foredeck and crashed into my chest, filling my boat with water. One, particularly huge, not only slammed me head on, but also clobbered me straight down from above. Soon I was sitting in water up to my waist, and my deck was level with the river's surface. Fortunately my boat's bow and stern held inflated flotation bags which gave the craft positive buoyancy, keeping it afloat even when swamped. But my long, skinny vessel wallowed out of control, unstable, sluggish and unresponsive, deep in the water.

Working feverishly with my double-bladed paddle, I fought to stay upright and to keep my bow pointed downstream. The dark shape of a hippo-sized boulder screamed by on my right, followed by another exploding past on my left. Then my bow slid straight up the broad sloped face of a flat mid river rock. Tripnee was gone. I stayed there long enough to empty my boat, then got back in and headed after her. Again and again I slammed into ice-cold waves and rocks of all sizes.

Then it happened. A gigantic wall of water turned me broadside and a second flipped me over. Upside down, swamped, I came out of my kayak. Fortunately, I at least had a life jacket and expected to gain the surface soon. But the rapid went on and on until I thought it would never end. I tumbled deep below the surface. My lungs were about to burst, as I was mashed underwater against the upstream face of an undercut rock. The relentless current pounded me down and down, hammering me into a black, wet, coffin-like dungeon. With my lungs screaming, I kicked, stroked and clawed, trying desperately to scramble out of that deadly crevice. But my efforts were to no avail. I was stuck tight.

At my wits end, with my very last bit of strength, I reached out, felt a strong jet of current moving around and past the rock, and cupped my hands in it to grab it like a mini sea anchor. This, combined with me wildly twisting, kicking and slithering, working my body in caterpillar-like undulations, moved me bit by bit, inch by inch. Finally I got far enough to be fire-hosed off and around the rock and back into the downstream current, which promptly swept me off and away. I reflected that air or no air, as long as I was moving, I had a chance, but getting stuck, wedged or entrapped meant death.

I surfaced in a big, smooth calm. It was all I could do just to gasp over and over for air in the darkness. Suddenly there was Tripnee with my boat and paddle! Thrilled and relieved, I grasped them both with numb hands as a rush of feeling, mostly pain, swept through my banged up limbs and scraped flesh. When I suggested we try our luck on land, she said we had been flushed through the biggest rapids and things would get easier from here on. So on we went, and things did improve.

About midnight, exhausted but exhilarated, Tripnee and I floated out onto Lake Isabella. I used our paddles, a nylon poncho and a small bag of half-inch diameter tubular webbing that the guides called hoopi—stuff I had grabbed as we jumped into the kayaks back at base camp—to tie our boats together into a makeshift catamaran and rig a sail. The space around us opened. A big hemisphere of bright stars glimmered above us. The wind, as it often does in canyons at night, had shifted and was blowing downhill, downriver, toward the south. I kept my old friend Polaris, the north star, directly behind us, as we sailed south back across the lake toward the Dream Van.

Tripnee caressed my chest with her palm and widespread fingers and said, "You were really something back there. Half the time I wasn't sure where we were, but you somehow picked out runnable lines in the total dead of night."

"Interesting," I said, snuggling against her, "It seemed to me that again and again you were the one who knew which way to go."

CHAPTER SEVENTEEN
AIRPORT

Sailing silently along in the dark, we were passing the Kern Valley Airport runway, which stretched along the lake's eastern shore, when we heard what sounded like a small jet come in for a landing. I thought it odd that although we heard the whoosh and hiss of what must have been high-tech, super quiet jet engines, we saw no lights, nothing.

"A dark landing," said Tripnee. "Let's check it out."

Turning from a run straight downwind to a broad reach across it, I sailed for shore.

"The thing about this little airport," said Tripnee, "Is that it's close enough to the Mexican border to be convenient for smuggling, but far enough north to escape drug-enforcement scrutiny. Also, the runway right on the lake makes it easier for heavy planes to land and take off."

"Right," I replied. "I'm guessing this plane came in now for a reason—it's not just using the cover of night—but also landing into the wind, which requires less runway. And, come to think of it, that dead pilot earlier today probably thought he could get away with being overloaded because he was taking off into the wind."

"Good points," said Tripnee.

We bumped aground on a sandy, grassy beach, and pulled our kayak catamaran into a nearby waist-high thicket of brambles. Keeping to the rough outskirts of the airport grounds, where random clumps of vegetation provided cover, we carefully made our way around the north end of the runway and past an area crowded with parked Lear jets, G4s and G5s, which were most likely owned by patrons of Indian Rock Resort.

"Hmmm," I mused in a whisper, "Rook's high-end clientele provide a nice screen for cartel planes."

"I guess," she said quietly.

Just then I made out a familiar shape in the darkness. "Well, what'cha know?" I whispered. There four feet in front of us was a black humvee, concealed among low trees well away from any of the airport's roads. "Anyone hiding their vehicle here," I said, "must be up to no good." We recognized the dents and scratches; it was Rook's!

I considered stealing the behemoth vehicle again, just to tweak and rattle the cartel. But I knew that Tripnee's—our—chances of apprehending the cartel kingpins would be decreased if we spooked them and improved if we could lull them into complacency.

We continued, moving slowly, silently, deliberately through the night. One step at a time, we crept past three well-spread-out fixed-base hangars. Then, as we approached the fourth building, we heard muffled sounds of people moving and talking. Tripnee and I, side by side, snuck up to a back window and stole a quick look.

Inside the window was a small office. The door connecting this room to the hangar beyond was ajar enough to give us a glimpse of a handful of men moving fast, quickly passing what looked like bags of heavy-duty drugs from a

Lear jet to two ordinary-looking Winnebago RVs. As soon as the plane was empty, it was loaded with an arsenal of heavy and light weapons and ammo, including stinger missiles with shoulder launchers, no doubt destined for cartel use south of the border. All of the men, it seemed, were wearing shoulder holsters with Glock pistols. Sure enough, there were the two crew-cut shooters Mack and Hektor. Within minutes the transfer was complete, the lights inside the hangar went dark, the big doors rolled open, the plane backed out of the hangar, and men drove off in the RVs. As the jet taxied out onto the runway, the hangar doors closed and the place went quiet.

Realizing that the slightest sound would betray our presence, Tripnee and I, very, very carefully, crept back into the nearest semblance of cover, a swath of knee-deep grass that ran along behind the hangars. Sensing imminent danger, we lay down, getting as flat as possible. As several men came fast around the back corner of the building, heading straight for us, I don't know about Tripnee, but I held my breath.

Even though our situation was hopeless, I tensed to spring up and mount some kind of defense. The men were literally a split second from stepping within a foot or two of us, and could not possibly have missed our presence, when, just then, thank the universe, the darkened Lear jet emitted a sudden low yowl and took off like a bolt of black lightening. At precisely the essential moment, the men all looked toward the jet, and away from their feet, where Tripnee and I could, in the starlight, make out the double-tied laces of their thick black shoes. By the time the men took their eyes off the jet, they were past us, moving away toward the humvee hidden in the trees.

Tripnee and I lay there, drawing long slow breaths, barely able to believe our luck. Carefully we moved into deeper cover. We heard the faint sound of the humvee start and move away. Gradually the crickets resumed chirping and, again skirting the runway, we made our way back to our kayak catamaran.

On the homeward voyage through the night across Lake Isabella, a steady twenty-knot breeze kept our jury-rigged nylon poncho sail taut and straining at our rickety paddle mast. With my left hand I controlled it by maintaining tension on two strands of hoopi, one running to the mast head, the other to a corner of the poncho. At the same time with my right, holding a paddle mounted with hoopi as a rudder, I steered a course back to the Dream Van on Engineers Point. The lights of the town of Wofford Heights slid by on our right, and the distinctive belt and sword of the constellation Orion rotated overhead. Yes, we were immersed in dangers both natural and man-made—but somehow eclipsing this was a deep appreciation of being with this woman in this place.

I turned and looked at her. "I've got a problem," I said.

"What's that?" asked Tripnee, with a note of concern.

"Whenever my navy buddies talk about their relationships with their wives and girlfriends, there's always strife, issues, tension and struggle," I said. "Of course, you and I just met, so everything I'm going to say is premature. But anyway, here's my problem: Sure, we're in a life or death fight with the cartel. Sure, we, or at least I, have had to struggle to survive the river. And sure, you're a rogue agent who disregards her own safety. But between you and me, in our personal relationship, I don't feel any tension. It just feels so good between us, so good to be with you."

"So what's the problem with that, Bozo?" asked Tripnee.

"The problem is twofold, Ms. Clown. First, it seems too

good to be true. And, second, if I tried to tell my friends about us, how it is being with you, they would think I'm being saccharine, or leaving stuff out, or seeing it through rosy glasses."

Tripnee settled in beside me, her hand squeezing my thigh, and said, "Some problems are good to have, idiot."

CHAPTER EIGHTEEN
GIANT SEQUOIAS

Navigating by starlight meant blundering through the night largely blind. For much of our lake crossing, we weren't sure where we were. Endless gradations of darkness, from greyed-out murkiness to solid pitch-black, obscured the shoreline in the entire semicircle before us.

Then, finally, gradually, out of the inky gloom ahead came the distinct sound of waves lapping against shore. I pushed my steering paddle down and felt bottom. A moment later our little craft hit land. We climbed out, astonished to find ourselves on the beach directly below the Dream Van! Tripnee and I loaded the kayaks onto the van's roof racks, and tossed the other gear in through the back doors.

"If I know us," said Tripnee, "We both memorized the plane markings and those RV license plates."

"It's nice to be known," I replied.

"Let's put out an all points bulletin on the cartel RVs and plane, but tracing their owners may lead to a dead end," said Tripnee.

We climbed into the van, fired up the com system, sent out the APBs, and researched the registered owners—including the lease holder of the jet under Lake Isabella.

Not surprisingly, the ownership trails dead-ended in several Mexican holding companies, faceless corporations with myriad interests, some perhaps legitimate, some otherwise.

"The key thing right now," I said, "is for you and me not to get killed. When the sun rises in a few hours, we won't want to be out here in the open."

"My thoughts exactly," said Tripnee. "I know the perfect place. Mind if I drive?"

"Sounds good," I said, handing her the key.

Lithe, strong, passionate, a force of nature, Tripnee climbed into the driver's seat, fired up the big engine, thrust the tranny into four-wheel-drive, and punched the gas. As she pounded her way along the rough roads leading off Engineers Point, I relaxed back into the shotgun seat, exhausted but euphoric.

Gradually, though, my euphoria was replaced by a brand new terror. Jerking the van out of four-wheel drive, Tripnee raced north on Hwy 155 through Wofford Heights and into Kernville. We skidded to a stop in the Fulfillment Voyages yard, offloaded the kayaks, then accelerated north toward the high Sierra back country. At first I made excuses for her, but after a while I could no longer deny it: Tripnee's driving was reckless and dangerous!

Four-wheel-drive vans have a high center of gravity and are known to roll over on sharp curves taken too fast. We were barreling around tight mountain bends at such blistering speeds the van was literally going up on two wheels. Frequently our tires left the pavement, spitting dirt and gravel into the underbrush. As the Dream Van pitched and careened, I found myself gripping the arms of my high-backed captain's chair with white knuckles.

"We're eating up the miles," I shouted above the engine's roar, "but at this rate we'll roll over. We need to slow down."

She looked at me with a gleam in her eyes, and eased our speed only slightly.

"With driving skills like these," I asked, "how did you ever keep your Prius right-side-up and make it down that cliff yesterday?"

"Hey," she said, "I made it because I drive like this."

"Insane," I said, "but I see your logic."

In the middle of whipping around a hairpin curve with one hand on the wheel and the other on her hip, she glanced at me with that fiery light in her eyes and said, "You want to hear something crazy?"

"From you? Definitely." I replied. "But will you please keep your eyes on the road and your hands on the wheel!"

"When that humvee first attacked my Prius, I was overwhelmed with fear. Then—and this is the unbelievable part—just as it rammed me over the edge, at the very moment I looked into your eyes, I felt calm and remembered an old saying my dad taught me: 'Fear is excitement that has forgotten to breathe.'" With a playful laugh, Tripnee squeezed my leg, and my leg loved it. "So," she continued, tromping on the gas, "I took some deep breaths and decided to enjoy—and rise to the occasion of—what might be my last moments alive. And you saw the results."

"Wow!" I moved her hand back onto the wheel. "You truly are the shaman, and your father must have been amazing too."

"Actually," she said, "my dad was a Choinumni tribal shaman and had the title 'tripne.'"

"So your name means shaman? How great is that!"

Smiling broadly, she cast those huge blue eyes upon me.

"This is all wonderful, but would you please watch the road—and slow down for Pete's sake!"

In what seemed like only a few minutes, but was actually much longer, we found ourselves in a remote corner of Sequoia National Forest not far from the Golden Trout Wilderness. As the first glimmer of dawn lit the eastern horizon, Tripnee re-engaged our four-wheel drive and left the pavement. Like a busy ant scampering into a bamboo jungle, the Dream Van jolted and bounced along a tortuous, little-used Forest Service road as it wound and climbed deep into a vast grove of giant sequoia trees. Soaring hundreds of feet above us, thirty feet and more in diameter, the ancient gargantuan trees stood thick, swollen and erect as far as the eye could see in every direction. It was as though, in this place, the earth itself was rising in full turgid arousal.

At length, Tripnee, her tongue caressing that contoured upper lip, brought us to rest in the exact center of a natural cathedral, a perfect circle of the towering giants.

"Welcome to my secret place," she said. "Until this moment, I've always come here alone. This is where my higher self and innermost depths merge and soar."

As beams of morning sun probed the primeval forest around us, we popped the van's top and unfolded the commodious double bed. Tripnee drew me to her, pressed herself against me and kissed me deeply. My fears fell away and my entire body responded as never before. A tsunami of sustained passion lifted, engulfed and flowed through us. Even banging wounds was like ecstasy. Our clothes vanished. With arms, legs and bodies intertwined, with me inside her, we moved as one through rolling landscapes—and whole mountain ranges—of wild, undulating rhythms. We soared, surged, bucked, throbbed, peaked and flowed, then took flight again, rocked, swooped, climbed, and summited all over again. Finally we pulled blankets over the two of us and, wrapped in each other's arms, collapsed into a deep sleep streaming with rich and wonderful dreams.

I awoke feeling recharged, alert and content. The thought came to me, *So this is what it feels like to be alive, to be me.* I experienced a suspension of my tendency to yearn, to yearn to be somewhere other than where I was. With that veil lifted, I felt neither bliss nor disappointment, but rather a deep, good, clear feeling—a simple acceptance of what was, of being wide awake right there in that moment.

Lying close beside me, the contours of her body glowing in the suffused forest light, Tripnee rubbed her breasts against me, caressed me with a leg and snuggled her lips and tongue into my neck. On second thought, I was overflowing with excitement and bliss. The touch of Tripnee's smooth skin was heaven. She ran her hands down over my chest, my stomach. She slid onto me and we moved slowly, wonderfully. I felt reborn, brand new, as though I was seeing, feeling for the first time.

Afterward, we slept some more. When we woke, warmth poured in from the day outside. Like two giddy kids sneaking downstairs early on Christmas morning, we snuck outside, nude, and in the hollow of a giant sequoia we made sublime love again. What a world, what a place, what a woman!

At the Dream Van's outside shower, we took turns soaping and washing each other, with both of us laughing on and on at how the other dragged out the process, making it last far longer than any rational human could imagine. Then, toweled, combed and dressed, we worked side by side to prepare sizzling steak, eggs over easy, toast, fresh blueberries in yoghurt and hot coffee.

As we ate, Tripnee, gestured toward the old star-shaped mark on my upper left arm, and asked, "How did you get that scar?"

"It happened when my parents were killed, but I don't remember, actually," I said. "It's part of so much that was taboo to talk about when I was growing up."

Something that had long been dancing in and out of my awareness suddenly struck me with bold new clarity: How little I knew about my parents, their murder, my roots—the whole thing. For as long as I could remember—beginning before even the trauma of war—a part of me had lived submerged in pain, in a permanent feeling that something huge was missing. And I realized the next thing I needed to do was to finally, once and for all, get Peace to open up.

CHAPTER NINETEEN
UNCLE PEACE

The investigator in me kicked in. Peace had information he had never told me, and I needed to know what he knew. Revving up the van's com system, I placed a Skype video call to Peaceful Mountain Weldon, who lived in a little house overlooking a creek in El Sobrante, an unincorporated town in a scenic, grass-sloped valley near Richmond in the East Bay hills across from San Francisco.

As Peace's worried face appeared on my screen, he said, "Adam, are you OK? What's happening? How are things going with your quest?"

"In some ways wonderful beyond imagining!" I replied. "In fact, on that note I'd like to introduce you to Tripnee." Tripnee came over briefly; I introduced them; and I could tell Peace was charmed.

Then I said, "In other ways, though, things here are red hot and incredibly dangerous. Which brings me to the urgent purpose of my call: Peace, Tripnee and I are in serious, serious danger. You've got to—you've absolutely got to tell me everything you know about my mom and dad's murder."

"Oh dear boy, this search of yours is going to get you killed—just like your folks!" Peace's face contorted with agony. "Break it off! Get out of there!"

"I love you, Peace," I said. "But your way is not my way. I've got to do this. Both Tripnee and I are in this up to our necks and are going to see this through—or die trying. Now, once and for all, will you, for the love of god, help us? Our lives hang in the fucking balance!"

Peace blew out a big breath. "Okay, okay, okay, I get it. Against my better wisdom, I'll tell you what I know, but only because you're already down there in the thick of things. I can see there is no way to get you out of there, other than by helping you move forward on your own path."

I breathed a huge sigh of relief. "Thank you, Peace. I know you've always meant well. What you did might have made sense when I was little. But that time has long past. Now I need the full story."

"There's a lot I don't know," said Peace, "But I'll do my best, my boy. Let's see, where to begin?"

My zen monk uncle was silent for a while and then began, "Your dad, my brother Abraham, met your mom Sarah when he went down to teach high school in Lake Isabella. Those two lovebirds had a wonderful, magical bond. You could tell just seeing them together: The electricity, the way they looked into each other's eyes and touched each other. And how they doted on you! You were the center of their universe!"

Hearing this both thrilled and killed me.

"I lived in the Santa Lucia Mountains near Carmel at the Tassajara Monastery for seven years before Abe and Sarah's death. You were five when you and your folks visited me about six months before they were murdered. They told me then that they were very concerned about a drug cartel that was starting to operate in the Kern Valley, but they didn't tell me any details," said Peace. "There was something strange. Something about the cartel threat was deeply affecting both of them—but it was especially devastating to Sarah, and hitting her very close to home."

Peace went on, "Sarah was half Tubatulabal Indian, which makes you one quarter Tubatulabal. And you have another uncle: your mom's half brother. Sarah had inherited a big ranch in the Kern Valley that was very special to the Tubatulabal Indians. After your mom's death the property went to your uncle, who wanted it because it was sacred tribal land.

"After the murder, I meditated for a month on what to do. It was then that I decided to leave Tassajara and go back to being a school librarian so I could raise you. When I went down to Bakersfield, first, I picked you up from the Kern County Child Protective Services people. Then, at a title company, I signed papers that released your interest and transferred the tribal land to Sarah's brother. That seemed like the right thing to do because it was sacred to the tribe. Also, the fact is I wanted nothing to do with the place where your folks met such a violent end. I wanted to put it all behind you and me. I never did meet the brother, your other uncle.

"Before I left Bakersfield I talked with the Kern County sheriff," Peace continued. "According to his reconstruction of the crime scene, you were in the same room with your folks when that hail of bullets smashed through the window and killed them right in front of you. In that attack a jagged shard of glass ripped into your upper left arm, causing your star-shaped scar. It's always puzzled me that no one was ever charged or arrested."

My uncle and I talked for a long time. Even though he had had limited contact with them, just hearing Peace finally, after all those years, talk about my folks fed a voracious, life-long hunger within me—and at the same time reignited my agony, my childhood sense of loss.

At length it was time to bring our conversation to a close. "It's good to see you, my uncle," I said. "You mean the world to me."

"Here in El Sobrante the universe smiles, my boy," said Peace. "I sat down by the creek all morning. And with school starting tomorrow, my library will be overflowing with kids! Just how I like it!"

After we said our goodbyes, and Peace asked me for the umpteenth time to be careful and head home as soon as possible, he shared one more thing, and it was a doozy. In closing, he said, "Oh, by the way, your other uncle's name is Reamer Rook."

CHAPTER TWENTY
SEQUOIA WALK

For a very long time after my talk with Peace, I sat and took it in, and walked and took it in some more. Tripnee was an attentive listener when I needed to talk, and wonderfully patient when I needed quiet. At times I had tears streaming down my face. My body and soul filled with understanding and appreciation for all I had gone through and become.

No wonder I had always been a voracious reader with an unquenchable curiosity and thirst for knowledge. No wonder, despite uncle Peace's zen pacifism, I had worked so hard to perfect my skills in kung fu and chi gong. No wonder I had a passion for justice, had always felt driven to confront schoolyard bullies, and had become a Navy SEAL captain specializing in criminal investigation. No wonder I was here right now deep in Sequoia National Forest determined to solve the mystery of my parents' murder.

I looked closely at the world around me and felt it come into sharper focus. In the late afternoon, Tripnee and I walked among the giant sequoias, which I knew from my reading formed one of thirty-eight similar groves in the forest. The trees around us approached and perhaps surpassed 270 feet in height, thirty feet in diameter, and 2000 years in age—and were the largest living things on earth. Gargantuan yet soft and vulnerable, they radiated a hushed aliveness, a genuine, natural holiness. Hand in hand, Tripnee and I moved as though down the aisle of earth's own blessed cathedral. In the distance all around us, as in stained glass windows framed by sky-high columns, we glimpsed a mountain terrain of granite monoliths, glacier carved canyons, lush meadows and vast green forests.

It dawned on me that what had started out as a search for my parents' killers was allowing me to see myself more clearly, and begin to embrace my life with compassion and acceptance. I was at once astounded and filled with exhilaration at the prospect of finding real resolution.

As we walked, Tripnee whispered, "Being here with you is paradise."

"For me also," I squeezed her hand.

We looked at each other and nodded. It was time to move things forward.

I said, "I think we can crack this whole case wide open."

Tripnee said, "It's telling that Rook's humvee showed up so soon at the airport drop. I've been slow to see the man for what he must be."

"Yes," I said. "Something tells me that all three: dear uncle Reamer, the cartel and my parents' murder are all linked."

"And then there's Dog," said Tripnee. "His dad has to be cartel."

"Dog impresses me," I said. "Think of the pressure he's been under to follow in the path of his autocratic, cartel-kingpin father. Yet, he risked his life to save us. I think our next step should be to talk with him as soon as possible."

"Definitely," said Tripnee.

"The thing is he's down on the Forks with the school."

Tripnee said, "Hmmm, that's close to where we are now. And I do know where they'll camp tonight. Although I don't know anyone who's done it, it just might be possible to hike in there."

I asked, "How hard could it be?"

CHAPTER TWENTY-ONE
POT FARM

It was already well along in the afternoon, and we needed to move fast. Decamping in the Dream Van took no time. We put away a few things, dropped and clamped down the top, and were off.

The guide school had hiked into and launched onto the class 5 Forks of the Kern run earlier that day, and was planning to spend the night at Thimble Camp, a remote, inaccessible river beach opposite the confluence of the North Fork of the Kern and Thimble Creek. Both creek and camp took their name from an eponymous nearby group of sheer-sided, 8254-foot thimble-shaped rocks which drew rock climbers from all over the world.

As we drove along Lloyd Meadow Road toward Thimble Creek, I reflected on recent news reports about trouble all over these mountains. It was common knowledge that a lot of the green one sees is cartel pot plantations. Investigative journalists and Forest Service authorities alike estimated there were hundreds of outlaw marijuana farms on this forest alone. Many were known to be guarded by deadly booby-traps and campesino cartel gunmen who shot to kill. Not only did the cartel's meth and heroin destroy lives and bring on slow agonizing death, right here on America's most precious public land the cartel killed unsuspecting hikers who wandered too close to their pot farms.

It was late afternoon when we parked near Thimble Creek. Not far to the east the land fell away into the shadow-filled canyon of the Kern, while several thousand feet above us the Thimbles glistened and vibrated in the mountain air like Valhalla, the home of the gods. We realized it was too late in the day to begin a descent into the sheer-walled Forks canyon, but we decided to go for it anyway.

Strapping on a couple of small water-tight backpacks, one containing a lightweight double sleeping bag, the other some climbing gear and a few odds and ends, Tripnee and I began following the stream as it gurgled eastward through dense stands of ponderosa pine and cedar, and an occasional giant sequoia. The land gradually became steeper as it fell away before us.

We had walked only about a half-mile when we came to a shallow pond created by a small rock dam. My sixth sense told me something was out of place, and, sure enough, I noticed that a carefully concealed black plastic tube ran from the pond off down the slope angling to the south. I moved some sand and rocks to reveal a section of the pipe, which was a full three inches in diameter. Tripnee and I examined it and nodded at each other. We both understood that this was almost certainly part of a pot farm irrigation system. Judging from the size of the water line, it was probably a big one planted by the cartel.

We didn't have time to round up low level cartel pot "gardeners", as the cartel's undocumented campesino farmers were usually called. We were out to get the drug lords themselves and thereby bring down the whole cartel. So we did not follow the big hose, but continued down into the Forks Canyon.

Thimble Creek sliced into the speckled granite Sierra bedrock to carve out its own narrow, twisting mini-canyon, within which it plunged over a series of five- to fifteen-foot waterfalls. Following its tortuous path, we threaded single-file along narrow ledges, slid down precipitous inclines, side-stepped across treacherous traverses with our backs pressed to the gorge wall, and at times sauntered side-by-side across level spots. Graceful and silky, the sculpted convex and concave contours of the water-polished gray-white stone ravine flowed smoothly from one sensual shape to another. Many, undeniably, were suggestive of the dreamy folds and curves of the female body.

Bang! A gunshot rang out. Reacting automatically from both military training and my own war-hardened reflexes, I pulled Tripnee down and covered her with my body even before the reverberating echo died away. Next, from somewhere nearby came a second gunshot, and then, a few seconds later, a third. Looking around, I saw no one.

"I don't think they're shooting at us," I whispered.

Tripnee nodded and whispered back, "I wouldn't mind staying in this position, but something tells me we should check it out."

After stowing our packs in a stone alcove, we found hand and footholds in the gorge wall and climbed up. Poking our heads above the rim of the creek's inner gorge, we looked around. No one. But, on a small densely wooded terrace twenty feet away, I saw the faint trace of a path.

As we approached the terrace, the hair on the back of my neck stood up. I froze and Tripnee halted next to me. Stopping and just standing there, sensing my surroundings, I gradually became aware of a deadly hazard, a clear, almost invisible fishing line stretched taut across the trail at ankle height. A shudder passed through me as I traced the line and saw that it was wired into a sawed off shotgun aimed square at my midsection. If I had taken one more step, my guts would have been blown to smithereens.

The stench of old death hung in the air. I looked twenty-five feet down the slope and saw a bear carcass crumpled and caught against a rock. Where the bear's face and much of its head should have been, there was only putrid bear flesh and spilled noodle of bear brain. Judging from its partial decomposition, a few days ago this once magnificent creature must have tripped the line and gotten its face blown off.

Pointing out the line and shotgun to Tripnee, I said softly, "There're probably other lethal traps. I've done this before. I'd prefer it if you'd take cover here, and let me scout ahead. I'll be back."

Nodding assent, Tripnee gave me a hug and quick kiss, then moved up the slope a few yards to conceal herself in a group of giant granite slabs which formed a maze of passages, crawlways and hiding places.

Carefully stepping over the trip line, I crept ahead. As I moved along the path, I rounded a bend, stepped between some boulders and—oops!—very nearly stepped on a full-grown rattlesnake coiled in the center of the path. Knowing that rattlers usually do not strike—provided you don't startle or actually step on a them—I ever so slowly stepped over the reptile and went on. Looking back, I saw the six-foot diamondback slither into hiding.

Rounding another bend, I emerged into a rustic camp littered with pot farm trash: empty 50-pound fertilizer bags, discarded pesticide jugs, a chest-high mound of empty food wrappers and soda and beer cans, animal traps, a rabbit hutch, the ash and blackened rocks of a cooking fire, three crude beds of cut cedar boughs, shovels, machetes, hoes, coils of irrigation tubing and a "Reconquista!" t-shirt.

I continued on, pausing now and then to listen and sense the space around me. I passed a massive outjutting of the canyon wall, and that's when I saw them: three dead men stretched out face down, side-by-side, a neat bullet hole in the back of each head. Beyond the bodies was a broad, level terrace of many acres. It was as though a great blade had cut a deep, flat notch into the butter of the canyon wall. The native ponderosas, cedars and oaks of the plateau had been stripped of their lower and middle limbs, leaving only a gossamer canopy of branches to provide camouflage from routine marijuana eradication aerial patrols. Chopped off at ground level were the stumps of hundreds, probably thousands of marijuana plants. I could see at a glance that the men were no doubt Mexican campesino gardeners who had planted, watered, guarded and harvested the crop grown here—and they had been murdered, probably moments ago, by the cartel as their payment.

Taking cover among some rocks nearby, I surveyed the place. The scent of fresh death mingled with the skunk-like stench of ready-to-harvest sinsemilla buds. But the plants were gone. The place was still and no one seemed to be around. I noticed another narrow, inconspicuous trail leading up the slope back toward Lloyd Meadow Road, and decided to check it out.

As I moved along this narrow track, I came to another shotgun, tripwire booby trap, this one with the muzzle pointing away from me. I noticed a spur trail angling back toward where I had left Tripnee, and took it as it wove among colossal granite slabs that had eons ago flaked off the canyon wall to form a labyrinth of nooks and crannies. Realizing I was back where Tripnee must be hiding, I moved slowly through the maze searching for her. I had explored most of the tangle of narrow passageways and was about to softly call out, when I felt the barrel of a gun jam into the small of my back.

"Hands out in front of you, on the rock!" barked a deep gruff male voice. "Feet back and spread 'em!"

After my initial surprise, I felt relieved not to be instantly shot and did as directed. The man frisked me for weapons, then pressed his gun into the base of my skull. "Try anything, and you're dead."

"I believe you," I said, looking straight at the rock in front of me and keeping any trace of irony out of my voice. "You mean business."

"Fucking straight," came the reply in a tone that was ever so slightly softer. I sensed the man backing away as he said, "Turn around—slowly."

Facing him, I saw that my captor was the black-shoed, square-headed Mack Dowell. The taller of the humvee riflemen, the guy was about my height—six-foot-two—and had the swagger and look of a bodybuilder. Strangely, though, the man's clothes were several sizes too small and exposed pillar-like expanses of ankle and wrist.

"The fun is over for you and your friend," he said. "Too bad. I can tell you eat right and take good care of yourselves." Mack then sniffed the air. His mouth and nose twitched and scrunched up, pinching his small, dead, wide-set eyes into narrow slits. "Most of the people we whack are in terrible shape, ready to drop dead on their own."

My mind raced with thoughts of Tripnee. The fact that I had not been shot straight off—and something in the way Mack spoke—suggested that she might still be alive. I was possessed by an overwhelming urgency to get free, find her and help her. But I knew that my chances of doing so depended on me right now appearing utterly defeated, docile and hopeless.

Standing ten feet back, Mack Dowell gestured with his Glock toward the trail I had first taken. "That way. Any fast moves, and I pull the trigger."

I nodded and moved as I was told, letting my shoulders slump and my whole body droop. I considered putting the cartel booby trap to good use by lunging to one side and tripping the wire to blast my captor, but realized the plan was likely to get us both killed. The downside of that, from my perspective, was the part about me being killed. I, followed closely by Mack Dowell, stepped over the trip wire.

Then I remembered the snake. I hoped that, like most of us earth critters, it was a creature of habit. If I had encountered it on its favorite spot, and it had returned to that spot, there was hope. I would have to step over it fast to minimize the chance of it striking me, and then pray that it would either strike my gun-toting follower or provide a moment of distraction in which I could make a move.

As I neared the place where I had encountered the reptile before, I tried to time my strides to sweep me swiftly over it. Hitching between rocks on the approach, I saw only bare ground! No snake!

So what now? Feeling as defeated as I was trying to look, I kept moving, racking my brain for ideas. One part of me descended into a tailspin of self-criticism: What kind of fool was I to grasp at such straws? How pathetic! To hope that a rattlesnake would return to a particular place at the exact moment I needed him there?

Still, another part of me kept breathing and remained alert, ready for any opportunity that might present itself.

And, at the same time, with each step, a third part of me continuously sensed the muzzle of the Glock slinking along a foot or two behind me, aimed at my spine.

Suddenly there it was—the coiled rattler! This time in a new spot, which, bless its reptilian heart, was squarely centered on the path just beyond a narrow place between two boulders! I subtly elongated my strides to swing my left foot over and past my long, skinny friend without triggering his strike reflex! A moment later, the instant I heard a sharp intake of breath behind me, I tucked my torso forward, and lashed back with my right foot in a swift high ferocious kick that connected with something solid. Bringing my foot down fast and spinning around, I saw Mack Dowell fly violently backward and watched his head slam into a boulder, knocking him out cold. I also noticed with satisfaction that he had two small bloody puncture holes in his sockless ankle. Grabbing his Glock, and giving my friend the snake a wide berth, I moved with stealth and speed toward the pot-farm encampment.

Poking my head around a flying buttress-like outflaring of the canyon wall, I saw Tripnee, alive and apparently OK, tied with her back to a tree and facing in my direction. In front of her, with his back to me, stood a crew-cut, black-shoed figure that had to be Hektor. Tripnee betrayed no sign of my approach. Instead, she held his gaze and growled with animal intensity, "How can you live with yourself?"

As I crept up behind him, I heard Hektor say, "My dear, I'm doing God's work!" The man's pistol was constantly in motion. As he spoke, as if to emphasize various words, apparently at random, he repeatedly thrust its barrel into her face. "These are the end times, the end of days! All of this—me, you, your death—it's all written…"

Hearing this, I decided to take no chances, and as soon

as I was close enough, choosing a moment when his gun was lowered, I brought the butt of Mack Dowell's Glock down hard on the man's head, knocking him unconscious with a single blow. I untied Tripnee and without delay we hog-tied Hektor on his belly with his arms and legs pulled up together behind his back. We went back and did the same for Mack Dowell, who was showing signs of waking. We searched the two men, but found only extra ammo clips for the Glocks. We kept the guns and the clips.

It was getting late in the day and we had to get down the cliff without delay while we still had at least a little light. We disarmed the two shotgun booby traps, retrieved our packs and resumed our descent into the canyon of the Forks of the Kern. Maybe leaving the cartel men tied up was an unusual law-enforcement tactic, but under the circumstances I felt we were treating these two murderers better than they deserved. Most likely, the next day we would get to a place with cell phone coverage where we could call to have them picked up by the proper authorities.

CHAPTER TWENTY-TWO
THE CLIFF

Thimble Creek is what geologists call a hanging tributary because, in the heart of the Forks run, it enters the main canyon of the North Fork of the Kern over a waterfall. A nearly vertical three-hundred-foot cascade to be exact! The mouth of the creek at the confluence appears as a deep U-shape scooped from the vanilla granite inner rim of the main Forks Canyon.

At times wading in the creek itself, at times squeezing along the curvaceous sloping sides of the groove of the creek's mini-canyon, Tripnee and I worked our way down to the very brink of the cataract. Standing on the edge of the precipice, we beheld a vast open space. The cliff fell away before us into the increasing shadows like the taut pelvis of some vast earth woman-mountain. Instead of plummeting through midair, the crystalline waters of the creek hugged the smooth rounded lip and slid down the sheer glowing creamy granite face as if it were the ultimate water slide. I thought of trying to actually glide down it, but the slope was only, at most, ten degrees off vertical, and such a plunge would be akin to jumping off the Golden Gate Bridge.

Thanking my lucky stars that I had thought to bring them, I pulled my 120-foot climbing rope, a similar length of light cord, two climbing seat harnesses and some cara-biners and climbing chocks from my pack. I knew I should be beyond such things, but the appreciation I saw in Tripnee's approving nod and smile sent a thrill through me.

Moving carefully, because a fall here would be all she wrote, I found a deep crevice to hold a chock to provide a strong tie off point for the rope. With the rope end secured with a quick-release slip knot and the light cord rolling-hitched to the quick-release, I threw rope and cord far out and we watched them fall out of sight down over the bulge of the smooth cliff face. Once we descended the rope, there would be no way to retrieve the chock, but the cord would allow us to pull the quick-release and drop the entire rope and cord down to us, so we could use them again—over and over—to lower ourselves all the way to river level.

Tripnee asked, "What will we do if we get to the end of the rope and there is only smooth polished wall, and no place to stand or hold on?"

"We can always climb back up if all else fails," I replied, "but let's cross that bridge when we come to it."

We got into our climbing harnesses, which were little webbing seats with straps encircling waist and thighs with a clip-in loop in the crotch. The next sensible thing to do would have been for me to belay down the rope first so that if it had to be reclimbed, only I would have to do it. However, without wanting to say so out loud, I was feeling uneasy about leaving Tripnee alone at the top of the cliff so near the pot plantation. So I clipped both of our harnesses together into a short noose of webbing which allowed both of us to belay down together, side by side, hip to hip. Feet to the great wall, leaning back out over the chasm, trusting the rope, we walked slowly backward and down as we eased the rope little by little through a carabiner friction brake. Mild pressure on the line stopped us, while loosening it resumed our motion.

As we dropped into the abyss, I sensed our spirits lift, probably because we were finally putting some distance between us and our recent spine-chilling close-call.

"After what happened back there," I said, "I'm so thankful you're okay."

She squeezed my arm, "I was so thankful to see you appear back there!" she said. "When I was waiting for you, Mack Dowell somehow just materialized behind me, jamming a Glock into my back."

"Exact same thing happened to me," I said. "Those guys must know that terrain and maze of granite slabs like the backs of their hands."

Tripnee flashed a quick smile, "You were magnificent! Do you have any idea what it does to a woman to see her man overcome barbarians like that? You get a girl's mythic juices flowing!"

"I like primordial acknowledgements," I quipped.

"Yeah? Well, you're the guy who defended the cave from the saber-toothed tiger. You're the guy who brought back the meat that kept the tribe from starving." Then, with eyes half closed she whispered, "You make me so hot!"

As we rappelled in tandem ever deeper into the Forks Canyon, approaching the end of our rope, we no doubt looked from a distance like any two people descending into an abyss. But Tripnee and I, grinning from ear to ear, surged with excitement and mutual admiration. Every touch, every brushing together of hips, arms and legs was supercharged.

We were now within twenty feet of the tip of the rope and I gripped the line to bring us to a stop. The cliff face had subtle undulations and hollows, but no ledges, handholds or nubs—not even any cracks or holes big enough for a single finger.

I looked right and left. Nothing!

The prospect of climbing back up or just hanging with Tripnee actually didn't seem that bad. But I had a thought: Perhaps first we should check out the arc of our rope's swing side to side.

Sliding down the granite surface a few yards to our north, Thimble Falls emitted a fine mist and resonant white noise, but offered nowhere to perch. So we swung south, side-stepping left. The fine gritty texture of the granite surface provided good traction, allowing us to arc like a pendulum far over, out and around a projection of the cliff surface—and what do you know! There, fifteen feet below, was a small outcropping!

I let out line to ease us toward it. It was going to be tight! As we backed down, we had eight feet remaining, then four, then two! I stopped us with just one foot to spare. But we were there and it was enough. We rotated our bodies from horizontal, hanging by our seat harnesses, to upright, hugging-the-wall. Then we shifted our weight from the rope to what turned out to be a one-by-three-foot ledge. Pressed to the wall, wedged onto the narrow shelf, the precariousness of our situation sank in.

But a number of things heartened me. The south-facing cliff wall was warm from a full day's exposure to the sun. The slight slope of the cliff was a huge advantage because it made it easier to press ourselves against its coarse surface. And, I was very relieved to see at my feet a stout horn of solid rock that would make an excellent next tie point for the rope! Thank the universe we had the rope!

In order to drop it down so we could retie, and begin the second leg of our descent, I detached the end from the carabiner friction brake. I was about to reach for the cord to release the quick-release knot, when suddenly the rope and cord shot up out of my reach—and kept going! Someone out of sight above us at the lip of the falls was pulling them back up!! I realized instantly that it must be the cartel. Perhaps a third cartel man had freed the other two and, in a furious search for us, they had all come down to the creek mouth and found the chock tie point. By taking away our lifeline, they would condemn us to a dramatic death worthy of their enemies—a demise featuring an agonizing prelude of exposure and desperation trapped on a narrow ledge, followed by a final plunge into oblivion.

Instead of swearing at the top of my lungs, I forced myself to be calm and, hugging the rock beside Tripnee, I studied our situation. The good thing was we were hidden by the gradually bulging curve of the cliff eyebrow above us, and so were out of gunshot range. The bad news was the rock around us—above, below and to either side—was smooth and unclimbable. We could go neither up, down nor sideways.

But wait a minute. Did I know that for a fact? By having Tripnee press both our packs and herself into the wall, and hanging onto her as a counterweight, I found that I could lean far out and better study the stone face that was our immediate universe. True, for a diameter of at least ten yards in every direction there was not a single crack, handhold or finger hole. But, directly below us about sixty feet was a small protruding knob! I blew out a lungful of air. Was it even possible?

Coming back in to the wall, I mentioned the nub to Tripnee, along with the improbability of getting to it. Using me as her anchor, Tripnee leaned out and studied the protrusion.

"If we use everything we have, including each other, our clothes, everything, to form a ladder, I think we can do it," she said.

We set to work creating the longest string of stuff we could. With my knife I cut the waterproof packs and climbing harnesses into long strips. Using the webbing straps and carabiners, Tripnee tied and clipped everything together into a motley chain that included our sleeping bag, our sandals, and every stitch of our clothing!

"Hanging out with a woman who knows her knots has its advantages," I grinned. "This just might work!" I didn't want her to know my doubts.

Tripnee had put a loop in each end. She hooked one over the sturdy horn jutting up from the lip of our ledge, and lowered our makeshift ladder. Down and down it went, far further than I had thought possible, but it was still too short! Just how much too short was hard to say, but it didn't look good.

With me pressing my back to the wall, Tripnee, holding my hand, leaned far out and looked down.

"Gonna be tight," she said. "But if I go down first and hang onto the end, and you follow and hang off my ankle, we just might make it."

We shared an embrace on our tiny terrace. Then Tripnee started down. As she swung herself over the edge of our ledge, her strong hands latched on to my legs. Moving with finesse, Tripnee descended our motley ladder slowly, deliberately, being careful to avoid sudden movements which might put an extra strain on this diverse chain of unknown strength.

When I saw that she was in place far below, hanging from the bottom loop, clasping it with both hands, I started down.

Gripping the taut sections of fabric and webbing, lengths of sleeping bag and odd bits of doubled up clothing—including our canvas shorts, and even Tripnee's sports bra and panties—all stretched to the breaking point, I lowered myself inch by inch, foot by foot. When I finally felt Tripnee's head with my toes, I eased beside her and kissed the tip of her nose. Continuing down, I gripped her arms and then the camber of her shoulders. With my left hand hooked over her right shoulder, and my right arm tightly encircling her ribs, I eased ever so slowly along that magnificent torso until my arms hugged her narrow waist. Then, with her chest all free and jaunty just inches from my eyeballs, she turned slightly in my grip and bent her left leg at the knee, creating a sort of horizontal tree limb with her left calf. Clinging to her hip bones, I carefully moved onto her level calf just long enough to shift my hold to her right leg. Then, surely giving her a deep tissue massage in the process, I let gravity draw my hands ever so slowly down her right thigh over the knee clear to the ankle. Here I canted my head to look down at the proboscis. There it was! But could I reach it? I forced myself to extend full length, and felt for the snout with my toes. Nothing. Just vertical rock and air.

I let go with my left hand and hung with my right encircling Tripnee's ankle. This lowered my toes by several inches. They searched. Nothing! Still just flat wall and empty space!

"I must be close. Can you lower us an inch or two?" I called up.

"I'll go to one hand," she gasped, "But please be quick!"

I felt us slide down a good five inches, then stop. *She must be holding on by four fingertips!* Her ankle vibrated with tension—the strain of pushing those fingers past the limits of endurance. I felt for the carbuncle. Still nothing! It was time for what rock climbers call a dyno, a dynamic move or jump: releasing one hold to quickly switch to another. I didn't know if I could do it, but I had to try. I had no choice.

To increase friction and slow my slide, I flattened my body against the wall, pressed as much of my skin as I could against stone. With the inside of my right foot hard against the cliff directly above where I judged the bump to be, desperately trying not to think about the consequences of a miss, I released Tripnee's ankle and let myself slide, fall, fly. Down, down, down I went, heedless of the scraping pain. Where was that knob? Thump! A good two feet further down than it had looked. But it was a foothold with a level top. Thank god! I rested, breathing hard, and realized I was covered in sweat.

"Got it! And it's good!" I called, trying to sound calm. To shorten Tripnee's slide—and hopefully prevent her from picking up momentum that might sweep us both off the cog—I rose on tiptoe and extended my arms toward her. Struggling to keep my voice from quavering with the terror I was feeling for both our sakes, I shouted up, "My hands are two and a half feet below you. Come down when you're ready."

Tripnee pressed herself into the wall, almost as though suctioned to it, and came down in a controlled slide, bringing both feet neatly into my palms.

"Whew!" she said, "Do I like the feel of those hands!"

Turning sideways so I was facing southwest, I lowered her feet onto my hips. With her hands first on my head and then my shoulders, she slid the inside edges of her feet down my legs. As the length of her floated through my field of vision, I could not help but notice how the curves of her body harmonized with those of the greater canyon in the distance, now silhouetted against a breathtaking sunset.

She came to rest in front of me, with her right foot on top of mine, which was cherishing the feel of our wonderful new piece of real estate, the rock bump. We kissed, laughing with both relief and deep trepidation. Looking up we saw all of our belongings strung in a line, permanently out of reach.

"It's not often that one's stuff turns out to be a total and complete lifesaver," she said.

"Thank god for that!"

"Hey," Tripnee looked down, "This is, like you said, a really good foothold. But I'm the sort of gal who hopes, eventually, for a little bit more."

Stuffing down my terror, I grinned, "I knew it! Never satisfied."

Looking about, we saw that we were more than halfway to river level. But we still had a long, long way to go. I also noticed, beginning about ten feet below, a stubble of small moss nubs growing out of the granite! Also, that rock looked less gritty, less textured, almost polished and glassy—and ever so slightly less steep.

"Time to go," I said.

As I stayed put, pushing myself into the wall while balancing on my right foot, Tripnee wrapped her arms around me, and with sizzling slowness slid down—and down. When her breasts were against my legs, she tightly encircled my left leg with both arms, swung her own legs free and let gravity pull until she was eyeball to my ankle. I tipped my right foot so she could get her hands on the stone talon. She swung down and hung from our stone protuberance by both hands with fingers interlaced—and as she did so, for the view and the intensity of it, I think, she put her back to the wall. Letting her body stretch, she fully extended into the most mind-boggling rope ladder in all creation.

Keeping my balance, I eased into a one-legged deep-knee bend, and swung down to straddle the knob while facing the wall. In a reverse press, I lowered myself out and down over the barb until I too was hanging by both hands, arms extended, face to face with Tripnee. I shifted my weight onto my left hand. She swung out a little. I got my right arm and leg between her and the wall, brought my left leg across in front of her, and squeezed her tightly with my arm and both legs. Letting go with my left hand, I felt her lissome now sweat drenched frame take my weight. With my free left hand I brushed her hair out of her eyes. She gave me a trembling smile, and for a brief moment I caressed her cheek, lips and neck. Then, enveloping her with both arms and both legs, I slid down the full, long, slippery length of her until I was hanging below with my left hand encircling her right ankle.

In front of me at hip level I felt two of the tiny mossy buds. Two feet off to my right I felt another, and near my toes I found two more. Each was soft, springy and gentle on my bruised hands and feet, but so delicate I doubted they would hold me.

Gradually I transferred my weight to them—it was by the slenderest of threads, but somehow they held! Looking around, I marveled then as to why these exquisite tufts of moss grew here in such abundance. Was it the proximity to the falls? The particular slope, texture and chemistry of the rock? Whatever the cause, for Tripnee and me right then it was an incredible blessing.

With my toes dug deep into two moist clumps, I took

Tripnee's feet in my hands, lowered her, and placed her heels on two moss mounds at my hip level. With relative ease, we climbed down, staying flat to the wall, and taking care to transfer our weight gingerly, to reduce the chances of a mossy nipple giving way. But none did. And we descended steadily for about fifty feet until the moss grew scarce, and ran out completely.

We were now about forty feet above the river, and I guessed that the rushing water of Thimble Falls, from this elevation, just might make a survivable slide. It was growing dark. We had to get off this cliff—and fast. As we traversed over to the falls, I dreaded the coming moments: would the slide be smooth, or would it tear us up? Figuring it was better if just one of us got hurt, I pulled Tripnee onto my lap, my belly to her back bone, and, with my spine to the roaring cascade, took a big side step well out into the streaming water, and let it take us!

CHAPTER TWENTY-THREE
FORKS CAMP

We shot down the falls in an exhilarating acceleration. The water-worn stone was slippery and smooth, and in a heartbeat we plunged into the swift, cold river, which raced along the base of the cliff. Surfacing, gasping for breath in the icy flow, we swam hard for the far bank, powering with the last ounce of our strength across the current as it swept us downstream. At length, Tripnee, then I, reached an eddy, got to the river's edge, and stood up in calf-deep water where we fell into each other's arms, weak with relief. When we waded ashore, there was Becca!

"Welcome to Thimble Camp, you guys!" Becca beamed her gleaming smile. "Cassady and I noticed you when you were about one third the way down that cliff! In the twilight and with all these trees, no one else saw you, which is just as well. You guys were fabulous! You stuck to that smooth wall like limpets!"

"Wow! Are we glad to see you!" Then we eyed each other. Aware Tripnee and I were stark naked, we all three grinned and shrugged sheepishly.

"Cassady and I saw what you did with everything you had with you," Becca said. "That was very resourceful, by the way! So I brought you both some clothes and towels.

And I thought you could use the first aid kit. These are some of Kim's things for you, Tripnee, and here's some stuff of Cassady's for you, Mr. Yummy."

"You're a doll, Becca," said Tripnee.

"Thanks! This is exactly what we need!" I said. Tripnee and I plopped down together, opened the first-aid kit and began cleaning and dressing each other's scrapes and wounds. As we did this, we told Becca about our close call at the pot farm and my theory that cartel men stole our rope. At length, Tripnee wrestled into shirt and jeans, and I pulled on some pants, a sweatshirt and a jacket.

Becca seemed to reflect on everything we had told her, and said, "Wow, thank god you're okay! Come on. We have dinner for you."

Thimble Camp was a long wooded sandy beach wedged between the river and the base of the steep eastern canyon wall. Nestled here and there among the alder, willow and ponderosa pine were small sandy clearings where people had pitched their tents. In the biggest clearing, the entire guide school sat in a circle around an eco-friendly fire built in a rectangular fire pan designed to prevent ash from marring the immaculate sand.

The three of us joined them, Tripnee and I picking a spot with a boulder backrest.

"Hey!" "Holy Mackerel, Tripnee and Adam!" "Welcome!"

"Thanks," "Good to see you!" "It's great to be here!" We responded.

"Hey!" said Dog. "Am I glad to see you! How'd you guys get here?"

"Hiked and slid in a little while ago," I replied.

"Whooaah!" said Sparky, the tall, skinny instructor. "How was that?"

"It was steep," I said. "We made it, but barely!"

"You can say that again!" laughed Tripnee.

Reddy and Ludimila, who apparently had been on the dinner crew, handed us plates heaped with grilled wild salmon, stir-fried veggies, rice pilaf and salad, and cups of what turned out to be darned good wine poured from a bag. Looking around, I saw that everything in the camp was light-weight and compact. The cook gear, fire pan, food boxes, everything, had been carried by horses and people down a three mile trail, and then floated by raft to this pristine wilderness setting.

"I've gotta tell you, Adam!" gushed Dog. "The Forks is incredible! 'Course, the instructors captained the big stuff, but all of us students are doing great! I myself guided Nose Buster!! And look around, everyone's nose is intact!"

"Dog, your run really was fabulous!" said Cassady, to a chorus of agreement.

"Thanks, you guys," said Dog. "It was truly a great team effort. Everyone did their part. In fact, I want to especially thank you, Ludimila. It was you who kept me from falling overboard in that first big hole. Without you, I would have had to swim the whole thing."

Tripnee and I briefly exchanged glances and raised eyebrows. This guy was coming along!

"Way to go, Ludimila!" said Becca. "Ya know, for all of us, guiding brings up a ton of fear, and you've been ultra brave in talking about and facing yours. Now here on the Forks, you've really come into your strength and confidence! We all see it."

"Yes! We sure do!" said Cassady, to a general murmur of agreement.

Ludmila beamed and blushed, obviously moved.

Tripnee and I told the guide schoolers about the pot farm, the dead bodies, and our ordeal on the cliff—leaving out Tripnee's undercover FBI status. They listened in horror, asked a lot of questions, and at length, regained their irrepressible high spirits. Somehow our very openness had drawn the group closer together.

As the conversation flowed, Tripnee and I held hands. I felt an easy openness; everywhere I looked people met my gaze and smiled.

Mugs of rich, thick hot chocolate were passed out.

Tripnee said, "I'm going to just blurt it out: I love the nurturing support flowing among us! Right here, with you, I'm seeing the Really Big Picture in action!"

"Did you hear that? From the guru herself!" chortled Reddy. "We must really be doing okay!"

"I have to admit," I said, "Just being with you guys makes me want to guide too!"

Cassady's steel pan instrument, called a hang, emitted melodic rhythms which floated above the white noise of the river. Towering canyon walls above us framed a narrow, brilliant band of stars extending north and south. It occurred to me that our unique route into the untamed Forks Canyon gave Tripnee and me a heightened appreciation of the rugged inaccessibility and complete wildness of this giant crevice deep in the Sierra. Perhaps we were getting a glimpse of how our planet felt to the Tubatulabal Indians before contact with European settlers.

CHAPTER TWENTY-FOUR

DOG

When the group broke up for the evening, Tripnee and I walked with Dog down to his tent, which occupied its own private little beach. We sat cross-legged in a circle on the soft sand facing each other, close enough to touch. A crescent moon glistened on the black river racing nearby.

"I'm so glad you're here," Dog said, "There's so much I desperately need to say to you both. You'll probably hate me! I've realized a bunch of things. I've got to come clean. Got to tell the truth. Like Becca says, I gotta say it. If I keep it bottled up inside any longer, it'll strangle me, poison me."

Dog stopped and looked at Tripnee for a long time. Then he looked at me. In the moonlight I saw tears in his eyes.

"You guys have figured out," he half asked, half stated, "My father, Toro Canino, runs a Mexican drug cartel?"

"We guessed as much," I nodded.

"My family's been smuggling drugs forever," Dog said. "Grandfather El Jefe—he was full-blooded Yaqui Indian chief—well, he smuggled pot and peyote. Tough bastard and dangerous to cross, but he had a code of honor and a live-and-let-live way of doing things. Got him into trouble though. Let his guard down at the wrong time. Got his eyes gouged out. His throat slashed by Pescadero, a rival gang. Toro actually saw it. Went ballistic. Exploded on a rampage. He slaughtered Pescadero. Wiped out eleven other drug gangs and took over their territories. Built a single huge cartel—everyone calls it La Casa.

"It's been thirty years since El Jefe died, and Toro's still on a rampage. And getting worse. Growing pot was never enough for him. His focus is the hard stuff. Heroin and the deadliest, most life-trashing drug ever: crystal meth. And the killing is out of control! With Toro, you're either with him a thousand percent or you're dead." Dog made a throat slashing motion. "No middle ground. If he senses any ambivalence, even the slightest wavering, you're toast. I, for example, am toast."

"But you're his son!" I protested.

"Hey, my own mother got the ax when she stood up to him!" Dog gave an agonized movement of his shoulders.

"Holy shit!" I blurted.

Dog continued, "Toro was grooming me to play a role in the cartel. After I got my Stanford MBA, he ordered me to spend time here in Kern Valley, the key distribution hub for their smuggling operation. This actually appealed to me, not because I want to join the family business, but because I've always been drawn to the rafters working on the Kern."

Tripnee and I leaned forward, riveted.

"When I first asked Toro if I could train as a river guide, he turned me down flat. But—and this is really hard to confess—when I suggested it could prove useful for me to be an undercover mole among the river people, he let me do it. Now I was torn apart, not knowing what to do. And I did spy on the rafters."

Shaking his head, Dog said, "Oh god forgive me! Now

I've got to say it! I was hanging around the Lower Kern camp, and I overheard you, Tripnee, whisper to Becca that you're undercover FBI working with the Forest Service."

Tripnee just nodded and patted Dog's knee.

"Tripnee, Tripnee," Dog began sobbing, "I told them. I ratted you out! They know! It was because of me they ran you off the cliff! I drew the target on your back. And they'll kill you! And they'll kill you too, Adam!"

A wave of anger engulfed me. I wanted to pummel and strangle this kid, and yell into his face, 'You bastard! How the hell could you do this to Tripnee? Who the hell ARE you?' But I didn't, mainly because Tripnee nudged me, signaling restraint. Her face, as she looked at Dog, was full of a compassion that I at that moment did not feel.

His body shaking convulsively, Dog sobbed, "I'm so, so sorry, but sorry doesn't cut it! I'm a rat! A vile, cowardly, despicable rat!"

Tripnee said soothingly, "Oh Dog, you've lived in a crucible your entire life. But I can see your courage, your goodness. The very way you're talking to us now is something very few people could do. You, all of us, we're going to get through this together." And with her eyes riveted to his, she said, "I know you're a good man, and I'm honored by your friendship."

Tripnee's words doubled the flow of tears pouring down Dog's contorted face. His mouth worked, but nothing came out. Finally, between sobs, he stammered, "Tripnee … I .. love … you."

Hitching closer and grasping Dog's hands, I said, "I'll be honest, a part of me wants to wring your massive neck. But I can also truly say that last night, you were great. When Toro and his men showed up, and you told Tripnee and me we needed to escape, you saved our lives. You risked your own to do that!"

Dog's fingers dug into my palms, and his crying, if anything, intensified.

"When the chips were down," I continued, "you did the right thing. The fact is you're an incredibly brave guy!"

Not knowing what else to do, I held on and let the heaving whole-body sobs course through him. I realized this was only a boy, and gradually my anger subsided to be replaced by compassion.

Looking at Tripnee, I appreciated the life lessons she was helping me through, and feeling a growing closeness. This wretched young man was on a positive, healing path—and I was learning how humans should be.

We talked on into the night. As Dog poured forth feelings and information that he had concealed for a lifetime, he seemed to grow, expand and breathe more freely. In spite of this, he jumped at every little sound coming out of the darkness around us, and he talked several times about targets etched on our three backs—and nooses around our necks.

Then he dropped an H bomb: "Toro's partner, the other big kingpin, is Reamer Rook. You know him?"

Tripnee and I looked at each other, and stopped breathing. I was utterly stunned. The world seemed to go silent. I saw Tripnee's lips move but heard no sound. It was similar to some of the near-miss Afghanistan explosions I had just barely survived.

After a while I heard Dog saying, "Toro and Reamer have a rivalry of inventive badness. They're two vicious mother fuckers who will stop at nothing to protect and expand La Casa's drug empire. Their favorite pastime, what they do for fun, is to stuff people—usually people who have caused them trouble, but anyone'll do—into the penstock flume that leads into the KR3 turbine down near Kernville. They even have a special name for it: 'No muss. No fuss.'"

I asked, "Where do Toro and Reamer access this flume?"

Dog said, "Up Packsaddle Creek Road."

Just before we parted for the night, on a wild hunch I asked, "Do you know, by any chance, how Rook first got his hands on the Indian Rock Resort land?"

Dog shrugged, "That was before I was born. Don't know the details. But I remember Toro boasting, years ago, like it was an example of what I should aspire to, that he and Rook killed the previous owners by blasting them to kingdom come with AK47 machine guns."

CHAPTER TWENTY-FIVE
THIMBLE CAMP MORNING

In the middle of that night, I bolted awake wracked by images from that horrible time. I remembered it all. It was the day after my fifth birthday. Mommy and daddy had just taken turns reading me chapter seven of my favorite bedtime book "The Land of Noom." I was in my cozy blue flannel pajamas and mommy had just stood up from kissing me on my forehead—I loved it when she did that—and daddy was tucking me into bed. Without warning the window over my bed exploded, sending shards of glass everywhere. A line of red holes appeared across daddy's chest and he fell down. A single red hole appeared in mommy's forehead and she fell down. I sat up reaching toward them, then my arm erupted in pain. And after that, nothing.

I returned to the present and realized I was spooned with Tripnee under a borrowed sleeping bag. In the main clearing we had slid the fire pan aside and slept on the warm sand underneath. The unzipped one-person bag barely covered us, but we were toasty from our combined body heat and the warmth radiating off the fire-pan hot spot.

The memory had hit me like a thousand sledgehammers. Flattened by soul-wrenching despair, I had to do something, anything to fight my way back from the black void. I began telling Tripnee what happened—and I kept on talking—my mouth by her ear—pouring out my grief and misery. I heard her breathing change, felt her touch and knew she cared, allowing me to move through my devastation, to empty all my years of hurt. Finally I had hope that this long suffered despair was not to be forever.

Somehow with Tripnee's help, I was able to face the new day and see what it held. No doubt I would need many more such sessions of outpouring, but for now I was able to emerge from my dark abyss.

As night turned to day, I went alone down by the river and realized that the Forks surpassed any place I had ever been. The air and water were crystal clear. Every detail, near and far, even the cobble of the river bottom, stood out in sharp detail, as though magnified. I swear a passing golden trout eyeballed me with recognition, and I gazed back. The trees, the swirling water, the soaring cliff faces were brushed in with an utter disregard for subtlety. All stops had been pulled. All around me the hand of the creator let fly a flowing picture of beauty beyond imagining. Maybe it was my recent catharsis, maybe it was the place itself, maybe it was being near Tripnee, perhaps all three, but I had awakened into the Garden of Eden.

How, I wondered, could the world contain such beauty and at the same time such cruelty? How could the world contain both Tripnee and such men as Toro and my uncle? What kind of man would kill his own sister?

Not long after clear first light, I heard the sound of a sleeping bag unzipping nearby, and saw a long swath of pale skin rise up from the cold ground. Kim, who I remembered as the skills board instructor, pulled on clothes and then swept the camp with a bemused gaze. Her attention lingered on several prone sleeping-bag-encased forms, and then on me.

We silently smiled at each other, sharing the communion of early risers, relishing the calm before the hubbub of the day.

Kim fired up one of the stoves, and soon had tea water boiling and a giant pot of coffee brewing, sending tantalizing aromas wafting through camp. These seemed to give the breakfast crew the will to rise, and in short order, the camp was a beehive of activity. Both to do our part and because pitching in has to be the best way to bond with any group, Tripnee and I joined the breakfast crew.

"How can I help?" I asked, and found myself frying a truck-tire-size pan of bacon and sausage. Tripnee, Reddy and Ludimila prepared a similar-sized pan of scrambled eggs mixed with scallions, tomatoes and green and red peppers. Tall, skinny Sparky washed and sliced an enormous bowl of fresh fruit. Big-muscled Mark and petite Toni served up hash browns and French toast done to perfection. Kim, meanwhile, moved among us, helping find things, tending to details like heating up the maple syrup, mixing orange juice, getting the serving table ready, and setting up a four-bucket dish wash: first and second were soapy water, then came hot rinse, and finally a sanitizing dip with a few drops of chlorine. In about an hour everything was ready and we all sang in unison, "Breeaaaakfaaaasssttt!"

"Ooooohhhh yeeeesss!" "Deeeelicious!!" "Great job on breakfast!" Everyone was up now, enjoying the food, one another and our surroundings. The sky-high cliff to our east—which backed up against a towering mass of Southern Sierra high country—meant direct sun would not reach Thimble Camp for many hours. So we ate in the chill morning air, an upbeat energy infusing us all.

"Today," said Cassady between mouthfuls, "we'll see why the Forks is one of the very best whitewater runs in North America, maybe the whole world!"

"Just being here," said the fair-haired, well-proportioned Ludimila, "makes my heart pound!"

"Me too. Just look at that waterfall!" said Mark nodding toward three-hundred-foot-high Thimble Falls, directly across the river.

Tripnee and I smiled at each other, remembering—and savoring—the danger and sexiness of our unforgettable cliff descent the day before.

"Yes! And listen to roar of first rapid downstream!" said Toni while taking a big bite of fruit-covered French toast.

"I hear you," grinned the buffed but gentle Cassady. "This place has it all: outrageous beauty, total gnarly wilderness, and the ultimate in whitewater excitement!"

"More like whitewater terror!" smiled Ludimila.

"We all feel that to one degree or another," said Becca. "It's only normal."

"Hey, I'm normal, I'm normal!" laughed Ludimila.

"A few things," said Cassady, "that can help us normal people to cope: First and foremost, remember to breathe. And in emergencies, when the shit hits the fan, three questions to ask are: What is the situation? Where are we going? How do we get there?"

"I like how those questions focus on the positive and avoid blame," said Ludimila.

"When you mentioned them before," said Reddy, "I did some checking on the internet. Studies have shown those three simple questions make for peak performance."

"So, Cassady," Mark asked, "what's the toughest rapid on the Forks?"

Cassady sucked in a big breath and let it out slowly.

"Hard to say, there are just so many. But the single place that scares me the most is the Thing in Carson Falls, it's a perfect drowning machine."

I noticed Dog sitting slightly apart on a boulder overlooking the whole grand scene. As I sat down next to him, I asked, "How are you this morning?"

"Good," he said, as he balanced a well-stocked plate on his knees. "Amazingly good! As agonizing as it was, I feel so much better after our talk. I really appreciate you and Tripnee!"

"Our talk really helped me too." I said, feeling ever closer to this young man. I went on to fill Dog in about my parents, my relationship with Reamer Rook and that morning's vivid revival of my memories.

"Man that's fucked up," said Dog, "Reamer's your uncle and killed his own sister! I wish I could say I'm surprised, but I'm not."

I said, "I'll never understand how, how, how he could have done it!"

"Vicious monsters spewing misery and death is what we're looking at," said Dog. "You, me, Tripnee, all of us, just knowing what we know puts us in their crosshairs."

"Yeah?" I said. "Well, they're in my crosshairs."

Breakfast cleanup and preparations to head downriver were under way, and Dog and I pitched in. I was impressed by how smoothly and quickly it went. At this point in the school, everyone—by dint of much coaching, numerous seminar talks and plenty of sheer hands-on doing—understood the morning launch routine, and things flowed like a choreographed dance.

Clothes and sleeping bags that needed to stay dry were

sealed in watertight bags. Food and commissary gear was packed into ice chests and aluminum boxes. A last call went out for those needing to use the porta potty, and Becca brought this important container down to the boats with great care. I could see that the students and instructors were securing everything into the boats extra well—rigging for a flip—so that even if a load were subjected to the fierce upside down underwater wrenching that could happen after a flip, nothing would be lost.

Dog and I used a cylindrical high-volume pump to top off the five boats. Dog showed me how to evenly distribute the pressure among the air chambers, and get the boats drum tight. A stiff boat, I learned, was more responsive, performed better and had a much better chance of successfully navigating the ultimate whitewater test that was the Forks of the Kern.

I noticed that many of Dog's sentences began with the words, "Cassady says..."

"Cassady says," said Dog, "The right air pressure can transform your boat from a sluggish ox cart into a sports car."

"Like your Lamborghini?" I kidded.

"Exactly!" laughed Dog.

Dog, the instructors and the entire group attended to the details of rigging and preparation with a reverence for the boats and equipment. In this isolated place, where the only practical way back to civilization was downriver, our rafts and gear not only had a rugged utilitarian beauty, they were in a sense our whole world and were crucial to our survival. For some odd reason, I thought of Siddhartha ferrying people back and forth across the Ganges, and had an odd sense that his spirit was alive among us.

Becca handed me a lifejacket. "It's a swiftwater rescue

jacket with a quick-release harness and tether designed for what we call live-bait rescues. Those're extremely dangerous and require special training, so you won't be using those features. But the core jacket has great flotation and should serve you well. Besides, this and the one I gave to Tripnee are our only extras."

With the packing finished, we did a final camp and beach check, everyone strapped on lifejackets, untied, coiled and stowed bowlines, climbed into the boats, and pushed off.

Tripnee, Dog and I smiled at one another, glad we were together in Cassady's boat. Excitement filled the air.

"Cannonball heart of the Forks, here we come!" yelled Cassady.

"All right!" "Yee haw!" Came a chorus of replies from the various boats.

We were just crossing the eddy line and paddling out into the main current when I felt a sudden blast of air, actually, multiple jets of air—blowing up! One by one small round holes appeared around us in the tubes of our boat! Pssst! Pssssstt! Pssssssssssst! The boat was deflating under us. In the din of the approaching rapid, I barely heard a faint popping sound, and looked up to see two people shooting down at us from the lip of Thimble Falls. Within a few moments all but one of our rafts had deflated into uncontrollable shapeless blobs of blue material and baggage.

CHAPTER TWENTY-SIX

THE FORKS

A fully inflated whitewater raft is a thing of beauty: rugged, resilient, sleek in a bulbous sort of way, river-worthy, highly maneuverable, even elegant. But it is an illusion. Of course, good boats have multiple air chambers, so it takes a lot of leaks to pop the bubble.

But two machine guns, probably Uzis, did the job.

Within moments we all found ourselves neck deep—and deeper—in the river, being flushed down into the first rapid of the day. The very boats which moments before had been our islands of safety by virtue of their remarkable buoyancy and stability, were now sinking webs of entanglement and sources of extreme danger. As our boat, now an amorphous mass of high-tech plastic fabric, jumbled bags and ice chests, and tangles of lines and hoopi, sank ever deeper, our crew of seven extricated ourselves and swam free.

Powerful, fast, frothy white and ice cold—the rapid was so long that it extended out of sight down around a broad bend in the canyon. As I tumbled along underwater, I caught fleeting, submerged glimpses of other swimmers and sinking, deflating rafts. Surfacing, I gasped for air. Having no boat to swim to, and remembering my previous whitewater swimming lessons with Tripnee, I faced downstream, kept my toes up to prevent foot entrapment, used my feet to kick off rocks, held my breath in the wave crests and gulped air in the troughs.

At one point, down around the bend, the rapid grew quiet for a few moments, and something bumped me from behind. Turning, I saw Ludimila, her eyes wide and dilated in panic and pain. Gasping, hyperventilating and overwhelmed, she had blood pouring from a nasty gash in her left shoulder.

"Ludimila, you're going to be OK," I yelled into her ear, as I took her right hand and placed it over her wound, "Press tightly to stop the bleeding. Whenever you can, take deep, slow breaths..."

Suddenly we dropped into a reversal wave and were ripped apart. I was spun and pummeled as though in a washing machine. When I regained the surface, she was fifteen yards downstream, but—good girl!—still held her hand to her wound.

As I looked beyond her, my heart leapt to see one of our boats, still inflated, maneuvering in and out of an eddy picking up swimmers at the base of the rapid!

Someone—it was Tripnee!—was strongly towing an inert Cassady life-guard-style toward the raft. Many hands reached down and pulled the lanky, blond instructor into the boat, his face red with blood, and at the same time, off to one side, Tripnee pulled herself up and in, jumping aboard like a fish.

Ludimila was pulled in next, continuing, like a trooper, to clamp her hand over her gunshot wound. I was next to wash down to the boat. Exhausted from the bone-chilling swim, I felt boundless gratitude as caring hands lifted me from the water.

Once aboard, I took a huge, relieved breath, realized I still gripped my paddle, saw there was work to do, and jumped into a spot where I could follow Becca's clear, calm commands: "Right side only, forward." "All forward." "Stop." "Pull'em in! Pull'em in!" "Back-paddle. Back-Paddle." The boat moved back and forth across the eddy line, alternately darting out into the downstream current to grab thankful swimmers, then retreating back into the eddy to wait for more. Like a salmon trawler catching fish left and right on an ultimate, no-limit day, our boat overflowed with writhing bodies. And more kept coming.

Meanwhile Kim and Sparky had the first-aid kit open and were tending to Ludimila and Cassady, who, thank god, was showing signs of life.

And while all this was going on, people were beginning to crack under the pressure of our collective real-time nightmare.

Toni screamed, "Holy Shit! What hell is happening?"

"Who's shooting at us?" Someone else yelled.

"Let's face it!" A third person exclaimed. "We're all gonna die!"

Tripnee took Toni's hands, and, to calm everyone's fear as well as Toni's, spoke loudly enough to be heard throughout the boat, "We've been shot at out of the blue. No one could have foreseen it. You, me, we're all afraid, and with good reason. But right now we've all got to stay calm and pull together. Be a team. So, everyone, take long, deep breaths. Listen to Becca and the instructors. We're going to make it through this!"

There was a murmur of agreement.

After a minute, Reddy, perhaps to help lift the mood, piped up, "Holy mackerel! I just counted heads. We've got everyone! Twenty three people packed into one 16-foot boat! It's got to be historic!"

After another pause, someone asked, "To lighten the boat, maybe some of us should try to hike out?"

"Leave people to get shot? No way!" responded Becca. "Like Tripnee says, as a strong team we can do this! The thing is, right now, we only have one bend between us and the shooters. Before they work their way around to the cliffs above us, we—all of us—have to be gone."

As though taking a silent poll, Becca exchanged glances and silent assenting nods with each of the other instructors, including Cassady. I knew that in war zones, when survival depends on swift, coordinated action, a decisive leader can save the day. Still, good leaders find ways to build consensus, and at that moment, these nods of agreement, especially because they were observed by all, served to unite and reassure everyone, all in a few heartbeats.

"The wounded are going to be OK," said Kim, while she and Sparky, having finished with it, sealed and lashed down the first-aid kit.

"OK, then," said Becca, "Let's head downriver! Let's do this thing!"

CHAPTER TWENTY-SEVEN

VORTEX

In the stern, five-foot-tall Becca stood to see over the Gordian knot of humanity that was her crew—a crew, she told me later, that was several times larger than any she had ever captained in one boat anywhere, let alone on a class 5 river, least of all on the Forks of the Kern.

There is a physical limit to how tightly you can pack people together and still have them be able to paddle. We were, I figured, pushing past that limit. Seven people squeezed onto each long side tube, giving us fourteen main paddlers, who would I figured be providing most of our power. In addition, three people leaned forward belly over the bow, ready to do draw strokes by reaching straight out, plunging paddle blades deep, and pulling them straight back—literally stomach muscling the boat forward.

I knew about draw strokes. One person doing them in the bow of an empty boat can do amazing things, like ferry from one bank to the other, and back again. So three bow draw strokers were formidable—especially our three muscular specimens: Dog, Mark and a six-foot-five giant named Buck.

Six people packed the boat's center, and took on the job of holding themselves and everyone around them in. Because our overloaded craft seesawed from side to side low in the water, submarining under big waves, I could see that these central holder-on-ers were going to be crucial in keeping those of us on the perimeter from getting washed overboard.

It was amazing our boat floated at all. Even in the calm eddy, the tops of our tubes oscillated barely above the river's surface. Holes built into the inflated floor intended to make the boat self bailing, were instead allowing the river to flow in. Water twelve inches deep sloshed around our feet making our vessel all the more tipsy and sluggish. Our raft was a ponderous, unresponsive barge.

I was sure that captaining such an unbalanced population explosion down one of the steepest, most maze-like white-water runs in the world had to be nigh on impossible. Holy shit! My heart went out to Becca and all of us!

"Forward!" Becca boomed.

Seventeen paddles moved in unison, plunged deep, powered through water, and returned through air to again and again penetrate the river. It took four strokes to produce the first sign of movement. Then, little by little, we gained speed, propelling our overburdened boat across the eddy line and out into the powerful downriver current.

"Stop," shouted Becca.

The flow turned us, pointing our bow downriver. First up were two big holes, one right after the other. Becca took them down the center, with our bow pointed squarely into the six-foot back-cresting waves. She must have known that our sheer mass would carry us through, because she called no commands and simply let our heavy boat with its precious human cargo slide forward like an out-of-control freight train. Sure enough, the two big waves, which would have walloped and tossed any ordinary raft, flattened under us as we glided through with hardly a jostle.

Holy mackerel! So far so good!

Along with being awash in fear, I felt a wild surge of excitement to be jam-packed in with these intrepid souls—Tripnee, Becca, Dog, Reddy, Cassady, Kim, Ludimila, Mark, Toni, everyone—doing this thing that had to be historic. Brimming with aliveness, whatever happened, I was glad to be right where I was, with this stalwart crew, headed down into the whitewater adventure of a lifetime, of a hundred lifetimes.

At the same time, part of me silently screamed, *This is impossible! I don't want to die! I'm just starting to live!*

I was finally on the verge not only of bringing my parents' killers to justice, but also of coming fully into my own life! I was finding the huge part of myself that was lost when they were butchered. War, of all things, had shown me this inner void. My path toward healing was unfolding better than I could have dreamed, and now I wanted to embrace life and continue evolving, not have it all end here!

Aware that there are no coincidences, that all the threads of my life were converging at that moment, in that insane voyage, I inhaled deep breaths and rebraced my feet. Heart pounding, wiping sweat from my palms and paddle, I sat on the left side at the back of the boat, next to Becca and across from Tripnee. By being close, I thought maybe I could protect them, provide some extra muscle, some extra help at a crucial moment.

In the far distance I spotted a complex maze of boulders interlaced with narrow channels. My hands trembled and my heart sank. How on earth could an unwieldy whale of a boat like ours maneuver through such an intricate labyrinth? Bloody hell! This fast approaching rapid looked like a post-tsunami graveyard of jumbled tombstones, and I knew only one thing for sure: I was overwhelmingly thankful that I was not the one who had to make the calls.

"Left turn!" came Becca's voice, clear and calm.

I and the whole left side back-paddled, everyone on the right powered forward, and our three bow riders faced left delivering forward strokes. On the fourth, the boat began to turn.

On the seventh stroke, Becca yelled, "Stop."

A few beats later, our twig of a captain called, "One stroke right turn," which stopped our spin, leaving us perpendicular to the current, bow pointing left.

"Forward! Forward! Hard forward!"

The grizzly snarl of boulders closed on us fast. Too fast! A rock as big as a bus loomed closer and closer, and I thought for sure we were going to slam into it broadside. Miraculously, Becca's right-to-left course thrust us sideways through the slot just to the left of it. But my relief was short-lived, as ahead I saw coming at us fast a foam covered wrap rock. Then, that too, in the nick of time, slid to our right, as we lined up perfectly on the channel between it and the next boulder over.

It suddenly struck me that Becca was not only looking extra far downstream and starting her moves way early, she was actually thinking further ahead than one could see—drawing on her years of running the Forks, during which she must have etched every rock and chute into her brain. She was now combining this extensive inner map with exquisite timing to thread a diagonal line from right to left through the boulder tangle.

"Stop!" cried Becca. "Back-paddle!"

Holy bejesus! Now we slowly accelerated backward

diagonally from left to right, narrowly missing boulder after boulder, squeezing through one tight slot after another, all guided by Becca's rote memory and supernatural timing. As our ridiculously cumbersome boat cheated disaster again and again, our terror began to be replaced by hope, then confidence and even cockiness.

Awe and adulation for our extraordinary captain spread through the crew. I had seen it before. In extreme situations, people project an aura of infallibility onto their leader based not so much on a history of success, as on their own over-whelming need for reassurance. If our captain can do no wrong, our survival is assured. Right?

The reality, though, was multilayered. Becca's equanimity and brilliant paddle commands exuded mastery and inspired confidence. But from my vantage point at her left elbow, I glimpsed moments of imperfectly concealed confusion and dismay. This woman was as qualified as any human could be for this confrontation—but the scale of the challenge was off the charts. We were pretty much throwing ourselves off a very high cliff and hoping for the best. She simply had to wing it, to fly by the seat of her pants. And because, as she had told some of us earlier, 'Crews don't respond well to the commands of a panicked guide,' she knew it was imperative that she do so with aplomb.

Despite or perhaps because of all this, I was beside myself with appreciation for this woman who balanced between Tripnee and me. With all of our lives in grave peril, she, by the sheer skin of her teeth, drawing on inner wellsprings of nerve and ability, pushed and inspired us to success after success.

But the rapids were becoming more difficult.

"Next up is El Frijol Grande," said Becca, "Also known as Big Bean."

At first all I saw was a horizon line beyond which the river disappeared. As our wallowing behemoth sped tipsily, a wild, long steep runway of giant holes and leaping, aerated waves sprang into view.

"On this one, everyone hold on tight!" yelled Becca.

We were, by virtue of Becca's advance planning, perfectly positioned. Like a battering ram we pounded forward, bow straight downstream, headed for the rapid's deepest, straightest channel—but what a channel! Lying in wait directly down current were two monster reversal waves one after the next, each big enough to swallow us whole.

As our lumbering vessel swooshed into the first hole, everyone grabbed handholds and held on for dear life. A split second before blasting foam inundated the boat, I took a huge breath. I felt like I was holding onto a nuclear submarine plunging into the ocean depths. Explosions of spume stretched me out, knocked me around, and snapped, cracked and flogged me like the tip of a bullwhip. Feet, elbows, knees poked and stabbed my head and shoulders. When a whole body plowed into me on its way out of the boat, I grabbed for it with one hand while holding on with the other. Catching a wrist, I pulled it down to my handhold, where the person's fingers seized the webbing strap. As we careened along underwater, whipped and pummeled, two more swimmers, torn loose from the raft, crashed into me. I caught one by a life-jacket strap and the other between my legs in a scissor lock, then pulled each back to a handhold on the boat. Only later did I learn that all three—Ludimila, Buck and, of all people, Becca—had had their hoopi handholds literally break free in the deep underwater wrenching of Big Bean.

At last we surfaced. Our boat, amazingly, remained right side up, but was now completely spun around stern downstream. The crew was in a state of bedlam, with bodies intertwined every which way. Basically, though, everything seemed OK.

"Heads up!" yelled Reddy, "Two people are missing!"

Son of a bitch! Everyone's worst nightmare! We searched the undulating waters around us but saw no one.

Suddenly, two swimmers surfaced seventy feet down-stream. Tripnee saw them too, unclipped a toss bag, gripped one end of the rescue line within it, and prepared for her throw. With sinuous power, her entire body uncoiled to send the toss bag hurtling through the air—playing out floating line as it went—to plop directly between the two swimmers, an arm's length from each. A perfect throw!

"Well done! Way to go!" yelled Becca, as she sprang back into her standing captain's stance.

"If we'd been under any longer, I would have had to float up for air," said Reddy from midway up the right side tube.

"You and me both, and probably all of us," I said, to a general chorus of agreement.

While Tripnee pulled the swimmers toward the boat, Sparky made the "Are you OK?" signal by arcing his arm in a circle to tap the top of his helmet with his fingertips. When the swimmers, Dog and Toni, tapped the tops of their helmets to signal "OK," I sensed everyone's anxiety level drop several notches—from somewhere around "overwhelmed and ready to freak out" to "extremely stressed but hanging in there."

As Dog and Toni reboarded the raft and clambered back into their paddling positions, I noticed Becca and Tripnee exchange knowing glances, and heard Becca whisper in an aside meant just for Tripnee, "And that was just a 4 plus."

Becca brought out a mesh bag. "We're going to need bomb-proof hand holds. Here's some sturdy webbing."

I thought, way to go, Becca knows best, so I more than doubled the strength of my handhold with a length of the one-inch tubular webbing, and people up and down the boat did likewise.

Becca faced the whole crew, "Very well done, everybody! So far so good. Coming up, Vortex, a class 5 slash 6 waterfall, followed by a huge sticky hole called Gortex. Then comes the Gauntlet, hundreds of yards of continuous class 5 drops. Good luck!"

We neared the brink, and the river seemed to plunge off the edge of the earth. Effing shiest! Beyond the lip I saw nothing but empty space. Just mist wafting up, as though from Xanadu's measureless caverns! Suddenly, when we reached the very edge, a long expanse of precipitous waterfalls came into view, dropping away before us like a giant staircase down to hell.

Then something astounding happened. Maybe because everyone realized this was it and every square centimeter of our skin was in the game, we all became resolute and began to truly move as one and put our absolute all into every stroke. Through stroke after stroke, not only did our paddles stay in sync, but our torsos leaned forward and powered back together, like a single organism controlled by a single brain.

Poised erect to see over the low mountain of humanity that filled her boat, Becca seemed to be guided by an intuitive connection with the river. Much of the time, when it took us down the deepest channels, she simply went with the flow. When moves were necessary to miss rocks or navigate bends, she started so far ahead of time that I couldn't see why she initiated them when she did. Then, much later, we found ourselves in the perfect position, sliding neatly down narrow channels, missing menacing boulders by a hairsbreadth.

It might sound crazy, but I believe we were all experiencing an almost paranormal level of attunement to one another and the river. I felt something magnify my strength, and sensed the same happening to those around me. I remember reading that the Incas, sitting in human thought circles, were able to direct the noetic power of the human mind to literally cut stone—accounting for the phenomenal ubiquitous stone work accomplished throughout their Andean empire during their short history. In that boat, I felt us tap into an aspect of this human-earth-synergy potential. In no other way can I account for our survival, for the uncanny swiftness and surgical accuracy of our moves.

After diving over the entrance lip of Vortex on the far right, we dodged with jaw-dropping skill through one seemingly impossible maneuver after another, threading our way through an intricate series of narrow chutes. Then dead ahead was the vast keeper hole: Gortex. By dint of exceptional teamwork, we got up enough mo to skirt the hole on the right. Moments later, we entered Gauntlet, but I could see that we had to get left fast to miss another whopping reversal! Oh no! I realized it simply wasn't humanly possible to make the move! Then Becca, like an archangel tapping into a higher power, lined our right tube up on a giant diagonal wave that seized our whole boat and surfed us left, shooting us past the humongous hole. Next, with our stern pointed right, she called for the mother of all back-paddle strokes!

"OK then!" she hollered, "Back-paddle! Back-paddle! Need ya now! Need ya NOW! Back-paddle! Back-paddle! BACK-PADDLE!!!"

Holy bejesus frakking sheist! We hauled ass to the right, narrowly missing disaster after disaster!

"Take a big breath and hold on!" yelled Becca.

We then torpedoed stern first into the biggest bus-eating hole so far! All of us were stretched out, thrashed and flailed like flags in a hurricane. But this time all of our handholds held firm.

As we emerged from the rapid, I saw people looking at each other in amazement. Out of fear of breaking the spell, no one wanted to give voice to our astonishment.

Except Reddy, who chortled, "Holy Mackerel Andy! Oooooooooooo oooohhhh ooohh yeeeeaaahhhh! Brother Ben sat on a chicken, killed a hen! This is unbelievable!"

The rest of us quietly took in the experience, marveling at the symphony, the masterpiece we were part of—not just the Forks—but us, together—a team of earth people—at one with ourselves and our surroundings. I was blown away! It was wondrous! Unbelievable! Even with my war buddies, I had never felt so in tune as I did with this crew. We were a choreographed ballet, a Bach fugue, a vibrant human group performing at our peak!

"All I know is," said Tripnee, "there's something happening in this boat that I'm proud to be part of!"

Oh man did I love it! What I was doing right then satisfied a craving that had always been in me, but that I had only just then, in its fulfillment, become aware of. It struck me: It's all in how we inhabit our own skin! How I notice, accept and flow with my inner river! Not a simple formula, but a wide open invitation to embrace the wild universe within and without!

Defying all odds, this phenomenal groove continued rapid after rapid. Yet two points of discussion around the campfire that morning—which seemed like eons ago—increasingly stabbed at the back of my mind: Undercut rocks and the Thing!

CHAPTER TWENTY-EIGHT

WESTWALL

I had learned that undercut rocks—rocks with over-hanging upstream faces—are among the most dangerous of river obstacles. Most mid-river rocks have billowing water cushions which tend to shunt boats and swimmers off and around. Undercut rocks, on the other hand, not only gener-ally have no deflecting pillow, their downward-sloped faces can force floating objects below the surface and pin them underwater. Rafts and people—depending on the shape of the rock—can even be jammed clear to the river bottom.

"In all my years of rafting," Cassady had said, "the two undercut rocks that scare me the most—actually, they give me nightmares—are the Whale's Tail and the giant Dice Rock in Westwall. If you try to sneak left, the Whale's Tail can get you, and if you run the main falls, right there, dead center straight downstream, is the huge Dice Rock, a perfect cube, twelve feet on a side, balanced on one corner. Let me tell you, it's darned hard to miss. But you've got to, or you're going down!"

Oh oh! We rounded a bend to the right and I recognized Westwall in the distance. Even though I was seeing it for the first time, the legendary class 5 rapid was unmistakably marked by a massive vertical granite cliff towering over the river along its west side.

"Westwall, coming up fast!" yelled Becca. Then in a lower voice just to those of us around her in the stern, she said, "Oh boy, this is gonna be something!"

The riverbed fell away before us, and the current picked up speed. A medium-sized wave broke over the bow filling the air with grapefruit sized globs of foam, one of which caught me square in the face. Guided by Becca's clairvoyant commands, we began a series of moves, first right-to-left and then left-to-right, threading a route through the quarter-mile-long boulder-clogged entry.

Despite our continuous string of successes, I was wracked by apprehension. Far downstream I caught glimpses of the deadly duo: the Whale's Tail and Dice Rock. The gradient, I realized, was becoming just too steep, the current just too fast! Even for an ordinary raft, let alone our semi-submerged Titanic, there was no way not to pick up momentum—too much momentum. We raced toward the main falls—with the ominous Dice Rock dead center just beyond it—and I couldn't see how we had even a ghost of a chance. We might survive the main drop and its no-doubt fearsome hole, but the sheer inertia of our speeding super tanker would inevitably propel us straight into the underwater cavern that lay in wait below Dice Rock.

I thought of jumping overboard and swimming for it. If our boat and crew were entrapped underwater, wouldn't it be better to have at least one of us free to attempt a rescue? But Becca, except for the tension around her eyes and bulging veins in her neck and temples, looked calm and steady. Despite my inner voice screaming 'Jump!' I chose to take this ride to the bitter end, even if it meant being sucked down to a watery grave. At least I was in good—in fact, the very best—company.

Then, once again, Becca astonished me. First by taking

a monster wave, that she called the Catcher's Mitt, broadside—and then by calling for a forward straight into the right bank. The total result of these two actions was to slow our downstream motion and pick up enough left-to-right speed to send us, with exquisite precision, into, of all things, an eddy only slightly larger than our raft. Brilliant!

"This is the Waiting Room," said Becca, as our boat slewed to a stop. "This eddy is what makes Westwall runnable. Now that we've gotten rid of our momentum, let's take some deep breaths, shake ourselves and roll our heads around a little."

We did and it felt great.

"Now, we've got to bust a move like never before to miss Dice Rock."

We left the waiting room eddy by way of its upper end, with our bow angled upstream.

"Forward! Forward! FORWARD!" came the call, "If you've ever paddled hard in your life, do it now! Do it now! DO IT NOW!"

Still in glorious peak performance mode, we paddled furiously, like beings unified and possessed, as the current whipped our bow around, and swept us at breakneck speed toward the falls and Dice Rock just beyond. In complete sync, we accelerated our paddle rate from double, to triple and then to quadruple time, even as we shot over the falls. Miraculously—I have no idea how—Becca maintained a constant 45 degree angle with our bow downstream to the left even as we fell vertically and then plowed through the broad reversal. Throughout it all we crowded in stroke upon stroke upon stroke, all in ultra high-speed tempo.

Despite our Herculean efforts, the giant perfect cube of Dice Rock lunged toward us, its dark grey polished underbelly garish and beckoning. Whaoww! It just didn't look possible. Still, determined to go down doing our extreme best, we poured on the strokes, our arms and bodies racing like pistons full throttle. And Oh god, Oh god, we somehow managed to get left enough! Just barely enough to scrape down the left angled surface of the cube, our right tube grinding on waterworn stone. Holy moly! Completely out of breath, our faces streaked with tears of relief, we looked around as though seeing the river, the canyon, the beautiful earth for the first time.

Then it struck me: What are the chances that a perfect cube, looking very much like a giant version of one of Reamer Rook's gaming dice, should sit balanced for who knows how many millennia smack dab in the wrong place in this rapid—turning every run into a gamble for one's life? Was this proof that a sense of humor was built into the very nature of things, or what?

Leaving Westwall behind, we glided on swift, smooth current, taking in the azure sky, gleaming granite canyon, clear, crystalline water, and one another's beaming faces.

"You're all truly awesome!" yelled Becca, "Let's do a paddle salute!"

We all raised our paddle blades high in the air, and stabbed them up and out, forming sort of a seventeen point crown, yelling en masse as we did so, "Yes!" Then we brought our paddles down for a moment, and thrust them skyward again, this time clicking them all together high above the center of the boat while yelling, "Way to go!" followed by, "Hurray! Yippee! Holy mackerel!"

Catching Tripnee's eye, I silently mouthed, "I love you!" And her lips answered, "Me too."

"Around this next bend is Dry Meadow Creek," said

Becca, "We're going to stop here for a short rest. The biggest waterfall of all is still ahead, so we shouldn't celebrate just yet. But so far, so good! I am so honored to be here with you guys!"

Rounding the bend, our jaws dropped. A stream of ethereal clarity, like an idyllic fantasy, sparkling like a string of diamonds, tumbled down a staircase of waterfalls in a gorge of smooth, sensually flowing sculpted granite, to, finally, descend a zesty waterslide right into the river.

A few yards up from the tributary mouth, we eased into a tranquil eddy adjacent to a white sandy beach. Our bottom touched and we all clambered out, picked up the boat and lifted it onto shore. With twenty-three of us crowded around, our vessel looked dinky—way too small to have carried so many of us so far!

"Wheeeewww! Can you believe this?!" exclaimed Mark. "Getting blasted out of the water! All of us making it this far in this one boat!"

"I'll say this: Thank god for this boat!" said Ludimila.

"It's a miracle this one didn't get shot like the others." said Toni.

Cassady replied, "Becca was the first to pull out from camp, and must have been out of range when all hell broke loose. Great job, Becca, on what has to be the most epic captaining in Forks history!"

There was a huge chorus of agreement, "Thank you!" "You're so awesome!" "Oh, Becca, thank you!"

Chilled and exhausted, a bunch of us went up the beach a ways and plopped down on the warm, dry sand, while others, including Tripnee, went off into the woods. Becca, meanwhile, stayed with the raft, checking it over. Later, I saw her sit on the stern, open a watertight Pelican case tied to the rear cross thwart, pull out a satellite phone, and make a call.

Stretching out spread-eagle on his back on the beach, Reddy reflected, "Ya know, that attack was over the top. I guess cartel pot growers are known to kill intruders, but shooting from the cliff top at us down on the river is going to draw a lot of attention. That'll bring down the law, and be bad for business."

"They probably went berserk," I said, "Because Tripnee and I surprised them and left them hog-tied on their bellies. To put it mildly, we left them very uncomfortable."

"They must have been really pissed off," said Dog, with a knowing look.

"Those murderers terrify me," said Toni.

"Me too," said Ludimila with a shiver. "Do you think they'll attack us again?"

"Hard to say," I said.

"I think Becca is calling the cops right now," said Cassady. "There's not much the cops can do for us here deep in the Forks Canyon, but they could meet us at take out and offer some protection there."

"I have to say," I said, "You guys are handling extreme risk way better than some trained soldiers I've seen."

The lanky instructor Sparky sat up and said, "This whole thing is incredibly fantastic! Everyone here is amazing! There's an old saying, 'We can't always control our circumstances, but we can determine our response to them.' All of you are rising to the occasion. Instead of freaking out, we're coming together as the best paddle crew I've ever seen!"

"The risks are scary. But to me, this crew, this river, this place—all so wonderful!" said Toni as she ran her toes and fingers through the fine sand. "Maybe I crazy, but all of it, I love it!"

Tripnee and several other people returned just as Becca came over.

Becca stood over us as we stretched out on the sand basking in the sun. "OK everyone. So far, so good! Despite obvious problems with an overloaded boat, it's safer if we stick together and raft on out of here. I just talked with the deputy sheriff, and he'll be waiting at take out. But I'm still worried about us getting shot between here and there. We need to keep moving, so let's head downriver in a few minutes."

As Becca spoke, I noticed Tripnee register a look of surprise—and something else, exactly what I wasn't sure.

Going over to her, I asked, "Is everything OK?"

The odd expression returned for an instant, and then was gone. "Yes," she said, "but there's something I have to do. I don't have time to explain, but I'm going to hike out from here."

"We'll hike out together," I said. "I'm going with you…"

Grabbing my hands, she pulled me toward her and we gently touched lips. Then holding me there, she said, "I need you to trust me. I've got to do this alone. I'll meet you at sunset back at the van."

Alarmed, I said, "What if something happens…"

"I'll be OK. I'm an FBI agent, remember?" she said with a smile. "But it's good to have a back up plan. So if for some reason we don't meet before dark at the van, I'll see you at noon tomorrow at the Audubon Kern River Preserve, where the South Fork of the Kern enters Lake Isabella. Branch Terwilliger, the manager there, is a trusted friend."

"But…"

"And one more thing," she said, slipping back into that odd expression. "It's crucial that you not do anything to confront Reamer Rook or the cartel until we meet. I'll explain everything later, but right now we've both got to get moving."

She kissed me lightly again, then after talking for a moment with Becca, ran downriver to the water slide mouth of Dry Meadow Creek. Like a force of nature, Tripnee then bounded up the steep but climbable canyon wall, and in a minute or two disappeared over a shoulder of the undulating granite face.

What in the world could make her take the risk of heading off alone? Sensing there was something huge she was not telling me, and feeling uneasy and a little abandoned, I rejoined the others and helped lift the boat back into the water.

Soon my mind went to Carson Falls and the Thing.

CHAPTER TWENTY-NINE
CARSON FALLS

If I were on death row, my own impending execution would very likely become an obsession that would blot out all else. In the same way, the closer we got, the more Carson Falls and the Thing took over my mind and emotions. Perhaps because of this growing preoccupation for all of us, just getting there proved hair-raising and almost beyond our ability. One very tricky rapid—appropriately named Respect—very nearly nailed us, but not quite, and we continued to dodge downriver.

Carson Falls, I knew, was the infamous Big One, the single biggest waterfall on the Forks. If the enormous rapids that had been stomping, grinding and spitting us out all day long were the Himalayas, Carson Falls was Mt. Everest. It was a colossal double drop: Two immense cataracts jammed together, one plunging into the next, with the second even more treacherous than the first because below it lay the Thing—the biggest keeper reversal on the entire run.

Keeper holes loomed large in the minds of Cassady and the others. They form when downriver current pours over a drop and dives deep to charge a good distance along the river bottom, leaving a low pressure zone on the surface which is filled by white foam and spittle surging up at what is known as the boil line and raging back upstream. These two opposing currents—the free-falling blast and the surface back flow—form a voracious, sucking mouth which can hold and recirculate floating objects, including logs, boats and swimmers.

I knew from the campfire stories that what sets the Thing apart—and largely accounts for the forbidding reputation of Carson Falls—is the sheer size and violent power of this recirculating zone. The boil line is a full fifteen feet downriver from the falls, and the surface back flow rivals the downstream current in speed and power, forming a perfect drowning machine. Anyone unlucky enough to find themselves in the Thing between the falls and the boil line would be thrust at breakneck speed back upriver into the face of the falls, where they would either be tumbled in place or, very likely, sucked down, scraped along the river bottom, then lifted by their buoyancy to the surface, only to again be swept back up into the mouth, in a horrible repeating process known as being Maytagged. Human beings can undergo only so much underwater flailing; even if they get an occasional breath of air, the prolonged thrashing and repeated submersions over and over finally result in what is aptly called flush drowning.

Guided by Becca's calls, our jumbo crew pulled into a big eddy on river right and wallowed over to a rocky bank.

"Welcome to the Big One! Carson Falls is about two hundred yards downstream," said Becca as she picked her way to the front of the boat, stepping skillfully between bodies.

Turning in the bow to face us, she continued, "Running this class 5 falls and the Thing, as we've discussed, involves a higher level of inherent risk than anything we've done so far. For this reason, we always give everyone the option of walking around Carson. Today, with our overloaded boat, the probability of problems is extremely high, making walking, really, the saner option. Running is very risky."

Making eye contact with each of us in succession, Becca continued, "The thing is I have an intuition that if cartel shooters are going to ambush us again, they will do it here. Which could make walking more dangerous than running."

As a frisson of fear ran through the group, Reddy asked, "What about setting safety? Don't we need some people to walk down with toss bags and get in position to rescue any swimmers?"

"My next point exactly, Reddy," replied Becca. "Despite the risk of getting shot, we still need some people to walk down to provide rescue support. I'm sorry if I'm scaring you, but I feel you deserve to know—and can handle—the truth as I see it. I realize this is a lot to take in. Anyway, I appreciate and treasure you all, and I welcome your thoughts."

There was a moment of silence in which I saw a lot of very wide eyes and big intakes of air.

"Whatever you need me to do, I'll do it," I said.

"Same goes for me," said Dog.

"Me too." "Whatever you need." "I'm here for you, Becca. Anything."

Literally everyone volunteered to do whatever was needed. I had never felt closer to a group of people.

"Well, in that case," said Becca, her eyes glistening, "Let's have everyone in the middle of the boat get out, walk down to the falls and get in safety position. That way we're not changing paddlers right above the Big One."

"If there's shooting, hit the ground and take cover fast," I called after the toss baggers as they climbed out of the boat.

As we watched our rescue team scramble over gnarly

boulders and bedrock outcroppings to get down to the falls, Becca prepared us for our run. "OK, this is a double waterfall with a monster reversal, the Thing, on the bottom right. Our goal is to enter right and move left …" She went on to explain the intricate moves we'd need to make. "… As always, follow my commands and be prepared to hold on tight! If you do find yourself in the Thing, remember everything we've taught you about swimming holes, and watch for a toss bag."

When Becca returned to her spot in the stern, I quietly asked, "Why do you think they'll attack us here?"

She responded in a low voice, to just the few of us near her in the stern, "Two reasons: I know there're trails into the falls and into places that could be used as sniper positions. And, to the cartel's way of thinking, just forcing us into the water here we're more likely to drown—which, come to think of it—is, in fact, true."

We pushed off from the bank, paddled out into the downstream current, and, keeping well to the right of center, maneuvered down toward the legendary falls, the source of so many stories. My heart pounded like a racing pile-driver. Was this it for us? Was this approaching horizon line the last thing we were going to see? What a horizon it was! With nothing at all visible beyond it, not even mist or the river in the distance, it looked like we were about to shoot off the edge of the planet.

We were far right, a hundred feet from the brink, when Becca yelled, "Left turn." One, two, three turn strokes. "One stroke right turn," stopped our pivot with our bow angled slightly left, setting us up for Becca's move.

Fifty feet from the lip, a blast of cool up-canyon wind hit us. This gigantic falls generated its own wind and micro-climate!

Twenty-five feet from the precipice, I still could see no river beyond the lip! My heart was in my throat. Jesus, the stories were true. This waterfall was humongous. How could people even think of running such a thing? What fool, dare-devil or wild-eyed adrenaline junky could have possibly thought up the idea that it might be runnable? People did this for fun???

Then it sank in: How could we hope to pick up speed from right to left like Becca had told us? We were going to be literally falling. What kind of purchase could our paddles get on falling water? It was impossible! My mind reeled, only sheer muscle memory kept me in the boat, following Becca's commands.

"FORWARD!! All Forward! Need ya now! Need ya now!"

Paddling like madmen, we crested the edge. The deafening roar, the enormity of the abyss, the insanity—all struck me! Then, amazingly, there actually was a right-to-left current and, we were catching it, moving laterally, and we were going to miss the Thing! Holy, holy, HOLY!!! Becca knew something after all!

Just then Toni doubled over in front of me, blood spurting from her neck! Holes appeared in the tube under us! Ambush! I pressed my hand to Toni's geyser-like wound to stop the flow of blood. But the boat under us rapidly lost shape. All of us plunged into the churning foam, on our way, I realized, into the Thing!

Everything was chaos and tumult, like being thrashed in a giant tumbling drum with seventeen other people. Someone's foot clobbered me square on the nose, maybe breaking it, but this was the least of my worries. I was deep and spinning and getting the living daylights beat out of me by not only feet, knees, heads and elbows, but also by jets of current blasting from every direction.

Tucking into a ball, I felt myself go deep. The bodies struggling around me thinned out. It got pitch black and I became completely disoriented. My back slammed into what must have been the river bottom. Still tucked in a ball, I spun. Then everything grew lighter. I must be getting close to the surface. I rose and rose, the aerated water grew lighter and lighter. My lungs screamed for air. Where was the surface? The bubbles around me brightened to luminescent, then to glaring, dazzling white. Finally, the surface! Gasping, I sucked in air, and with dismay realized I was moving upstream back into the falls.

With every ounce of strength, I threw myself into an all out crawl stroke heading downstream. If I could just cross the boil line, I could get away. Stroking and kicking as fast as I could just wasn't enough! The flow racing upstream in that brutal pressure cooker drove me inexorably into the wall of plummeting water.

The cascade again hammered me downward, smashing me deep into the raging blackness. Spinning and banging, I again hit the riverbed, this time over and over, until I got shot up—and up. Surfacing, I swam hard toward the right. If I couldn't escape by going straight downriver, maybe I could break free out to the side. But even as I fought to move in that direction, the wall of down blasting water pounded me back into the depths. Around and around I went inside that blender from hell, how many times I have no idea.

Asphyxiated, exhausted and beaten to a pulp, I found my normal cluttered thoughts power washed away. Suddenly there was only the simple, crystalline realization that *I loved Tripnee*.

Surfacing for the umpteenth time, I was gasping out of control and half blacked out. Out of nowhere, a toss bag struck the foam a foot in front of my battered face. I seized the line and held on for dear life. It was Dog! His short powerful arms reeled me in, pulling me from that seething cauldron of death. Crawling up on the scalloped, polished rock I was about to collapse when I looked back to see someone else still caught and tumbling in the terrible maw.

It was Ludimila! Dog coiled and re-threw, putting his rescue line inches from her face. But she didn't grab it. She had been knocked around and recirculated too long. As she disappeared into the watery gullet, I saw that she was deathly white and unconscious.

There was absolutely no time to waste, I grabbed the end of Dog's line and clipped it to the tether attached to the quick-release safety harness built into my life jacket. Dog saw what I was doing and played out the right amount of slack. Summoning reserves of strength and perhaps insanity from somewhere, god knows where, I took several running steps and threw myself back into the Thing.

Within moments I was sucked into the killer reversal and blasted down and down. Instead of tucking into a ball, to find Ludimila somewhere in that boiling volcano, I stretched out spread-eagle, and let myself spin like a helicopter blade, at times twirling through pure raging foam, at times smashing along the rocky river bottom. Suddenly there was something. Yes, an arm! I grabbed it tight. A moment later something collided with my already mangled face. A second person! Pulling the two swimmers together, I encircled them in my arms, and held on tight. Our ball of bodies, all the while getting whiplashed and whomped, rose and rose toward the light. At last we reached air. Holy Jesus, I had Kim and Ludimila, both unconscious! Dog saw us and with several others started heaving on the line. As we reached the bank, Dog took Ludimila and I lifted Kim up onto a level rock shelf. Just as I started to check her pulse and breathing, Kim coughed violently. I rolled her on her side and she continued to hack, spewing up drool and vomit. Looking over, I saw that Ludimila also was regaining consciousness and taking in huge breaths, her chest vigorously expanding and contracting.

"Way to go!" I exclaimed to Dog. "You rock!"

"Actually, Adam," he yelled back over the roar of the falls, "You totally rock!"

"Do we have everyone?" I asked, as I closely monitored Kim.

"Yes!" said Reddy, scrambling over to me and Kim. "With you, Kim and Ludimila okay, that's everyone!"

"How is Toni? Did anyone else get shot?" I asked.

"Becca and Sparky are with her now," said Reddy. "She's lost a lot of blood and needs a hospital. Amazingly, Toni seems to be the only one hit."

"What about the shooters?"

"Thank god the sheriff showed up right after the first big volley," said Cassady, who was among the first team of toss baggers. "The snipers stopped shooting, and seem to have faded away."

Cassady nodded toward the other bank. Across the river I saw a man in a deputy sheriff uniform with a rifle standing on a high boulder overlooking the falls. He smiled and waved. I grinned and waved back, wondering how he had managed to arrive so fast, since, as far as I knew, there were no roads in to this spot.

"Wow! Thank god!" I said. "Cassady, how was it for you toss baggers when the shooting started?"

"Wild!" he replied. "At first we all dove for cover, but with swimmers in this drowning machine, we said 'What the hell?' and started pulling people out."

"At great risk to yourselves!" I said. "Showed real guts!"

Cassady grinned sheepishly and said, "Fortunately, it was about then that the sheriff showed up and the shooting stopped."

Surveying the whole scene, I saw our people spread out along both banks below the falls. Many, it seemed, had managed to avoid getting caught in the Thing and had swum ashore. I counted eight drowned-looking rats, including myself, who looked like we'd been pulled from the death machine. I took in a huge deep breath and gave thanks that we were all OK. It was a miracle!

To Dog I said, "Your toss bag saved my life, thanks!"

Dog beamed with pride. Just looking at this troubled young man in a happy state filled me with similar joy.

"Hey, Dog," I asked, "How'd you go from the bow to being a toss bag hero?"

"Incredibly lucky, I guess," he said. "Somehow the Thing spit me out quick. I swam to the bank, and saw that the toss baggers needed help."

"Man, you should be real proud of yourself!" I said, with a lump in my throat.

"Amen to that," said Kim, who, like everyone around me, looked battered but radiantly alive.

As we were getting ready to hike out, an amazing, ser-endipitous thing happened. A regular six-boat Fulfillment Voyages guided trip floated into view, and stopped above

Carson while some of their people walked down to set up safety. Then, like it was no big deal, they ran Carson Falls smoothly and matter-of-factly! Each boat entered right of center, caught the right-to-left current, missed the Thing, and eddied out just downstream. Seeing these calm, professional, smiling guides and excited, happy paddlers all obviously having a great fun time was like peering into another universe—parallel to ours, but normal, joyous and free of trauma.

To put it mildly, they were surprised to see us, and astounded to hear what we had been through. Their poised and courteous trip leader Brian used his trip's powerful satellite phone to have an ambulance waiting at the Johnsondale bridge river access trail a mile downstream. With Toni needing medical attention fast, all of us with the guide school, along with the sheriff, quickly divided up into their six boats and we all floated on. I noticed Becca and the sheriff's deputy talking in one of the boats, while everyone else was quiet and kept looking anxiously toward Toni.

CHAPTER THIRTY
THE SHERIFF

As our new flotilla made its way downriver, the rapids grew milder and the canyon walls spread apart, signaling a transition from pristine wilderness to the wider world. Rounding a bend, we saw the steel framework of Johnsondale bridge arching high across the river. Someone whispered, "Thank god," as we floated closer and saw an ambulance, a Fulfillment Voyages bus and the deputy sheriff's SUV parked near the western end of the span. Brian's boats dropped off our bedraggled group, and, after thank yous and farewells, re-entered the current to continue to their regular Willow Point take out, another two and a half miles downriver.

Two ambulance medics met us on the beach under the bridge, and put our weakly smiling Toni on their gurney. Our other casualties—Ludimila, Kim and Cassady—wanted to walk, so all of us, gesturing and churning with a mixture of distress, relief and euphoria, followed the gurney up a wide path to the vehicles.

"Near drowning victims," said Sparky, "Sometimes seem OK, but later drop dead on land in what are called 'parking lot drownings.' So we've got to have anyone who was unconscious in the water checked out. Better safe than sorry. Also, Cassady, let's have a real doctor take a look at you."

The military-style ambulance had upper and lower gurney bunks on each side, allowing all four of our wounded shipmates to stretch out in relative comfort. The four were shot up and bone-tired, but basically seemed happy and okay. Within minutes the boxy ambulance swung onto the highway heading south.

A few people started getting into the bus. In the middle of saying my goodbyes, standing there alone for a moment, I realized I was feeling a constant pang of missing Tripnee and wishing she were here to share this moment.

I noticed Dog standing alone with shoulders slumped looking north back upriver into the defile that was the Forks Canyon. I walked over. "Thanks, my friend! You were great! You're coming into your own here on the river!"

"And you're hella cool, Adam," he said with intensity. "These people really listen. They're all so positive." He gestured with open hands toward everyone boarding the bus, his voice quavering with emotion. "It might sound wacko, but I loved this trip. For me, the river is way less terrifying than the rest of my life. I can tell you, living with Toro and the cartel is pure hell."

Turning to look south down the canyon in the direction of Kernville and civilization, he shook his head, "Coming back to reality is a bummer."

Resting a hand on his shoulder, I nodded. "Hang in there," I said. "You're not alone. We'll see you soon back at base camp."

Upon hearing this, Dog's spirits—and his head and chest—seemed to lift a bit, and I felt buoyed by his response. But when I added, "Tripnee and I are going to need your testimony to stop the cartel," he whirled, looking alarmed. "Adam, you, me, and Tripnee—all of us—have got to be super careful. You've no idea how diabolical and resourceful those guys can be!"

"We'll do our best," I said, trying to hide my unease. "Together we'll get through this."

Dog, shoulders now sagging again, headed for the bus. I stood there looking after him, feeling both kinship and foreboding.

The deputy sheriff came toward me. His massive physique completely filled his sheriff's uniform. Although older with greying hair, the man exuded strength and quickness, and seemed very much at home decked out in full police regalia including Glock pistol, handcuff pouch, extra ammo clips, a police issue SWAT team rifle on his back, and a name tag reading, "Brewster Cockburn, Deputy Sheriff, Kern County." Looking at me with steady, bright eyes that appeared to take in every detail, he said, "Son, I need to talk with you."

"Of course, sheriff," I replied. "And I want to thank you for meeting us at Carson Falls. Your timely arrival saved the day!"

"No problem. Just doing my job."

It turned out, as I had anticipated, he was headed up to the cartel pot farm crime scene, where he would be joined by some volunteer search and rescue people who would help him deal with the dead bodies. I asked if I could ride along so we could talk en route. As the bus headed south, the deputy, with me in his shotgun seat, pointed his four-wheel drive SUV north, toward the headwaters of the Kern. As his turbo-charged truck climbed deep into this remote corner of Sequoia National Forest, we talked at great length. Something about the man's straightforward, down-to-earth manner made me want to believe deputy Brewster Cockburn was on the level and had no hidden agenda. But still there was the troubling fact that the cartel had apparently flourished for decades during this man's watch.

Being careful not to reveal Tripnee's status as an undercover FBI agent, I told him about our encounters with Mack Dowell, Hektor Torrente and the cartel.

At one point, the sheriff exclaimed, "Wait a minute! Your name is Adam Weldon! Your parents were Abraham and Sarah Weldon?"

I nodded.

The man's chiseled face softened into an expression of tender sympathy. "I knew your folks. Very, very wonderful people. I'm so sorry for your loss, son. To this day, I puzzle over who was behind their deaths."

I asked, "How well do you know Reamer Rook?"

"Interesting you should ask. He and I grew up together poor right here in this valley. Reamer had one mean father who hated him, and he had to lay low. And my own folks weren't much account, so me and him took care of each other and fished the river together every day. We joined the marines as buddies, and fought elbow to elbow in Viet Nam. We fought for the American way of life." The sheriff chuckled. "Sure Reamer gets carried away and goes too far a lot of times. But he's done well for himself." One of the deputy's big hands slapped the dashboard. "He's now far and away the richest man in this valley. He owns a ton of land, three gas stations, the newspaper, the radio station, a used car lot, three hardware stores, five restaurants, a huge mansion overlooking Kernville and that incredible Indian Rock Resort. His fiery Sunday radio talks are popular. The man is resourceful and determined. I admire that."

I asked, "Are the two of you still close?"

"Over the years," Brewster replied, "we've grown apart. Me, I'm just a deputy sheriff working for a good but no-big-deal salary headed for a modest retirement. Reamer has made things happen for himself. Reamer is what America is all about."

"So," I asked, "are you guys still friends?"

"It only makes sense that he doesn't have time for folks like me," said Brewster. "He's on a whole different level now."

"You think he's honest and basically a good man?"

"A lot of people resent success," said the deputy. "So lots of people badmouth Reamer. I ignore them."

I asked, "If someone produced hard evidence that Reamer engages in illegal activities, would you look at it?"

"Of course, but no one ever has. So, until there is proof to the contrary, Reamer is okay in my book, even if he does stir people up with his radio sermons."

Brewster paused for awhile, seemed to weigh a decision, then said, "Adam, let me ask you something: How well do you know Tripnee?"

"I met her just three days ago," I replied, "but she's one of the most amazing women I've ever known. To be honest, I'm completely swept away."

"Son, there's something you need to see. This video, on a pencil drive, was dropped anonymously into my Kernville PO Box."

With one hand on the wheel, the deputy deftly used the other to open the laptop on the seat between us, hit a few keys, start a video clip, adjust the sound level, and turn the monitor toward me.

Puzzled and intrigued, I studied the screen: The scene looked like it had been shot by a hidden wide-angle camera.

Incredibly, it showed Tripnee doing a drug deal! After handing over a briefcase of cash, she and others loaded loaf-sized bag after bag of what looked like methamphetamine into her Prius, until the little car was packed to the gills. No faces other than Tripnee's were visible, though I did see some thick black shoes.

I sat speechless. I couldn't see how I could defend this girl I had grown to love, and explain what I wanted to believe was a sting operation, without revealing she was with the FBI.

The deputy said, "I know everyone in this valley, and I even know, pretty much, what they think of each other. Tripnee has a solid reputation. In fact, the river people see her as a sort of guru of something called the Really Big Picture, which has to do with kindness. So, I thought she must, without me knowing it, have been doing a sting for the DEA, FBI or Forest Service. But I've thoroughly checked out this possibility—after all these years I have close contacts in all these agencies. I've definitely established that Tripnee is not connected with any of them. I'm afraid, Adam, this woman is dealing drugs and is mixed up with the cartel."

"Sheriff," I said, "The idea of Tripnee dealing meth makes no sense. There has to be some other explanation."

"Son," said Brewster, "I can understand this is very hard for you, but we have to face facts. Fact: The video shows her doing a drug deal. Fact: She's not with law enforcement. And another fact: You've known her for only a few days. I gather these four days have really been something. But the fact is you hardly know this woman."

Slowly, the reality of the video and what he said sank in, and I had to admit it did not look good. Aloud, somewhat to quell my own doubts, I said, "This video alone is not solid proof. There needs to be a lot more evidence." But I felt stunned, sick and flattened, like I had been hit by a locomotive, a planet-sized locomotive. The color drained from the world around me. Brewster sounded far away. My mouth felt dry and leathery. Swallowing became painful, and a huge lump in my throat compelled me to swallow again and again.

The sheriff said, "Adam, I'm showing you this to let you know the truth about the people you're mixed up with. And also because I need your help. We estimate that in Sequoia National Forest alone over 200 million dollars worth of pot is grown and a similar street value of meth is manufactured or smuggled through each year. I sense you're a fine young man. You've already become involved with these people. First of all, be careful and don't get into any trouble. But as long as you're in the middle of this, I need you to keep your eyes open and pass on to me anything you learn that could help me stop this flow of drugs."

"You and I both want to stop the cartel," I said. I told him about my criminal investigation experience in the navy, and asked if I could make a copy of the video. He agreed and lent me a pencil drive for the purpose.

Closing my eyes then, I tuned in to myself. My breathing was shallow and rapid, ineffective, like the oxygen had been sucked out of the air around me. I was desperate to reunite with Tripnee and clear up these questions. A fantasy flashed through my mind of heading back to our secret sanctuary deep in the giant sequoias, popping up the Dream Van top, and stretching out with her. But that was with the old Tripnee. Who was Tripnee really?

CHAPTER THIRTY-ONE
CRAZY MAN SHUTTLE

Brewster pulled off the pavement and parked where the road crossed Thimble Creek. Climbing out of the truck and stepping numbly onto black dirt, I felt somehow unsupported, as though I were falling into a dark void.

The deputy handed me his card, "Let's stay in touch, son. Call me if you need me or learn anything. And take care of yourself. With all the government budget cuts, in this whole valley all we have are one California Highway Patrol guy, some Forest Service feds—and me! That's it! So be careful!"

I said I would, and urged the deputy to be careful also. Watching him disappear down the creek toward the cartel pot farm, I reflected that I couldn't help but like this kindly old cop. At the same time, I was glad I had not told him Tripnee was waiting for me three hundred yards from that spot.

Heart pounding, frantic to clear up a million questions, bursting just to hold her in my arms and hear her telling me none of it was true, I sprinted through stands of ponderosa pine and incense cedar toward Tripnee and the Dream Van. But when I got to the spot, Tripnee was not there and my home on wheels was gone! I frantically searched the entire area for signs of struggle or clues to what might have happened.

I found only the van's wide tire marks, showing, on close examination, Tripnee's and my sedate arrival the day before, and a recent, hasty, loam-shredding departure.

Oh god! Oh god! My guts churned and my mind raced. Was Tripnee OK? Was she in danger? Was she hurt? Had something terrible happened to her?

Then thoughts of Brewster and his video rampaged through me. Had Tripnee stolen my van? Was I the blind lover, unable to see the real woman—someone I'd met only four days before? Was Tripnee, in fact, an FBI agent? What kind of FBI agent goes undercover long-term as a river guide? As a shaman no less? Did the government really do such things? It just didn't seem likely. Come to think of it, Tripnee's manner had been strange and downright suspicious when she suddenly decided to hike out the minute Becca said the deputy would meet us at the bridge. Also, how the heck did she know Mack Dowell's and Hektor Torrente's full names from the very beginning? These and other such questions devoured me.

In the midst of my agony, I thought of Tripnee's and my backup rendezvous plan. Maybe, in fact, very probably, she just needed to leave in a hurry and she'd show up at the Audubon Kern River Preserve. Yes, that must be it. By this time tomorrow, Tripnee and I would be back together, these questions would be cleared up, and everything would be okay again. But try as I might, I could not stop myself from falling into a black hole of loss and dread, a depression so deep, it took me all the way back to the bottomless terror of a screaming five-year-old whose mom and dad lay before him covered in blood.

It was late afternoon, and deepening shadows engulfed the forest around me. I stumbled back to the road, Brewster was nowhere to be seen, and no doubt would be tied up at the cartel site for some time. That death scene was the last place I wanted to go right then. Standing on the low bridge over Thimble Creek, a scene that a day before had overflowed with ethereal mountain loveliness, was now empty, clear cut of all beauty. The creek's chattering now menaced, carrying whispers of loss and death.

Beginning like a soughing of wind in the distance, a low hum gradually grew to become the metallic roar of a truck charging down the mountain. As it rounded a broad bend and hurled itself toward me, I read the words Wild River Crazy Men painted on its side. I stuck out my thumb and lo and behold, the truck screeched to a stop.

"Howdy Adam!" shouted the driver. It was Brushy with the huge mustache, one of the denizens of the KRV Recycling Center in Lake Isabella.

"Hi Brushy," I said. "Thanks for the ride."

"No problemo. I'm just driven' gear shuttle for the Crazy Men. Nice to have company."

Climbing in, I asked, "Hey Brushy, did you see Tripnee or a white four-wheel-drive van around here today?"

"Nope."

"What about Mack Dowell and his people? Seen anyone like that?" I asked.

"Nope," he said. Then, after a long pause, "Ya know, come to think of it, when I was coming up, I did see a van like that going down the canyon like a bat out of hell, almost tipping onto two wheels on the curves."

"Yeah?"

"Yeah! How could I forget!?" Brushy became animated. "It was wild! I had to swerve to miss'em! I was so busy trying not to crash—scared the crap out of me!—didn't get a look at the driver."

I pumped Brushy for more details, but he remembered only one: "I remember seeing Mack Dowell's black humvee barreling along out in front of that white van."

"You're sure the humvee was in front of the van?" I asked.

"Yeah, man. In front."

I shuddered, heart racing and mind churning. Sitting in silence, I swam in an inner avalanche of fear and endless questions. Try as I might, I couldn't extricate myself, but sank deeper and deeper into that maelstrom.

After I don't know how long, Brushy, reaching toward the truck radio, said, "Hey, it's time for Reverend Reamer Rook's broadcast."

I needed a break from my feverish imaginings, and besides, this might give me more insight into how this formidable, complicated man thought and, just maybe, some clues to Tripnee's whereabouts. Static blasted from the old dashboard radio and then Reamer's modulated voice filled the cab, apparently already launched into his talk:

"I'm going to level with you, my friends, I see more and more evidence that common sense has just plain died and no one knows anymore when to come in out of the rain.

"People have died right here in the Kern Valley trusting New Age gurus while seeking so-called enlightenment on vision quests in sweat-lodges. Right here in this valley we have pagan drumming circles and phallus worshippers.

"The Forest Service can't even mow the lawn outside their own headquarters without first doing an environmental impact study. But the problem is spreading. Truth, trust, discretion and reason are all dying."

Brushy yelled, "Hey, I'm homeless, but I dig this guy."

"Churches have become businesses," Reamer continued. "Criminals receive better treatment than their victims. Teachers get fired for reprimanding unruly students. A six-year-old boy was charged with sexual harassment for kissing a classmate. Teens have been suspended from school for using mouthwash after lunch. Schools are required to get parental consent to administer sun lotion or an aspirin to a student, but can not inform parents when a girl gets pregnant or wants to have an abortion.

"Today, people have unrealistic expectations of government. They think that government can protect them from the consequences of their own actions. Then they get angry when it turns out that it can't."

Brushy pumped his fist in the air, "Right on reverend! Tell it like it is!"

"Kids today are ashamed to take manual jobs. A college education no longer guarantees a good job. Kids don't even go outside any more.

"Everyone thinks they're a victim. Everyone wants everything now. Someone else is always to blame. And everyone knows their rights—but forgets the responsibilities that make those rights possible."

Brushy did another vigorous fist pump and yelled, "Right on, man!"

"Real happiness and success, my friends, is found not by claiming entitlements, but by realizing one's full potential through long, hard effort. I'll leave you with this wise old saying: Whatsoever thy hand findeth to do, do it with thy might."

Although I myself liked drumming circles and vision

quests, I had to admit that in many ways Reamer was urging a return to basic common sense that our country needed. If this guy was the honcho of a murderous cartel—which included the End-of-Days fanatic Hektor—how could he be so rational? Was this man a diabolic master of deception? Or had all my suspicions—and my entire investigation—gone astray? Barely penetrating my haze of anxiety, these thoughts left me in a sort of stupor, hollowed out and alone.

Turning off the radio, Brushy brought me out of my trance. "Hey, you see that sloping line slicing across that mountain?"

We were wending our way down the canyon. The river charged along on our right and an imposing peak towered skyward on our left.

Pointing, he said, "Way up there the KR3 flume cuts through Yellow Jacket Peak. It's called that 'cause when they dug that tunnel, they blasted through yellow bands of gold—real gold!—like the stripes on a yellow-jacket bee. That's a fact, man. Ask the museum in Kernville!"

Recalling what Dog had said about this being the cartel's favorite 'no muss, no fuss' murder venue, I asked, "You ever hear of anyone falling into that flume?"

"God no! Drop into that borehole and that's all she wrote." Brushy made a great rushing, bubbling sound by blowing through his clenched, saliva-drenched teeth and over-hanging mustache. Then he winced. "Ohhh! I just thought of Bud Birdsong. Still no sign of that dear, crazy old guy."

As we drove on, I caught glimpses of the flume. Although underground for much of its route, the aqueduct burst into view above grade here and there on it's straight-as-an-arrow course. I imagined people flushing along the length of this manmade stream bed, and then, high above Kernville power-house, abruptly plunging down a pressurized waterfall inside penstock pipes to be atomized by massive spinning turbines. Like unending YouTube nightmare videos, these images tore through me, merging with the blood throbbing through my own arteries, filling me with unease.

"Well," said Brushy, "we're almost to the Voyages camp."

CHAPTER THIRTY-TWO
DOG GONE

Brushy pulled over. Fighting up through my inner purgatory, I thanked him and climbed down out of the truck. Before me, in the gathering dusk, was the low forest of tombstone-like boulders and beyond them, down by the river, the tarp awnings of the temporary Fulfillment Voyages guide school base camp. The place was eerily quiet, not even a bird chirped.

As I made my way among the chest-high stones, I pressed the back of my forearm against one and leaned into it, appreciating its solidity. This felt good, so I did it with another rock, and then another. Eager to see Dog, I walked over to his car and tent, but he was not there. His chariot-of-the-gods Lamborghini Estoque sedan, though, seemed somehow almost alive. Leave it to the Italians to breathe life into an inanimate machine through sheer aesthetics.

As I entered the main camp, Becca, Reddy and others rushed up.

"Adam!" exclaimed Reddy, "Dog's been kidnapped! We called the sheriff but he hasn't come."

Thoughts of what the cartel might do to Dog if they knew he was cooperating with Tripnee and me caused my blood to run cold. I said, "Tell me what happened."

"An hour after we got back," Reddy replied, "We were all down here by the river, except Dog, who stayed up by his tent. I looked toward the parking area and saw a bunch of cartel goons leave Dog's camp, pile into a black humvee and speed away! Dog was right there, then he was gone. They took him! They kidnapped Dog!"

I explained the deputy's likely whereabouts. Then I asked if anyone had seen Tripnee or my van, but no one had. I kept mum about Tripnee's drug dealings.

Toni and the others were still at the hospital, with no word yet on their condition. The fact that they were still there might mean nothing, or it could be a bad sign. We talked over the whole situation and reflected on our wild trip. All the while a dreadful sinking feeling gripped me. People carried their heaping dinner plates to the square tables, but I had no appetite.

Becca looked at me, "Adam, we're all worried about Tripnee and Dog, and I can tell you're really feeling the weight of it."

Nodding and giving her hand what I hoped was a reassuring squeeze, I told her about Tripnee's and my back-up rendezvous plan and asked if I could borrow a vehicle.

"Of course, take my Explorer."

"Thanks. I'm going over to the nature preserve now. She might be there already, or be trying to reach me."

CHAPTER THIRTY-THREE
KERN RIVER PRESERVE

Wrestling with despair, I drove the 18 miles or so to the Audubon Kern River Preserve. If Lake Isabella shimmers in the shape of a pair of pants, my route took me south along the inside of the long, skinny north-to-south leg, down around the crotch and out beyond the foot of the billowy west-to-east leg. Turning off the highway onto a long approach road, the powerful headlamps of Becca's hybrid Explorer lit a tunnel through the darkness.

Ahead, a commotion of beasts moving with a shambling yet agile gait filled the road. As a huge mama brown bear and two cubs turned to face my headlights, their eyes glowing, I stopped and turned off the engine a respectful distance away, fascinated. Sniffing the air, the three regarded me—and I them—for a long moment. Suddenly, at a signal from mom, the three bolted into the night, quickly disappearing into the surrounding pasture of perennial grasses, rushes and reeds.

Moments later, as I swung into a parking spot in the middle of a group of rustic, one-story, wood buildings, my vehicle's lights panned across an apparition: an extremely skinny man of about sixty, with a beaked nose and giant eyes peering out through thick glasses. The man, who was sitting in the dark on a rough-hewn bench, in his brief moment in my headlights, wore a beatific grin. I climbed out of the Explorer.

"Welcome to the preserve," he said in high, flutey tones that reminded me of the cry of a distant loon.

"Branch Terwilliger?"

Nodding, he placed his index finger to his lips, "SSShhh," and waved me into the seat next to him.

Easing onto the bench, I took some deep breaths and let myself tune in to my new surroundings. Stars lit up the warm night around us.

"Whoooo, whoooo, whoooooooo," came a resonating call from the shadowy shape of a nearby cottonwood.

My companion expertly mimicked these sounds, then whispered, "That's Harry, one of my dearest friends, a great horned owl."

As we sat, not only did the owl, Harry, hoot back, but the space around us reverberated with murmuring and chattering, hissing and bellowing. About half the racket came from Branch himself, who, I noticed, was not mimicking, but was carrying on conversations with a host of unseen critters.

At length we moved inside. I summarized the situation for Branch, whose careful listening and occasional insightful comments confirmed that he was indeed a kindred spirit and caring friend of Tripnee's. He had not seen or heard from her, but I expressed hope that she would come the next day, as per our plan.

"Adam," said Branch in his cry-of-the-loon voice, "For Tripnee's sake, the best thing you can do now is keep your strength up and get some rest. Any friend of Tripnee's is a friend of mine. My house is your house. Let me fix you some dinner and show you the guest bedroom."

The very fact Tripnee had a friend like this heartened me enormously. Taking this sound advice, I ate two cheese quesadillas, which even in my distressed state I could tell were delicious, and headed to bed.

In the middle of the night, in a cold sweat, I started awake out of a macabre dream: I was half of a baked potato, with no arms and no legs, and a match-head-sized thinking unit attached by a thread. In order to have any chance at all of survival, I had to travel twenty-six miles through a mountainous landscape of precipitous cliffs and swollen, overflowing whitewater cataracts to go I didn't know where. I felt hopeless, helpless, doomed. Finally, some survivalist part of me jolted me awake. Gasping for air, I lay there in the dark, my heart racing, as I clung to the hope of seeing Tripnee in the coming day.

My state of mind the next morning sank further when I went outside to find hundreds upon hundreds of turkey vultures. Like a Hitchcock movie, the immense birds sat with their backs to the rising sun, wings outspread, tip feathers splayed like gnarly fingers. As I paced through the nature sanctuary, the ghoulish creatures sat atop every fence post and pole, crowded every rooftop, and occupied every available perch in the thickets of black and red willow and Fremont cottonwood.

I headed back to Terwilliger's tongue-and-groove wood frame house, hoping against hope that Tripnee had arrived during my walk. But she was not there. I was crestfallen. Branch, it happened, was going to spend the day simultaneously leading a bunch of sixth graders on nature walks and coordinating a group of volunteers working on the preserve's trails. At the sound of each approaching vehicle, I rushed to see if it was Tripnee, only to have my hopes dashed again and again.

As the day wore on, my spirits sank lower and lower. I descended into a cold lonely place that I knew all too well. It was the universe of loss, loneliness and abandonment that had tormented me since age five. As I waited, using Branch's computer, I watched Brewster's video of Tripnee's drug deal again and again, each viewing another blast of shrapnel ripping into my heart.

Was I in love with a woman who existed only in my mind? Who was the real Tripnee? Did she really care about me? Could Tripnee have squealed on Dog? Why else would the cartel grab him? Was my love for Tripnee just a set up for more loss and disappointment?

Why the hell was I so glad Tripnee had a friend like Branch? Seeing this endearing but goofy bird-man as proof of Tripnee's sincerity and goodness was just me grasping at straws, putting myself through any contortion to avoid the conclusion that Tripnee was not the person I thought. Branch, I had to admit, was so lost in his own world, that his friendship was really no proof at all that Tripnee was not leading a complex double life with a very dark side.

How bizarre—yet how appropriate—that I was surrounded by vultures, birds that ate the eyeballs and the flesh of the dead! Was this a sign from the universe or what?

At that moment, in the depths of my emotional caldera, I noticed a Rumi poem mounted on a plaque on Branch's wall. It read:

The Guest House

This being human is a guest house.
Every morning a new arrival.

A joy, a depression, a meanness,
Some momentary awareness comes
As an unexpected visitor.

Welcome and entertain them all!
Even if they are a crowd of sorrows,
Who violently sweep your house
Empty of its furniture,
Still, treat each guest honorably.
He may be clearing you out
for some new delight.

The dark thought, the shame, the malice.
Meet them at the door laughing and invite them in.

Be grateful for whatever comes.
Because each has been sent
As a guide from beyond.

—Jelaluddin Rumi

I had just finished reading this when Branch burst into the house, sputtering and gesturing.

"Isn't it magnificent!" he chortled. "It was a cold morning, so thousands of vultures hung around today! Woweee! Now it's warming up, and they're on the move. As soon as the sun dries and warms their feathers, and heats the air to rise in great bubbles and columns, these magnificent beings will lift off en masse."

As the man talked—his words tumbling out in rapid bursts—he moved from door to window to door waving his arms in wild excitement. "These guys are nature's ultimate glider pilots. Huge wingspans. Incredible light weight of only three pounds. And an almost supernatural ability to find thermal updrafts of hot air. Pretty much without effort, ya know, they'll rise to about two thousand feet, then glide out to search for food and continue their migration. They're so good at finding the thermals, if you watch closely, you'll see hawks, ravens and for that matter human glider pilots follow their lead."

Behind his thick lenses, Branch's eyes looked as big as ostrich eggs. "As scavengers, vultures don't kill, but find and eat the dead. Hey, they're earth's clean-up crew. Peaceful, dedicated, green-party recyclers."

Strutting now like a peacock, he continued, "Their migration, which begins earlier each year due to climate change, comes in staccato crescendo rhythms. Stop, move en masse, stop, move en masse. When the weather is warm and clear, they go. When it's cold and wet, they stay put. We're in for a hot afternoon, so they're on the move. Come on!"

Branch leapt into the air, banging his head on his own ceiling. "Adam, what greater proof could there be that creation is magnificent beyond imagining? I'm so glad you're here to see this!"

The man's excitement was infectious. With him tugging on my sleeve, we rushed outside to see winged creatures lift off by the dozens, by the hundreds, by the thousands, filling the air around us and the entire sky as far as one could see.

The sight triggered something huge within me: an opening, a lifting off. Somehow grabbing myself up by the scruff of my own neck, I rose above the pain that had enveloped my life. Suddenly, instead of my feelings having me, now I had them.

In a sense it was simple: It had to do with rising up to a higher perspective, and seeing, understanding and accepting my life just as it was. Each and every one of my thoughts and feelings were understandable and had good reasons to be just as they were. But they were not me. I was the place where they showed up and stayed for awhile. I was the space they moved through. I was the riverbed, my thoughts and feelings were the river. Lifting off within myself, I saw this, and became calm.

Nothing had changed, yet everything had changed. I still had all the same thoughts and feelings, but I was flying, soaring, seeing things in a whole new light.

CHAPTER THIRTY-FOUR
CARTEL COMPOUND

I stepped back into the low-slung house and once again viewed Brewster's video of Tripnee's drug deal. This time, however, I studied it in a state of inner tranquility, scrutinizing every frame, every detail with the powerful concentrated beam of my full attention.

There was the lithe and athletic Tripnee handing over the briefcase brimming with cash. There were the two squarely crew-cut men with thick black shoes, seen from the back, loading the Prius. I could tell it was Mack Dowell and Hektor Torrente, but because their faces were never revealed, this video would be useless in court.

Wait a second! For a fleeting frame or two the camera panned sideways, revealing a distant background. With image enhancement software I'd used in some of my investigations in the military, I magnified and sharpened the picture. Lo and behold, it was a view of Lake Isabella, including, ever so tiny, Kernville airport. Getting out one of Branch's detailed maps of the area, and extrapolating from the position of the salient landmarks and topography, I narrowed down the location of the drug deal to one of the ravines on the west side of Lake Isabella somewhere between Wofford Heights and Kernville.

It was time to get moving! Outside, I profusely thanked

Branch, who was basking on his bench with that beatific smile, his ostrich-egg eyes following the vultures as they wheeled through the air far overhead. Then I jumped into the Explorer and was off.

After driving back around the lake, before turning left to go through the heart of Kernville and on toward Wofford Heights, I followed the road winding along the Upper Kern and took a little detour to the KR3 pennstock flume. There, in a few minutes, I set up a little insurance of my own.

Soon I was once again in the Explorer driving back into Kernville. The Kern River Brewing Company slid past on my right. Judging from the array of raft- and kayak-laden cars, trucks and vans eddied out around it, this enterprise deserved its reputation as a high temple of worship for river people from far and wide. As I moved on through the center of town, the riot of signs offering everything from river trips, mountain biking, fly fishing, kayaking and rock climbing to guided nature walks, spa treatments, drumming circles, horse whispering, chess mentoring, writers workshops and even earth-energy vortex tours left no doubt that this town and the Kern River were a recreation wonderland. The outdoor adventure vibe was magnetic, and the quaint western architectural motif throughout added tremendously to the charm. But I was on the mission of a lifetime—and drove on.

Between Kernville and Wofford Heights, I cruised slowly along studying the contours of the land. Judging as well as I could, I tucked Becca's hybrid vehicle into an inconspicuous spot and set out into the hills, taking with me, on impulse, Becca's multi-bladed Swiss Army knife.

Resorting to my old standby tactic of going to the high ground, I scrambled for almost an hour up and up, to the top of the highest hill in the vicinity, really a low mountaintop. Studying the angle of the airport, I judged I must be near the drug-deal location. But the ravines below revealed nothing. Thinking I must have missed something, I scrutinized them again, yard by yard, taking in every detail. Still nothing.

Lying down, with my back to the ground and looking up into a sky of brilliant azure—with, yes, vultures floating effortlessly far above me—I took some deep breaths, closed my eyes, and again visualized the enhanced image from the video. Then, sitting up and checking the scene before me, I sensed the need to move south.

After half an hour, in the late afternoon, coming up from the back side, I trudged out onto the summit of another peak. Peering down into a small canyon directly below, I thought, Whoa! and fell to the ground. The secluded property spread out below was clearly what I was looking for. The black humvee was there, along with three RVs, a van, a bobtail truck and about a dozen cars. There were two double-wide mobile homes, a big house, a barn and several smaller out-buildings. Everything was tucked way up this canyon and well hidden from the road far below. But no Dream Van.

I took some time to study the individual buildings and memorize the whole layout including approach and exit routes. The site was an elongated oval, with the vehicles at the upper end, the house and double-wides in the middle, and the barn and other buildings at the lower end. From the air, or to someone who stumbled on it by mistake, the place would look at first glance a lot like a thousand other motley Kern Valley homesteads with extra in-law quarters. But this place was different. It had a military neatness. There was a lot of activity down there; I estimated about twenty or so men. The barn seemed to be a vehicle maintenance center, and had two guys out front working on an RV. One building, separate from the others, looked especially fortress-like and had a heavily barred window. This looked like it could be a jail. Most telling of all, two men were doing guard duty; one walked an ordinary-looking barbed-wire fence surrounding the perimeter, and another occupied a hilltop between the compound and the highway, overlooking all of the likely approach routes.

A prolonged frisson of fear passed through my torso and limbs as it dawned on me that it was only through dumb luck that I had found this place without being seen and very likely killed. If I had judged the location more accurately and climbed up from the highway close by, I would have been seen by the hilltop sentry. It was only because I had goofed, and climbed up to this high ridge well to the north, and then worked my way south behind the ridge, that I had made it here alive!

Given the number of men down there and the level of care the cartel devoted to their security, I reminded myself I'd better be extremely cagey or I'd wind up dead, and be no help to Tripnee or anyone else. I began by re-examining the high hilltops around me, to make sure I had not missed any sentries. Satisfied, I settled in to watch the compound's comings and goings.

It was about an hour later, and my heart raced as I saw what I was looking for. A latino man wearing an apron and thick black shoes was carrying a tray laden with what appeared to be food from the house to the structure with the barred window. Several minutes later he carried an empty tray back. Had I struck gold? Could this be Tripnee's jail? If so, thank god she was alive and they were apparently feeding and treating her well.

I crawled back from the brink, standing only when I was sure I would not be visible, and headed for a wooded gully that spiraled from behind the hill down into the cartel hideout.

Along the way I found what I was looking for, a willow sapling about twenty feet tall and about two inches in diameter at the base. Felling the willow and removing the skinny top half with the saw blade of the Swiss Army knife, I fashioned a bow using the sturdy laces of Cassady's shoes as my bow string. Cutting several willow arrows, I continued slowly and carefully down the gully in the diminishing light, keeping to the cover of scrub oak, mesquite, manzanita and willow.

At one point, I surprised three coyotes, a tawny mama flanked by two juveniles, who, with hackles erect, put their heads down, bared their teeth and growled with ferocity. I backed off. They backed off, then turned and, with mama covering their rear, headed up a side ravine. Soon after encountering the coyotes, I found a hefty log about three inches in diameter and six feet long. I added it to my arsenal and kept going.

It was almost dark when I reached the perimeter fence, where I waited, concealed among clumps of ceanothus, braced and ready. Sure enough, it wasn't long before the perimeter guard, walking the fence, stepped close enough for me to knock him out cold with a single violent swing of my club, catching him on the back of his head. Stripping the large, olive-skinned man down to his shorts, I stuffed his t-shirt deep into his mouth to keep him quiet, and used his belt, shoelaces and the strap of his AK47 to tie him up on his belly, feet and hands bound tight together behind his back. Once I had the man gagged and trussed, I checked his vitals; his pulse and breathing were steady, though he would be damned uncomfortable when he came to. The man carried no identification, but he did have a set of keys, a cell phone and a cigarette lighter, all of which I pocketed. With the man's socks, cloth strips from his shirt and some dry perennial grasses, I made two arrows ready to be flaming incendiaries.

It was now as dark as it was going to get, and, grabbing my weapons which now included the AK47, I was ready for my next move. Occasional bursts of raucous yelling and guffawing mixed with mariachi music drifted up from a covered patio between the two mobile homes. Hoping these sounds would mask mine, I crept among the cartel vehicles, filling the exhaust pipes with dirt and stuffing rags I found in a pickup bed and pieces of the guard's clothing into the fuel tanks, leaving a tag end hanging out of each. This way, I figured, however things unfolded, the humvee, van, truck, RVs and diverse assortment of cars would be disabled, either by not starting or, if I could manage it, by exploding.

Keeping to the shadows, I crossed toward the jail and was twenty feet from it when its door suddenly burst open, flooding the area with light. Two men—it was Mack and Hektor—tromped out. Caught in the open, I dropped low and brought up the machine gun ready to shoot. By some amazing piece of luck, Mack, in the lead, didn't see me because he was looking back at Hektor, and Hektor's view was blocked by Mack's muscled, taller body. They both pivoted to face the building, switched off the interior light and closed the steel door. Turning a key in the deadbolt, they then rattled the door to make sure it was locked tight. In the meantime, I sidled into deep shadows nearby. When the men swung back around, their eyes still had not adjusted to the dark and, though I was exposed in their field of vision, they did not see me.

"Shut up, you holy roller numbskull!" Growled Mack's voice as they walked past in the dark.

"You shut up, you food nazi!" That was Hektor's voice.

"Before or after I pound you into the ground?" Replied Mack.

The pair receded into the night, arms waving, barking at each other. Crouching low, I waited and slowly let out a big breath, as they strolled up to and entered the house. I got out the guard's keys and tried them one by one on the deadbolt. None fit. I went around to the back to the barred window, which, because of the steep slope, was a good twelve feet off the ground. I leaned my six-foot club and ten-foot bow against the building to create steps at three feet and five feet. Pressing myself to the wall, I eased up, putting my weight first on one, and then on the other foot brace. Stretching, I grasped the heavy-duty wrought-iron bars and pulled myself up to peer into the dark interior. The opening had no glass.

"Tripnee?" I whispered.

I heard movement and a moment later her beautiful face appeared on the other side of the bars.

"Oh, Adam, Adam!" she whispered.

"Are you OK?"

"Yes, yes. Oh Adam, Adam, Adam. Thank god."

Chinning herself up, she pressed her face between the bars and we kissed, and in that moment I knew that everything was OK between us.

"The Dream Van's in the barn," she said.

"Excellent!" I whispered, quickly revising my plan to take advantage of this news. "I'll be back soon to pull off these bars. Be ready to come out fast and jump into the van."

Gathering up my odd collection of weapons, I moved silently to the barn and again tried the keys. Finally, voila! The last key slid in and turned. There, visible in the shadowy depths of the cavernous structure, was my wonderful machine, almost luminescent in all its brawny beauty. I slid underneath and retrieved the hide-a-key. I found my pen-light in its usual place under the driver's seat. Shielding the beam with my hand, I saw that, although everything had been tossed and gone through, it looked like most of my stuff was still pretty much OK. Seeing my favorite shoes, with actual laces intact, I put them on.

Suddenly, the barn door opened, and the barn's interior lights blazed! Yikes, I turned out my flashlight, dropped low in the van, and froze. Thank god some instinct had prompted me to close the van door.

"I could of sworn Jose locked this door," said a Mexican-accented, male voice. There was the sound of approaching footsteps. I brought up the muzzle of the AK47, my hands in firing position. Holding my breath, listening to every sound, I waited. My own heartbeat roared in my ears, but I didn't move, I just waited. Footsteps circled the van and then with-drew toward the door. Finally, the lights went out, the door closed and I heard the lock click.

Whoa! I thought, *That was close! Careful now, careful! I'm nearly there!*

After things had been quiet for awhile, I crept back to the door.

Damn! I thought. It was locked from the outside, with no way to open it from the inside. Still using the shielded penlight, I searched for another way out of the barn. The windows were old, painted shut and sure to make a racket if opened. Same with the big rear door. I climbed a ladder to the upper level. Aha! An old hay loft portal. I returned to the van, got a length of one-inch tubular webbing, and used it to descend silently down from the loft opening. Unlocking the door again from the outside, I retrieved my bow, arrows and the gun.

The bow and incendiary arrows were rough hewn, but would, I hoped, allow me to torch the house without being seen. At the far upper end of the compound, I got into position at the top of a steep slope adjacent to and well above the structure. Concealed behind a rock outcropping, I lit and shot my two arrows. Just as I had anticipated, it took a long time for the flames to catch and spread over the dry, cedar shake rooftop. Perfect!

I worked my way over to the vehicles and one by one began lighting the gas tank rags. I had just two more fuel-tank wicks to light when someone saw the roof fire and started yelling. Soon there was a huge hubbub and all attention was focused toward the house.

I lit the cloth fuses on the last two cars, and ran for the barn. I had just slipped inside when the first vehicle exploded. Beautiful! Throwing caution to the winds and counting on ongoing explosions at the other end of the property to draw all eyes, I pushed open the old doors at the back of the barn, ignoring the racket this caused. I jumped into the Dream Van, which was already facing the now open doors, started the powerful engine, threw it into all-wheel drive, and, steering by memory with lights off, charged out of the barn, wheeled toward the jail and backed up to Tripnee's window. Scrambling over my jumbled stuff, I got to the back of the van and dug out my heavy-duty tow chain.

Climbing the van's rear ladder, I handed one end of the chain to Tripnee, knowing she'd understand what to do.

"Are you good?" I asked.

"Fabulous!" she said as she tied the chain to her window bars. "It's ready!"

I secured the other end to my three-ball hitch, leapt back into the driver's seat, and floored the gas pedal to send the heavy van, with all of its multiple batteries, water and fuel tanks, and steel-I-beam chassis, accelerating downslope. When the chain came taut, I felt a major jolt and heard a crashing of steel and concrete. We'd done it! The window bars were off. I skidded to a stop. In a moment, the passenger door flew open, Tripnee bounded into the shotgun seat. I again gunned the motor to send us racing away into the night, dragging the window bars behind us. When we were a mile away, I pulled into a secluded spot, untied and stowed the chain, and we continued on.

CHAPTER THIRTY-FIVE
KNUCKLEHEAD

"I don't like it!" said Tripnee. "You walking in and confronting Rook is just too dangerous!"

Hidden in a dark, dense grove of broad-leafed sycamores on a secluded beach on the Lower Kern, we were talking over our options while restoring some order to the interior of the Dream Van.

"The whole reason I hiked out of the Forks," she said, as she put together a set of nesting pots and put the stack into a cupboard, "was to keep you from killing yourself in just that way. Before you got off the river, I wanted the FBI, DEA and the whole goddamned federal cavalry to be on their way to rounding up Rook, Toro and the cartel. But Mack and Hektor had staked out the Dream Van and stopped me."

"The thing is, now they've grabbed Dog," I said.

"If Toro suspects Dog is helping us," said Tripnee, "the guy's in serious danger. And without Dog we don't have enough evidence to bring down Rook and Toro."

"Yes," I said, "So with Dog needing our help right away, we have to move fast. Waiting them out and slowly gathering more evidence is not an option. We can call in the feds, but that alone won't be enough. Now if I can confront Rook with you listening in and recording everything—and in addition we call in the feds—we just might shake Rook's tree enough to bring him down and find Dog."

"How the hell are you gonna do that?" asked Tripnee.

"I have a few tricks up my sleeve," I said, trying to look convincing.

"Yeah? I actually believe you. But it still sounds nearly impossible and like a sure way to get yourself killed."

"The inescapable fact is Dog's in trouble and needs help. Delay could cost his life!" I said.

"But we also need to avoid outright suicide," she pleaded. "Adam, the cartel is more dangerous, more incredibly deadly than you realize. They would've killed me, an FBI agent, in a heartbeat. They kept me alive only to use as bait to catch and kill you."

"We outsmarted them there," I said. "You have to admit."

"Yes you, you outsmarted them. You big knucklehead," she said as she grabbed me around the neck and kissed me, pressing the full length of her body against mine.

More quietly, holding her and looking into her tear-filled eyes, I said, "This man murdered my mom and dad, and I'm going to bring him down. This is something I've got to do."

Her chest filled and she breathed out slowly, eyes blazing. "OK, OK then," she said. "I can't say I didn't see this coming. But since I can't talk you out of going in alone, I'm sending in the feds right behind you."

CHAPTER THIRTY-SIX
BLUEBERRY SMOOTHIE

Early the next morning, we awoke knowing what we had to do. First, we shared a blueberry and yoghurt smoothie. Next, I dug my backup weapon, a Sig Sauer Model P226 self-loading automatic pistol with a 15-round magazine, out of the small safe concealed so well in the bowels of the Dream Van that even the cartel goons didn't find it. Then, after I scraped the bugs off the windshield, we set off for Indian Rock Resort by way of Tripnee's house in Lake Isabella.

En route I asked, "So why couldn't deputy Brewster figure out you are law enforcement, and the tape was a phony?"

Tripnee responded, "Everyone knows the cartel's got judges, police and maybe even sheriffs on their payroll, so we made sure Brewster wouldn't learn about my undercover mission. Of course, the drug buy was a sting."

"So who made that video?" I asked.

"This might surprise you. I did," she said. "I dropped it in his mailbox to see if he was in league with the cartel. Now we know the man's honest and on our side."

"Devious," I grinned. "Remind me to be on my good behavior around you."

Following our plan, I shifted into four-wheel-drive to

climb a steep slope, and hid the van on a hilltop deep inside a mass of house-sized boulders a mile from the resort's outer perimeter. Taking up my first-aid kit and the FBI gear we had picked up from her house, Tripnee used gauze and wide cloth medical tape to incorporate a tiny, curved, wafer-thin, waterproof micro recorder-transmitter-tracking device inside the wound dressing on my left forearm. Her motions were those of the deft and controlled FBI professional at work, and the touch of her long fingers felt good. When she was finished, the bandage looked completely flat and normal. To test the gadget, and its companion gizmo, a powerful voice-activated receiver-recorder-tracker that would remain in the van, Tripnee said, "Love ya," and we could see from the flashing diodes that the system was working. To make sure, she hit rewind and play, and her sweet, "Love ya," floated forth like the voice of an angel.

It was time for me to go.

"Please be careful, Adam," she said, her eyes pleading.

"I'll do my absolute best," I said. "Thanks for going along with my need to do it this way."

We clung to each other for a moment.

"OK, I'm going in. You can make those calls now."

"Good luck. I love you," she whispered.

"I love you."

Tearing myself away, I set off through the woods toward Rook's extravagant resort. Looking back one last time, I saw Tripnee through the van windows starting to make calls: To the FBI, the DEA and the California state troopers. In some contrarian corner of my mind, I pondered the prospect of being dead by the time they arrived.

CHAPTER THIRTY-SEVEN

CONFRONTATION

I entered the resort overland. Steering clear of security cameras, I jumped the gleaming white fence far from the road, and took cover whenever I had to avoid Rook's guards and grounds people. I skirted the resort maintenance yard, where I glimpsed Mack Dowell, but got by without him seeing me.

On the final approach, I dusted myself off as I strode across the parking lot loaded with stretch limos and other flashy cars. When I bounded up the steps to the casino's grandiose front entrance, I saw looks of surprise and recognition on the faces of the two burly, black-shoed doormen. I pushed past them before they could react, and plunged deep into the main casino. Orienting myself in the vast room teeming with people in shimmering clothing all drinking and gambling with abandon, I maintained a swift but under-the-radar pace and made my way deep into the inner recesses of the complex, heading for Reamer Rook's personal office.

As I neared my goal, a Latin, broad-shouldered man with thick black shoes and a wire going to an earpiece blocked my way. Without losing momentum, I placed a round-house kick hard against the guy's left ear. Before the man hit the floor, I had barged past the voluptuous, scantily-clad receptionist and pushed through the heavy door into Rook's inner office.

Reamer was looking right at me, leaning back in an ultra-comfortable chair, feet up on his desk, leisurely smoking with an air of nonchalance. As the door closed softly of its own accord behind me, he said, "Come on in, young man, I've been expecting you."

Perching his huge cigar on an ornate ashtray, he got up and all six-foot-six of him came around his broad desk with his hands spread wide in a gesture of openness and welcome. "I've been watching you, Adam, and before you make the biggest mistake of your life, I want you to listen to me. How about we sit down?"

I steadied myself, drew a deep breath, and said, "OK. I'm listening."

He waved us toward a far corner of the spacious room, where we sat in a pair of overstuffed leather lounge chairs arranged side by side.

"Adam, you're an extremely clever and resourceful young man—and you're damned lucky—I like that. I've got a place, a very big place, for you."

My stomach churned. "Tell me more," I said.

"Well, for one thing, I can see why you've taken an interest in Tripnee. Oh yeah, I see why! Join me and you'll be surrounded by more beautiful women than you can imagine!"

Inwardly I seethed.

"And money. You'll love the money!"

What was with this guy who killed my family? My whole being reeled. Murdered his own sister! How could this asshole even live with himself?

"Go on," I said.

Keep talking you bastard and hang yourself! I thought. Despite my earlier protestations to the contrary, I didn't see many tricks as I looked up my figurative sleeve. I did know, however, that everyone's favorite topic is themselves, and that their capacity for rationalizing their own evil deeds is limitless. My plan, at its core, was simple: Get Rook on tape talking about anything and everything. Inevitably he would incriminate himself.

"You're an interesting guy," I said.

The deeper I got into this, though, the more my inner radar told me that this scheme might indeed turn out to be a good way to get killed. Drawing the man out without tipping my hand was going to be damned near impossible.

"I'm going to tell you something," Rook said, "Something very few people know."

At that moment his well-endowed assistant with the miniscule wardrobe entered the room. How Rook had summoned her I couldn't tell.

"Adam, this is Muffin," said Reamer. "What would you like to drink?"

"Hi Muffin. I'll have a Kern River Pale Ale," I said.

"Great choice. Make that two," said Rook.

Rook's eyes followed Muffin as she sashayed out of the room.

"My father," Rook began, "Was a crazy old Tubatulabal chief whose people had been killed by white settlers and the U.S. Army, leaving him boiling with hatred for anyone white. It had to be a love/hate thing though, because mom was white. My biggest mistake was popping out of the womb looking Caucasian. He pretty much disowned me and treated me like shit. He even beat my mother and sister when he caught them being nice to me."

"I survived by fishing and learning to fend for myself.

Turned out he did me a tremendous favor. I became self-reliant, and, just between you and me, I learned to live by my own rules."

Rook straightened up, "My motto: Life is what you make it—seize every opportunity." He smiled then. Behind that smile were icy, dark, empty, coal-black eyes—and behind those, I thought I saw the faintest hint of a vast pain.

Muffin undulated in with two frosty super-sized ice-cold mugs of Pale Ale. Again, Rook's calculating gaze followed the woman's rhythmic movements.

"Sounds like you've got a highly evolved philosophy there. How do your radio sermons fit in then?"

He twisted around, looked me straight in the eye and dug his fingernails into my shoulder. To keep from wrenching away, I concentrated on taking first a deep breath and then a swig of the ale.

"Now young man listen to me. Learn something. There's PR, and then there's reality. It's important to be perceived by the public as good, wise and well-intentioned. But what one does in reality, out of the public eye, is another matter." He said this with a chilling wink.

"How did you go from barely surviving and foraging for fish to all this?" I gestured at the casino and resort around us.

"Like you, I owe a lot to the military," said Reamer. "Me and Brewster—I still have a soft spot for our deputy sheriff—we were kids together and army buddies. He was the one who suggested we join, and it turned out great for me. I made the most of the opportunity, studied Sun Tzu and Machiavelli, and eventually became a captain. The army taught me discipline, organization, strategy and the use of force."

"Use of force?"

"Yeah, sort of my own version of the Powell Doctrine, after General Colin Powell. Use overwhelming concentrated force to get your way."

His smile sent icicles down my spine.

"Was that how you got this property?" I asked.

Rook just smiled.

This man was hard to provoke, so I tried a different tack, and asked, "Why are you telling me all this?"

"The fact is Adam, we have a very special connection. You might be surprised, for instance, to know that I know you have an unusual scar on your right arm."

I peeled up my sleeve, revealing the star scar. "You know about this?"

Rook said, "Young man ... I'm your uncle! Your mom's brother. You're my nephew. You could join me. I could do a lot for you. Together we could conquer the world!"

"Yes," I said, "And you killed my mother and father! How could you?!! How could you actually murder your own sister?!!!! What kind of monster are you?"

Rook looked surprised for the first time. Spreading his palms in a calming gesture, he said, "Easy there. Easy."

He passed his hands over his face and went silent for a while, then he spoke. "I really didn't want to do it. I took no action when Sarah inherited this land that should have gone to me, me the son, the man. For years and years I tolerated her rants about my business. But finally, she just went too far when she threatened to blow the whistle on my whole operation. I admit crystal meth is not pretty. But if my organization doesn't provide it, someone else will. It's business. It's nothing personal. Just fucking business.

And your head-in-the-clouds mom, my fucking sister, just couldn't get it, so she had to be dealt with."

He leaned back, sighed, smiled and looked at me, "And me getting this land has worked out well, as you can see."

I pulled out my Sig Sauer pistol from the holster at the small of my back, and said, "You and your whole fucking, goddamned drug operation are going down!"

Reamer just smiled and looked at me. Suddenly from behind me I heard, "Drop your weapon."

Turning, I saw Mack and Hektor, each with an Uzi, standing in a doorway. Considering there were two of them, each heavily armed, I thought it prudent to do as they said.

I was actually glad to have two guards, because this meant each was counting on the other to be alert. I noticed that each allowed his own attention to ease slightly, assuming the other would take up the slack.

"Oh shit," I said, gradually taking on the body language of demoralized defeat. Slowly, I let my entire body slump and my head loll forward. As though I was sinking into hopeless-ness, I adopted the manner of someone who was utterly done in, with no fight left in him.

Hektor, his black pants and white guayabera several sizes too big, and the taller Mack, his jeans and t-shirt way too small, sneered at my cowering manner—and came in too close for their own good—but just right for mine. I sensed that Mack and Hektor were treated sort of like the field hands on the old antebellum plantations. Relegated to outside work, they guarded the perimeter and did the dirty jobs outside the posh inner universe of Indian Rock Resort. When the voluptuous Muffin, busting out of her skimpy outfit, walked across the room, their heads followed. That moment of distraction was all I needed.

Moving fast, drawing on both my military and kung fu training, I seized and twisted the barrels of both Uzis, pointing and pulling them left, while in the same moment I launched my right foot toward Hektor, catching him in his solar plexus. Next, while wrenching the Uzis free, I simultaneously jerked my head back and to the right just enough to dodge Mack's right hook. As Mack's fist shot past, taking him off balance, I swung both Uzis up and clocked him hard on both temples with the two guns, and he went down in a heap.

I forced Rook and Muffin at gun point to drag Mack and Hektor over to one wall, and as the two thugs recovered, I had the four of them spread-eagle police-shake-down-style against the wall.

I said, "You're a sick son of a bitch, Rook. Over thirty years of killing people. On some level even you must know that your whole operation needs to go down."

Rook, amazingly affable, said, "I'm impressed. I'm proud that you're showing some family talent. We really could have conquered the world. The fact remains, however, that you have no idea who you're dealing with. You just don't know who I am." He turned then to face the muzzles of my two Uzis. "The thing is, Adam, you really underestimate me. You show talent and promise, but I'm afraid you're completely out of your league. You see, I know all about you and your other uncle, and unless you put down those guns, my team in El Sobrante will obliterate Peace and his entire school—with all of the children in it. I'm sure you'd like proof. For that, use the remote on my desk to power up that screen." He indicated a flat 4- x 8-foot screen on one wall of his office. "I already cued up the video call."

Once the call was initiated, Rook said, "Show the situation." The screen split. On each half, there appeared a man in a ski mask holding both a camera phone and what looked like a shoulder-fired stinger missile. Each man stood next to a nondescript RV—with the door open and a supply of rockets in view inside each. The RVs appeared to be adjacent to one another about 50 feet apart on a hilltop. Slowly, simultaneously, both cameras turned to zoom in on a school several hundred yards away at the base of the hill. As the cameras closed in, my uncle Peace's school came into focus—along with his library dead center—and the place was swarming with kids.

My heart sank. Rook had indeed outmaneuvered me. I said, "If I release you and drop these guns, how do I know you'll call off the attack?"

Rook said, "You wound me, nephew! I'm a business man. Blowing up school librarians and whole schools is generally bad for business because it brings down too much heat. I'd only do it as a last resort, but at the moment, you're giving me no choice. These men can obliterate the school and every child in it in one minute. However, if you lay down those guns right now and surrender to me immediately, I'll call off the attack and my team'll drive away."

"I can see I did underestimate you," I said. "You leave me no choice." I put down the Uzis and stepped back. Muffin ran out of the room. Mack and Hektor advanced cautiously, picked up their guns, and moved away in different directions, covering me like hawks, with no intention of being fooled twice.

Moving to his big padded chair, Rook leaned back, propped his feet on his desk and stroked his smooth round head as though searching for the finger holes in a bowling ball. "You're just like your mom," he said. "Too blind to see golden opportunity when it knocks! I figured you'd be. That's why I set up insurance. Don't get me wrong. I'm not a terrorist. I'm a practical businessman. I bought those rockets under the table from the manufacturer, who happens to be a patron of this resort, for just this sort of situation."

My mouth had gone dry.

"Adam, I'm afraid you're just too clever and too intent on causing me trouble. You've got to be dealt with. And I know just the thing for you! No muss. No Fuss."

The three men cackled. Rook opened a cabinet and got out a third Uzi. He and Mack kept me covered—from twenty feet away—while Hektor grabbed me roughly, his eyes gleaming with sadistic fury, and cuffed my wrists tightly together behind my back with heavy-duty police-style plastic cuffs. They then marched me down a long hallway into what looked like Rook's private six-car garage.

Hektor opened the trunk of a big car and stepped back, motioning with his Uzi for me to get in.

"Before you stuff me into this black Cadillac," I said to Hektor and Mack, "I want to know if you two ever considered switching clothes?"

Rook roared with laughter, but his two goons scowled unhappily.

Mack snarled, "The joke's on you, asshole. No muss. No fuss."

Hektor growled, "Man, we'll teach you to mess with La Casa."

With their gun barrels jammed into my back, all three pushed me into the trunk, and slammed the lid shut.

CHAPTER THIRTY-EIGHT
THE FLUME

It was pitch black in that trunk and stank of gasoline, piss, shit, and vomit. Fighting back the urge to retch, I slid from side to side in slimy ooze as the car raced around curve after curve on smooth roads, then I began bouncing around like a dice in a moist cup as the caddy jumped and jolted up an endless, rough, uphill stretch. Eventually, the big car skidded to a halt.

The trunk popped open, daylight blazed in and I struggled out, slowly unfolding my cramped limbs. Behind me, the plastic handcuffs cut deep into my wrists. The men stayed well back holding their Uzis cocked and ready. As my eyes adjusted, I realized we were midway up the eastern wall of the Upper Kern Canyon. A hundred yards up the incline from where I stood, the powerhouse flume traversed the canyon slope. Although much of the aqueduct ran through underground tunnels, its straight-line route was visible where it burst out of the earth here and there as a massive enclosed concrete trough resembling a giant elongated coffin.

My uncle Reamer Rook said, "Son, you can get thrown into that flume with bullets in your legs. Or you can go in healthy for your last swim. It's your choice."

Hektor and Mack motioned with their Uzis for me to

head uphill, and I started walking. My mind raced. Even if I was about to die, why not get as much evidence as possible on tape?

I said to Rook, "I realize this is it for me, but humor me. I'm amazed by the scale and ingenuity of your organization. Was it you or Toro Canino who thought all this up? And how do you move such a huge volume of drugs without attracting attention?"

"OK, I'll indulge my dying nephew's last question. What's family all about, anyway?" grinned Rook. "First of all, Toro is a great partner. He's ruthless and unstoppable dealing with our enemies—he even helped me deal with your folks. Also, he's great at handling things south of the border. But make no mistake, this is my baby. I thought it all up. The secret is RVs and planes. Recreational vehicles are everywhere, and so they're invisible as they move around the country making their drops. They can even camp overnight in any Walmart or Costco parking lot, among all the other nomadic RVs, without being noticed."

"Diabolically clever, I must admit," I said.

Beaming like a child receiving praise, Rook continued, "What's really cool are the planes. The very same G4 and G5 jets that ferry elite clients to and from Indian Rock Resort also carry drugs. Usually not at the same time. But the two cargoes combine into one very profitable whole."

Rook stuck out his chest, pulled his head back and up, and walked tall, looking satisfied with himself. "Adam, did I tell you I've always believed in wholeness—and also nothingness? That's where this penstock flume comes in. After you go through that KR3 generator down there," he gestured toward the massive monolith of the powerhouse visible in the distance, "It will be just like you never existed.

Perfect nothingness. But don't worry. You have several miles of flume to replay your life, and the final descent will go fast. Very likely, you won't feel a thing."

We arrived at the flume. My knees shook and sweat poured off my face and back as I looked down through a four-foot-square steel hatchway at fast, smooth, black water streaming past in a relentless, continuous current racing from left to right. Anyone caught in that swift laminar flow would have no chance. Man-made flumes and penstocks were notorious inescapable, smooth-walled drowning machines. Fully enclosed, with no calms, eddies or even hand- or foot-holds, they offered none of the escape routes or opportunities for self-rescue provided by natural stream beds. Looking down into that opaque relentless flow, I saw obliteration. A one-way trip into thousands of small blades covering a massive spinning turbine wheel. I glimpsed the atomization of my body down into its separate cells, with few of these remaining intact. Was I to be liquidated, then discharged out the bottom of the powerhouse back into the Upper Kern River? No muss? No fuss?

Rook and his men stood in a semicircle around me. A savage, primordial blood-thirst filled the air. I hesitated.

Hektor broke the silence, "Say your prayers, man. It's the end of days for you."

Rook said, "Which will it be? With bullets or without? You choose."

Mack said, "Bullets mean lead poisoning, man. Go in healthy. Anyway, you stink and need a swim."

Suddenly, from behind the men, came Tripnee's loud, absolutely commanding voice, "Freeze. First one to turn or move dies!"

CHAPTER THIRTY-NINE
THE BIG SWIM

"Drop your weapons now, NOW!!!" The raw, naked force and authority in Tripnee's voice left no doubt whatsoever that she meant exactly what she said, and at that moment the men froze and let their weapons fall.

Being careful not to block Tripnee's line of sight—or the path her bullets might take—to any of the men, I quickly kicked the guns away from them and moved to her side.

"First man to turn his head or move a muscle DIES!" Tripnee barked.

I watched as she kept her eyes and her Beretta M9 glued on Rook and his crew, while with her free hand she produced a Swiss Army knife, which she opened with her teeth, pulling out a razor-sharp blade. Studying the three men all the while, she reached behind me, and I felt her slip the blade carefully between a plastic cuff and my wrist. With a fierce downward thrust, she sliced through, freeing my arms. Then in a flash she folded and put away the knife, retrieving three pair of plastic handcuffs from her pocket.

Tucking the cuffs into my belt, I went over, reached down, grabbed the nearest Uzi, checked its settings, and aimed it at the cartel gang. Whew! Breathing slightly easier, I checked all around us making sure we weren't going to be surprised from behind. Keeping both of our weapons leveled at my former captors, we quickly rounded up the other firearms.

Tripnee said, "OK, each of you, very, very slowly, go face down onto the ground right where you are. Any sudden movement and you're dead! Get down on your stomach. Spread your feet wide. Get your arms behind your back. Slowly. Move fast and you're dead!"

I breathed deeply and a steely, tense calm came over me. I knew these men were waiting for the slightest slip up on our part, and had to be immobilized fast. Pulling out one of Tripnee's FBI handcuffs, I stuck the Uzi into Mack's neck, my finger on the trigger, and, with my other hand, I cuffed his wrists, pinning his arms behind him.

I had just handcuffed Rook, when shots reverberated past my head, and a voice rang out: "Drop it!" More shots whizzed past. A bloody groove appeared in Tripnee's shoulder. We looked at each other, nodded agreement and dropped our weapons.

Toro Canino, armed with a machine pistol in each hand, stepped out from behind some head-high bushes. Hektor quickly freed Rook, then Mack. The men grabbed their weapons and covered Tripnee and me, leaving no opening whatsoever for us to make a move. Color returned to Rook's face. His eyes were no longer popping out of his head, but looked colder, harder and crazier than ever. Like men recently scared out of their wits, then given a miraculous reprieve, he and his band were now taking zero chances. The time for words was past. We were on the fast track into the real-life nightmare that was the penstock flume.

With both of us standing side by side facing the hatchway opening, I turned slightly and gave Tripnee an eye roll and head tilt intended to intuitively convey a complex message that might be summarized as: 'I'm-going-to-do-something-off-the-wall but trust me I-hope-it-works-but-if-it-doesn't-please-forgive-me and above all I-love-you.' Tripnee, despite her wound, smiled and winked with understanding!

Turning further, I saw Rook aim his Uzi straight into my upper body and begin the barely perceptible tensing that precedes pulling the trigger. In that instant, I stooped and cowered, mimicking the body language of the terrified, and pleaded, "Reamer, whatever you do please don't send us down this flume alive! Make it quick. Please, please shoot us first!"

Rook's beady eyes widened, and he hissed, "You being family, I was gonna make it easy for you and shoot you and your sweetie before dropping you in. But you're a weak moron! Your sniveling shames me! Makes me ashamed we're family, ashamed we're both Tubatulabal!"

Rook emitted a blood-curdling laugh. "Ha, ha ha ha HA HA ha ha HAA HAAAAA!" More clearly than ever, I realized that I was dealing with a man who was truly mad.

"Aaahh, nephew, I'm gonna give you and your woman one last life lesson. I'm gonna stuff you both into this flume alive—so you can learn to master your fear! Just like I silenced my sister, now I've got to silence you. But at least I can give you a learning experience, an opportunity to deal with your emotions! Ha ha ha HA HA!"

And with that, the four men—with a ferocious, sadistic anger--shoved, kicked and gun-clubbed us down into the tunnel hatchway. Tripnee, in resisting the hail of blows, was knocked unconscious and went down fast. Her form dropped like a lead weight through the opening into the black flow, to be swept away in an instant. Both to stay with her and to get my head out of range of their furious blows, I dove in head first—but found myself hanging upside down dangling from my right leg. One of Rook's men had grabbed my ankle, suspending me in the hatchway! Bone-bruising blow after blow battered my already severely chafed foot and leg, I lashed upward with my left boot, connected with something solid that seemed to break and give way, felt my ankle come free, and plunged into the wet darkness.

At first, I tumbled disoriented underwater. Everything was pitch black. The rough, abrasive tunnel walls, when I blundered against them, tore chunks out of my flesh. The tunnel, which had been blasted out of solid rock, seemed to be about 6 feet square, and had an air space of about six inches above the water line. Surfacing to breathe was dangerous, though, because low spots in the irregular ceiling conked me hard on the skull again and again. Ooohhh! In the total and utter darkness it was impossible to know how far I'd come or how far Tripnee was ahead of me.

I had to catch her before it was too late!! I kicked and stroked like a madman, cracking my head over and over. I ignored, no, I used the pain ... to propel my limbs into double and triple speed. If I couldn't catch Tripnee everything would be for naught.

I gave it everything I had. On and on. It seemed an eternity. I sensed something ahead! A few more frantic, gut-busting strokes and YES it was Tripnee! Semi-conscious but alive! Thank god!

I got us into position. Keeping Tripnee's face above water, I encircled her chest tightly with my left arm, and got my right arm free and up and ready. Just then I saw the shaft of daylight ahead! We'd cut it close, but we could still do it! The last open hatch and the grab loop—that I'd placed the day before—were coming up fast. I knew I'd get just one shot at this: A single instant on which our lives utterly depended.

There it was! I tightened my grip on Tripnee, and reached and grabbed with my right hand. The sudden wrenching nearly pulled my arm from its socket, but we stopped, we were saved, we were not going down that penstock!! At least not right now.

Spreading my feet wide and searching for any kind of purchase, I found nothing but slick, water-worn flume bottom. The strain of holding the two of us in place against the charging current made the muscles of my forearm vibrate and then quiver uncontrollably. I sank my teeth into the webbing strap. This allowed me to re-grip the line and pull us up a few inches. In this way I hauled us further and further up the strip of tubular nylon. Oooooh my teeth hurt, my jaw ached and I could taste blood, but eventually, finally, we were directly below that beautiful, final hatchway.

The cerulean square of sky above us looked like heaven, and fed my strength. We were going up toward that glorious paradise no matter what, anything else was not an option. Cradling Tripnee with my left arm and still holding us in place with my teeth, I used my right hand to tie a series of loops into our lifeline at two-foot intervals. With my teeth, jaw and left arm screaming in agony, I started up. I got my feet into the loops, and with a combined effort of legs, quivering arms and bleeding jaw and gums, we rose upward bit by bit. Tripnee's full length dangled against me, her head lolling on my shoulder, her face inches from mine. As we rose, she gradually regained consciousness, first one eye, then both opened. Still woozy, but game, she grabbed the hatch threshold and helped pull herself up. Hand in hand, wobbly but very much alive, we stood up into the warm sunlight. Seized by the same impulse, we spread our arms wide, inhaled huge breaths and took in the resplendent scene before us. A honey wind caressed our faces. In the distance far below, the river sparkled and danced as it traced the valley's meandering central groove. I pulled Tripnee into my arms.

"Nephew, you figured me out!" it was Reamer Rook's booming voice. My heart stopped.

CHAPTER FORTY

THE REALLY BIG SWIM

From behind a large mound to our north, four armed men stepped into view: Reamer Rook, Toro Canino, Mack Dowell and Hektor Torrente.

Reamer said, "Very good, Adam! I have to give you credit. You outwitted me. After sending you down that first hatch, I had an uneasy feeling. Then it dawned on me how you'd played me. Just thought I'd check this last hatch and, sure enough, here you are!"

As my feelings dropped from ethereal heights into an abyss, Rook concluded, "Well, this is the very last hatch, so there'll be no more clever escapes for you! Now it's time to die!"

Rook seemed to lose control of himself as his voice exploded into a guttural howl, "Get back in that fucking flume now!"

He opened fire with his Uzi, and a line of bullets traced a tight semicircle around Tripnee and me, missing us not by inches, but by fractions of an inch. The meaning was clear: Rook and his men didn't give a shit whether we went into the flume dead or alive--they just wanted to be done with us. When I looked at Tripnee, amazingly, I felt okay. This was the end, but I was glad to be here with her, and I told her so as we moved back toward the open hatchway from which we had just emerged.

The four men prodded and herded us with a sadistic, amped-up ruthlessness.

Suddenly, Dog charged out of nowhere. He threw himself onto Toro.

Tripnee and I had seen him coming and were ready. At the same instant Dog struck Toro, Tripnee ripped into Mack and Hektor with hellcat fury. Simultaneously, I grabbed and deflected Reamer's Uzi, which went off in a roar of automatic fire, and I drove my fist full force square into his face, sending him reeling backward. As Rook fell, I wrenched the red hot gun from his hands. Then I turned to see Dog and Toro, with fists and feet flying, careening from place to place, ripping into each other like two buzz saws, the son venting a lifetime of dismay and anger, while his father exploded with his habitual venom.

Suddenly without warning, they plunged together through the maw of the flume hatchway down into the swift black current. Holy Shit! I leapt toward them, and from the lip of the hatchway was just in time to grab and hold Dog by the scruff of his thick canvas shirt. Toro was holding himself in place by gripping the flume hatch rim with one hand, while with his other—and with both feet—he rapidly struck and kicked Dog, doing everything he could to send his own son down the flume of death. The younger man's fists flashed through the air also, but with more control and better aim. He blocked Toro's blows, smashing him hard again and again. Finally, Toro, in one final fanatical bid to kill Dog, let go of his handhold and flailed, clawing wildly, gouging and ripping at his own son, going for the head, nose and eyes. But Dog fended off the worst of the blows and soon the powerful current dislodged the older man and swept him away into the darkness.

I had just begun to pull Dog up to safety, when Reamer body slammed me from behind, sending me down the hatchway into the black, fast, now horribly familiar subterranean river. Dog and I, both of us neck deep in the current below the hatch, desperately grabbed for the rim, straining for any handhold that would keep us from being swept down to the penstock turbine, down to join the dispersed cells of what had been Toro Canino.

Blood streaming out of both nostrils, Reamer started stomping on our fingers. By switching our grips from one hand to the other, we did our best to dodge his bone-crushing feet, but several of his rapid-fire kicks connected, and our pulverized fingers couldn't hold on much longer. Dog and I were doomed. But if there's anything I hate, it's finger stompers, especially the kind who send their stompees down to oblivion through a giant Cuisinart. In a lucky last-ditch grab with my mutilated left hand, I seized Reamer's right boot and tugged with all the strength I had left. Off balance, looking surprised, Reamer fell forward and plunged over and past us deep into the black, racing water—and in an instant was swept away to certain, inexorable oblivion.

Dog muttered, "No muss. No fuss. And good riddance!"

Gripping the hatchway lip with our crushed fingers, we crawled up out of the flume just in time to see Tripnee subdue Hektor and Mack with an elbow to the neck of one followed by a roundhouse kick to the right temple of the other.

Tripnee, Dog and I then securely cuffed the two men with the plastic handcuffs, and called the sheriff and feds, who, it turned out, were en route a short distance away.

Looking out over the Upper Kern Valley, breathing deeply,

I was struck all over again by the grand scenic beauty of the place. At that moment, an iridescent hummingbird, like a blessing from the earth goddess Gaia herself, in a blur of shimmering greens and blues, darted up to me, hovered for a long moment looking me over, then buzzed off. Far below, I saw what looked like the guide school just then floating past the KR3 powerhouse.

Ever so faint, a call and repeat chant floated on the warm wind up from the flotilla: "He-epwa babba ... He-epwa babba ... Hey-yeay babba ... Hey-yeay babba ... Babba babba ... Babba babba ... Sango sango ... Sango sango ... Sango yamawa ... ... Obatala!"

When we returned to the Dream Van, which Tripnee had parked near the first flume hatchway, we replayed the recording. Amazingly, everything had been picked up and recorded by both the micro recorder concealed inside my arm bandage and the receiver in the van.

Dog, it turned out, had not been kidnapped by the cartel after all, but had been hiding in the big trunk of his Estoque.

Later that evening, Kim and Sparky mentioned that as the guide school flotilla passed the powerhouse earlier in the day, the water emerging from the generator, gliding smoothly out of the base of the massive edifice and reentering the river, had had, for a fleeting moment, the faintest pink hue—and that they had caught the whiff of fresh ground meat. Interestingly, Becca, who had been right there with them, reported no such thing.

CHAPTER FORTY-ONE

EPILOGUE

With Dog's help, and that of several cartel operatives who turned state's evidence, Reamer Rook's and Toro Canino's entire drug operation was rolled up and put out of business. Federal authorities generally confiscate the property of drug dealers because it was purchased with drug money, and this was done with the humvee, planes, souped-up hydroplane houseboat, much of the cartel's real estate and the entire fleet of RVs used for drug distribution, including the two with stinger missiles.

Because Indian Rock Resort originally and rightfully belonged to my parents, when the full story came out, the federal, state and local authorities agreed that it should pass to me. Plus, macabre as it was, as Rook was my uncle, I was his legal heir.

Tripnee decided to take a sabbatical from her FBI job, and she and I spent as much time as possible together, with a sense of wonderful, open possibilities between us for the future.

I hired Becca and Dog to help me run Indian Rock Resort. It turned out that many of the super rich patrons were in fact very nice people, plus we made it our mission to hire and spend locally, and do everything we could to contribute to the economic vitality of the Kern River Valley.

I attended a river guide school taught by Becca and Tripnee, and started gradually building my skills and experience with the goal of eventually guiding on the Forks of the Kern.

Peace preferred to stay right where he was, living, meditating and inspiring kids to read in El Sobrante.

Reddy, Mark, Ludimila and Toni fell in love with guiding, and eventually joined Cassady, Kim and Sparky as trip leaders and managers for Fulfillment Voyages on the various rivers it runs throughout California.

Tripnee and I fell deeper and deeper in love, not only with each other, but also with the Kern River, the surrounding Sequoia National Forest, and the wonderful people living and playing there. Our favorite passion, among so many wonderful passions, remained sneaking off in the Dream Van to what was now *our* secret place deep in the giant sequoias, the largest living things on earth.

DISCLAIMER: WORDS OF CAUTION AND ENCOURAGEMENT

The characters and events in this novel are fictional, while the world portrayed is real. The Lower, Upper, and Forks of the Kern exist, though a few rapids have been renamed, moved or altered. Sequoia National Forest, the giant sequoias, the supportive community of river guides, the hot springs and Indian petroglyphs, Lake Isabella and its surrounding roads and towns, the Audubon Kern River Preserve, the airport, the bands of gold within Yellow Jacket Peak, and the flora and wildlife—including the legendary turkey vulture lift off—all actually exist much as they are described.

Some place names have been changed. Indian Rock Resort, the cartel pot farm and compound, and Thimble Falls cliff were shamelessly invented to suit the needs of the story. The KR3 flume, penstock, and powerhouse are very real—however, in case anyone gets ideas, safeguards are in place to prevent a "no muss, no fuss" death.

Unfortunately, marijuana plantations defended by deadly

booby traps and armed guards are a serious problem throughout our national forests and parks. Drug cartels have indeed been known to kill rather than pay their campesino farmers. Cartel distribution of crystal methamphetamine, which has been described as the world's most dangerous drug, is an especially grievous real life nightmare.

Uncle Peace is fictitious and is not representative of Buddhism or the middle way, and, of course, Mack Dowell is not a typical vegan.

Do not attempt to do the things described in this novel—this is a work of fiction, a flight of imagination. This having been said, exploring, enjoying, and helping to preserve our precious public lands—our national forests, parks, monuments, seashores, deserts and BLM lands—is one of the great adventures to be found on this planet. These places overflow with real magic. Go there, delight and bask in them, let them lift and nourish your body, mind and spirit—but do so with respect and care.

Rivers can be dangerous. Swimming rapids, unless you're with a whitewater expert, is not recommended. Always wear a lifejacket. Don't swim or boat at night. Approach all rivers only with experienced people who know where—and where NOT—to go. In this regard, the reader could do no better than to go with the whitewater rafting outfitters mentioned in the back of this book.

Embrace and espouse the leave-no-trace ethic: Be very careful to avoid starting a wildfire. Leave no litter, human waste, food or fire scars. Leave only footprints, take only memories and photos. Leave each place cleaner than you find it.

Drive carefully—the most dangerous part of nearly all trips is the drive. When off-pavement, don't blaze new routes or tracks; stay on designated roads and trails.

Our public lands and rivers afford unparalleled opportunities to connect and bond with ourselves, our companions, and our planet. They are spiritual places, and comprise a sacred legacy for us all. Savor and luxuriate in them. Be safe. Be excellent to yourself and others. See you there!

♥ Bill McGinnis,

Founder & President,
WhitewaterVoyages.com

P.S. If you enjoyed this novel, please tell your friends! To keep print and ebook prices down, I am going the indie publishing route, which depends on readers spreading word via Facebook, Google+, Twitter, LinkedIn, etc., plus good old word of mouth and messages in ocean-going corked bottles. Thanks so much!—Bill

ACKNOWLEDGMENTS

First and foremost, I thank my writing pal and mentor Jil Plummer, the author of six novels including the post-apocalyptic thriller **Caravan to Armageddon**. Jil's extraordinary help and encouragement was invaluable and transformed the writing of this novel into a fun adventure.

For their computer wizardry, writing and editing suggestions, and so much more, I thank my son Will and daughter Alexandra, both richly gifted deep thinkers well able to achieve whatever they tackle with their full might. I deeply appreciate the affection and support of my sister Mary, my brother Neville, and my extended family Sherrin, Janet, Roy, Jude and Linda.

My dear friends and editing confidants Bud Robyn, Elizabeth Nichols, Barry Kruse, and Dave Arnold inspired and sustained me. Alan Rinzler's sage advice early on was key; a huge thanks to you, Alan! My good friend and neighbor Nalini Davison's suggestions, edits, encouragement and psychological insight greatly improved this novel. Her forthcoming book "How to Talk to A Woman: A Handbook for Men" is sure to be fascinating, valuable and popular. The warm enthusiasm, insightful suggestions and evolved perspectives of Michelle Mallary, Cathy Drew, and Deborah Barth deepened this book. Thank you Lisa Rotter for your wonderful proofreading, comments, suggestions, listening and so much more! For their inspirational nature interpretation past and present, I thank Alison Sheehey and Reed Tollafson of the Audubon Kern River Preserve. For his encouragement and suggestions, I give thanks to Michael Noel, whose mesmerizing murder mystery now in the works—the working title is "Paris and the Night"—is no doubt destined to be a bestseller. For the book's cover and interior design, ebook formatting, and much more, I thank—and highly recommend—the talented Polly Bernson and Molly Williams of Big Hat Press in Lafayette. And I thank Kevin To of the Progressive Printing Agency of Hong Kong for over twenty years of consistently fabulous printing.

I enthusiastically acknowledge and thank all of the wonderful, joyful souls who have taken part in WhitewaterVoyages.com throughout its history, whether as clients or staff. Since its founding in 1975, hundreds of dedicated, immensely talented guides and well over a half million clients have rafted with Whitewater Voyages. To have known and rafted with you has been a lifelong pleasure and honor! You know who you are! Thank you so much for filling my life with fun, learning, inspiration, and adventure! If there is playfulness and wisdom in this book, it is due in large part to you. Although I cannot even begin to name all of you who have contributed so much, I would like to express my appreciation and admiration for Brian Mauer, Sheri Cole Scallo, Sue & Michael Mooney, Wanda Cole, Kay Vallis, Lisa Hayes, Roland Stevenson, Jim Cassady, Mike, Brenda, Dan & Amanda Grant, Pete Angstadt, Toni Hall, Matt & Susie Downing, Todd Brownell, Mark Kocina, Ted & Ruth Kearn, Jib Ellison, Beth Rypins, Jon Runnestrand, Kathy Meyer, Kim Mansoor, Harry Chest, Kyle Noon, Dave Catechi, Dr. Glenn Etter, Dr. Steve Givant, Buck Beddie, Aaran Tippett, Toby Barmeyer, Josh Sher, Julie Green, Zdenec Skyvara, Mark Goddard,

Laurence Alvarez-Roos, Mark Bayless, Eric Meldrum, Cyrus Luciano, Gene Evans, Steve Messer, Kelly Wiglesworth, Bridget Crocker, Dave & Susie Slover, the amazing Sullivan & Natter brothers, Mark Vanbuskirk, Isabella & Spreck Salaverry-Rosekrans, Ronaldo Macedo, Susie Dodge, Bill Cross & Polly Greist, ED Denson, Wendy Keller, Simon Saichek, Alice Deisinger Jorgensen, Tim Hillmer, Stephanie Stewart, Richard MacFarland, Buck Swashbuckler, Bruce Fox, Josh Neff, Max Norton, Ken Klages, Rob Perkins, Tom Hicks, Juliet Wiscombe Starrett, and Tracy Vietta, to name just a few of the outstanding, stellar souls who are and always will be part of the Whitewater Voyages family.

I thank the members and staff of El Sobrante's Lakeridge Athletic Club. This place invigorates my body and spirit. With generosity and good humor, our diverse community of souls bravely, day after day, practices—with ever increasing skill and success—the arts of listening, acceptance, and human kindness. I enjoy how we talk about our lives and everything under the sun, and endeavor, at least in our own minds, to solve our own and the world's problems. It is possible that we thereby help keep our own inner rivers moving and also send ripples of positive energy fanning outward into the world. For their friendship, encouragement, advice, and support, I thank Scott Parkay, Jack Frost, William Rivera, Michelle Marcucci, Robin LemMon, songwriter and musician extraordinaire Randy Mayer, Dr. Chris & Saena Webb, Martino and Danyel Magid, Dr. Ali Alejandrina Estrada, Dr. Zuzanna Lilliental, D'Artagnan Lloyd, Jay Olson, Jim Parrott, Rita Barouch, Christopher Cathey, Saeng Keola, Davy Dacaho, Miko Delos Santos, Tom Weeks, Dev Paul, Jim Jackson, Mickey Connor, Steve Blow, Theresa Bucci, Lisa Wellhausen, Jennifer Caroff, Jordan King, Vanessa Alvarez, Markku Pelanne, Kistya Afanaslev, and all of the club's other wonderful members and staff.

My family and I deeply appreciate our Raftnet buddies and cherish our long history of shared adventures. Thank you Brian, Dena, Taylor, Dylan & Caden Merrill; Brandon, Melanie & Chandler Lake; Joe, Sue, Ben & Ethan Greiner; Peter, Mariah, Jonah & Betsy Bowen Grubb; Paul & Jennifer Breuer; and Bruce, Abby, Hannah & Karen Blom Lessels.

For embracing and celebrating rivers and river running, I salute Joe Kowalski, Russell Walters, Susie Hockmeyer, Rafael Gallo, John McDermott, Fernando Esquivel, Bill Zell, Chris Aston, Bill Mashek, Bill Bernt, Neil Hartling, Marty McDonnell, Chris Condon, Norm Schoenhoff, Bob Ferguson, Luther Stevens, Kenny Bushling, Dr. Dry, Gregg, Scott & George Armstrong, Jim Ritter, Bob & Will Volpert, Nate Rangel, Jerry Ashburn, Bill Center, Betty Lopez & Steve Lyles, Steve Welch, George & Tyler Wendt, Mike Martell, Beth Harper, Bill Parks, Guy Cables, Don Hill, Tom & Marianne Moore, Justin Butchert, Jim Sattler, David Brown, Mark Dubois, Kevin Wolf Cloud, Ron Stork, Jonas Minton, John & Rhonda Stallone, Rorie Gotham, and the members of American Rivers, America Outdoors, Friends of the River, the Tuolumne River Trust, and the California Floaters Society.

In recognition of our great shared saltwater voyages— and entertaining discussions literary and otherwise—past, present and future, I doff my cap to my sailing buddies Bill West, Jay Daly, Rick Galbreath, Chris Northcutt, Herman Haluza, Al Wallash, David Mahaffy, Julian, Amber, John & Phyllis Sutter, and Matt, Brandy, Todd, Angie & patriarch Butch of the Tradewinds Sailing Club.

I would like to express appreciation and a warm remem- brance to Bev Mayer, Patrick & Diane Noonan, Becca Foster, Paula Johnson, Sandy MacFarland, Gloria Lenhart, Toni Meurlott, Kathryn Ackland, Nick Voorhees, and to my focusing pals Yshai Hope, Jeannette Perez, Ann Weiser Cornell, and David & Joyce Curry. Lastly, I thank, unnamed, my friends who need to remain under the radar because they are shy, publicity phobic, and on the lam. ;-)

RECOMMENDED WHITEWATER OUTFITTERS

Aggipah River Trips, **aggipah.com**, Idaho

Canadian River Expeditions and Nahanni River Adventures, **Nahanni.com**, Alaska, Northwest Territories, Yukon, Nunavut

Northern Outdoors, **northernoutdoors.com**, Maine

Rios Tropicales, **riostropicales.com**, Costa Rica

River and Rock Adventures, **riverandrockadventures.com**, California

ROW Adventures, **rowadventures.com**, Idaho, Oregon, Montana, Alaska, British Columbia, Baja, South America, Europe

Rubicon Whitewater Adventures, **rubiconadventures.com**, California

Sierra Mac River Trips, **sierramac.com**, California

Trinity River Rafting, **trinityriverrafting.com**, California

Western River Expeditions, **westernriver.com**, Grand Canyon, Arizona, Utah, Idaho, Oregon

W. E. T. River Trips, **RAFTWET.com**, California

Whitewater Excitement, **whitewaterexcitement.com**, California

Whitewater Voyages, **whitewatervoyages.com**, California

Wilderness Aware Rafting, **inaraft.com**, Colorado, Arizona

Wilderness Tours, **wildernesstours.com**, Ontario, Canada

Zephyr Whitewater, **zrafting.com**, California

Zoar Outdoor, **zoaroutdoor.com**, Massachusetts

Note to outfitters: If your organization should be listed here, but is not, I can include you in future editions. Please contact me at **bill@whitewatervoyages.com**. Thanks, Bill

Books by William McGinnis

Whitewater: A Thriller

Sailing the Greek Islands: Dancing with Cyclops
(*An Amazon eBook*)

The Guide's Guide Augmented

River Signals

Class V Briefing

The (*original*) Guide's Guide

Whitewater Rafting